HAPPILY
Ever
AFTER

JANET DAILEY

ZEBRA BOOKS
KENSINGTON PUBLISHING CORP.
http://www.kensingtonbooks.com

ZEBRA BOOKS are published by

Kensington Publishing Corp.
119 West 40th Street
New York, NY 10018

All Kensington titles, imprints and distributed lines are available at special quantity discounts for bulk purchases for sales promotion, premiums, fund-raising, educational or institutional use.

Special book excerpts or customized printings can also be created to fit specific needs. For details, write or phone the office of the Kensington Special Sales Manager. Attn.: Special Sales Department. Kensington Publishing Corp., 119 West 40th Street, New York, NY 10018. Phone: 1-800-221-2647.

Zebra and the Z logo Reg. U.S. Pat. & TM Off.

ISBN-13: 978-1-4201-3222-9
ISBN-10: 1-4201-3222-9

First Mass-Market Paperback Printing: July 2005

10 9 8 7 6 5 4 3 2

Printed in the United States of America

CONTENTS

SIX WHITE
HORSES

CHAPTER ONE

The horse moved restlessly, his coat shimmering with blue-black hues. Its midnight color contrasted with the white saddle and bridle, stitched with black leather and inset with black roses. White stockings were wrapped around the horse's legs and his impatient, dancing hooves were painted silver.

An old man stood at the black's head, neatly dressed in a Western suit that fit his lean build. His pepper-gray head was turned to the boyishly slim girl hurrying toward him.

"What kept you, gal?" he asked with a patient sigh. "They're ready to start the Grand Entry."

"The zipper got stuck on these fancy pants," she explained quickly, vaulting without effort into the saddle and taking the reins he handed her. The white outfit she wore matched the leather trappings of the horse, black roses embroidered on the pant legs and the shoulders and back. Her dark brown hair was caught at the nape of her neck and plaited into a single braid.

"Knock 'em dead, honey!" he called out to her as she reined the horse away.

"I will, Gramps!" Her hand raised in a cheery salute as the powerful hindquarters of the horse muscled to leap into a canter.

Not until they neared the rodeo stands did Patty King slow the black horse's pace. She wove through the congestion of horses and riders, mostly rodeo contestants. Patty smiled at the friendly teasing about her tardiness from those she knew, and tried to calm the butterflies in her stomach as she halted the black horse behind a pair of golden palominos whose riders were carrying the flags.

The gates into the arena were closed. Already there was a commotion in the bucking chutes and an excited hum coming from the crowd in the stands waiting for the rodeo to begin. Patty laid a soothing hand on the black's neck, quieting him with a few softly spoken words.

"Hey, Princess!" a voice called out to her. A lanky cowboy jumped from the rail and walked over, flamboyantly dressed in a bright Western shirt with leather chaps and jangling spurs. He stopped at her side.

"Princess?" Patty laughed, her brown eyes dancing at the sight of the young, handsome face that looked up at her.

"You're too little to be a king, so you have to be a princess." He winked. Grabbing the oversized saddle horn of her trick saddle and sticking the toe of his boot in the stirrup, he pulled himself up to her level, balancing himself with his other hand placed on the cantle. "I need a kiss for luck, Princess."

"Jack Evans, the last time I gave you a kiss for luck,

you were bucked off the first jump out of the chutes."
Twin dimples appeared in her cheeks.

An expression of mock seriousness spread across
the face so near to hers. "You didn't put your heart
into it that time. We'll just have to keep on tryin'
until you get it right."

She gave a rueful shake of her head. Arguing
with this cocky cowboy was hopeless. Besides, Patty
King had known him too long to be taken in by his
considerable charm. But she didn't protest when
his mouth covered hers in a light but lingering kiss.

"Much better." Jack grinned and swung away from
her onto the ground.

"If all that mushy stuff is over," a growling voice
said from the arena gate, "we'll get this rodeo
started."

A faint, embarrassed pink colored her cheeks as
Patty glanced at the grizzled, battered-looking
cowboy at the gates, his left arm in a plaster cast.

"I'm ready, Lefty," she said.

Grumbling softly, he nodded an acknowledgment. But her brown eyes had slid past him, caught
by the mocking gaze of a big man just mounting
the top rail of the arena fence. The look in his eyes
made her stiffen with resentment.

He was tall with powerful shoulders, and not
one ounce of spare flesh on his frame. Everything
about him seemed to radiate a sensual masculinity,
from the jet black hair that curled under the brim
of his Stetson to his thick black brows. Sooty lashes
outlined his metallic blue eyes. As Patty met his
gaze, she glared her dislike of their owner, Morgan
Kincaid.

The arena gate swung open and the rodeo announcer proclaimed the start of the rodeo in a

booming, echoing voice. The Grand Entry parade got started, swiftly proceeding to the presentation of colors and the playing of the National Anthem.

When the rest of the horses and riders in the Grand Entry left the arena, Patty followed, pulling her black horse to a stop just inside the gate. Her smoldering sense of irritation flared up at the sight of Morgan Kincaid swinging down from the rail fence and walking toward the chutes.

He was the antithesis of what she liked in a man. He had none of the quiet courtesy she admired—in fact, his manner was abrasive, setting her teeth on edge as effectively as the whine of a dentist's drill. He was too aggressively male to be handsome, with none of the rough edges smoothed. Patty scowled at his back, but couldn't help noticing the sheer breadth of his shoulders. She nearly missed her cue from the rodeo announcer.

"Our special attraction for this evening, ladies and gentlemen, is Miss Patricia King," he boomed out, "a native of New Mexico, a truly fine trick rider and Roman rider. Patty, give them an example of what they'll see later on this evening."

Reining the black horse in a full circle to the right, its signal for the flat-out run, Patty took him into the arena. She went once around in a hippodrome stand, falling away on the second circle to a side drag that left the crowd gasping before they broke into applause.

She rode out. There was no opportunity to stay and watch the first rodeo event, which was saddle bronc riding. Patty had to return to the stable area to help her grandfather harness the six white horses she used for the Roman ride. By the time the black leather trappings were on each horse and Patty had changed into a black outfit with white roses, she was due in the arena for her performance.

With her grandfather Everett King walking at the head of Liberty, the left horse in the front pair, Patty sat bareback astride Loyalty, the right horse of the last pair.

The arena lights caught the sparkles dusted over the hindquarters of the six white horses as they pranced into the arena to the tune of "She'll Be Comin' Round the Mountain." Patty's stomach was twisted into knots of nervous excitement.

Rising to stand on the rosined back of Loyalty, she clucked comfortingly to the horses, taking an extra wrap on the six black reins, three in each hand. Oblivious to the announcer's words, she shifted her left foot to Landmark's back, easing the horses into a slow canter while she adjusted herself to the rhythm.

Circling the arena twice eased her attack of jitters. While Patty guided the three pairs of horses into a series of figure eights that required a flying change of lead, her grandfather supervised the setting of the hurdles. There was one jump on one side of the arena and a double jump on the opposite side.

Deftly checking Landmark's habit of rushing the jump, Patty kept her balance as the horses cleared the barrier with faultless precision, one pair following the other, her feet placed on the backs of the last two horses. The double jump was trickier on the opposite side of the arena. As the last pair of horses was landing from the first obstacle, the first pair was making the second.

When all the horses had cleared the last jump, it was once around the arena to a sliding stop in the center where they all took a bow with Patty standing triumphantly on their backs, a hand in the air to acknowledge the applause. A refusal at any of the jumps would've meant a nasty fall for Patty as well as for the horses.

Wheeling the horses toward the gate, she slipped astride Loyalty's back. A beaming smile split her face as she met the congratulatory look in her grandfather's eyes. With the agility of a much younger man, Everett King caught Liberty's halter, slowing him to a walk through the gate and forcing the rest to do the same. A cowboy grabbed Lodestar's head while another took her grandfather's place with Liberty.

"You did a great job, Patty." He winked at her as he laid a hand on Loyalty's shining neck.

"You did the training. You get the credit," she replied in a breathless voice. "Thanks, Grandpa."

His gnarled hand closed affectionately over hers before a somber look stole over his face. "He's here, Patty."

For an instant she froze, unable to speak or breathe. A twisting pain stabbed at her chest. There was no need to ask who *he* was, Patty knew. She knew her grandfather was talking about Lije Masters.

"Where?" Her voice was choked. Her eyes fluttered closed for the briefest of seconds, to try to shut out the pain.

"In the fourth row on your left." A touching sympathy laced his words. "His wife is with him."

A sob rose in her throat and Patty forced it back with a quick gulp. *Smile,* she told herself sternly, *smile and wave at him even if it kills you.* Some of her panic was communicated to the white horse and it shifted nervously beneath her.

Touching the silky neck with a soothing caress, Patty deliberately let her gaze stray to the fourth row of the stand, forcing a smile of false surprise onto her mouth when she saw him. Lije's gray eyes studied her from a lean, tanned face as he returned her smile. Its effect on her heartbeat . . . devastating.

Her gaze flickered to the perfection of the blond woman beside him, envy squeezing nearly all the breath from Patty's lungs. Lije's wife was a flawless example of femininity. Not a tomboy turned into a cowgirl like her, Patty thought miserably. But she waved at them anyway.

"Magnificent performance as usual, Patty," Lije called.

"Thanks." The shrill edge to her voice was painful to her pride.

She heard a resounding slap on the rump of her horse as Everett King waved to the cowboys holding the front pair to take them to the stables. She and her grandfather were too close for Patty not to realize that he was silently asking her to end the conversation with the man she still loved, who had married another.

At the stables, Patty slipped from Loyalty's back and helped her grandfather remove the leather trappings from the six white horses. Their travel trailer was parked a short distance away, where Patty changed quickly out of her costume into faded blue jeans and a knit top of olive green, not allowing herself time to think in case she lost her grip on her shaky composure.

The horses were cooled off when she returned to the stable area. Shouts and applause from the rodeo crowd could be heard in the distance along with the announcer's booming commentary. It was all so familiar to her—rodeo was her life, thanks to Lije Masters.

"I'll finish up the horses, Grandpa," Patty said softly.

His alert brown eyes regarded her thoughtfully, seeing past her calm façade to the pain beneath. "You want to be alone, don't you, honey?"

"Is it that obvious?" She smiled ruefully.

"Only to me," he responded as he walked away.

Patty watched his lean figure disappear and sighed. It was strange that he was the only member of her family who instinctively understood how she felt. Both her parents assumed that her interest in rodeo came from her grandfather, who had actively competed as a young man. But her motivation had always been Lije Masters. As long as she could remember, she had loved him and only him.

When Lije had started following the rodeo circuit to save his father's ranch and keep it after his father's death, Patty had been determined to follow. She didn't have the patience to wait in New Mexico for the day he would return. It was her grandfather, Everett King, who had suggested trick riding, since she couldn't exactly support herself as a barrel racer.

Fate, unfortunately, had played a few tricks of its own that Patty never expected. Her bookings hadn't included the San Antonio rodeo. Liberty had been ailing and Patty had been at her parents' ranch in New Mexico before going to the Houston rodeo. She would never forget the bitterness of walking into that restaurant in New Mexico . . . and suddenly seeing Lije Masters with his new wife.

Nice of you to tell me, Lije. But to this day, she knew

she had carried the scene off beautifully, never letting him see how crushing his news had been.

A tear slipped from her lashes as she pushed the straw around in Liberty's stall. She was using the pitchfork more for support than anything. Reminding herself that Lije had never given her any indication that he looked on her as more than a friend or a neighbor was cold comfort.

Still, she had lived in hope of more. She had adored him, worshiped him, loved him, content with the smallest crumb of his attention. *You're an idiot,* she told herself fiercely.

Her hope had been sustained by knowing that Lije didn't believe in riding the rodeo circuit and leaving a wife at home. He'd said that he would never expect someone who loved him to experience the agony of watching him compete when every rider ran the risk of being badly hurt or crippled.

Yet Patty had lived with that fear for three years, biding her time, knowing that Lije intended to quit after another two successful years of rodeo.

Never in her wildest imagination had she believed that he would fall in love and marry someone else after only a few days of knowing her. But he had. A year and a half had passed since Patty had found out, but the pain was as intense as if it had only happened this morning.

Her grandfather's shoulder had been drenched with her tears. He had been the one who'd convinced her to continue the circuit when she wanted to curl up and die. Maybe he'd known that the constant training necessary to keep the horses in top form would keep Patty from dwelling too much on her shattered dream.

She did like the work, but it was just that—work. Riding in rodeos and fending off amorous cowboys who'd had one too many Lone Star beers wasn't all she wanted out of life.

Patty had wanted a home and children—Lije's children—and a ranch that she could help him run. She was as capable as any ranch hand around. That had always seemed a factor in her favor, a reason she was sure that Lije was bound to choose her eventually and no one else.

Wrong.

Lije's wife was a model who had never been on a horse in her life, city-born and city-bred, the exact opposite of Patty in every way.

The salty taste of tears covered her lips and she realized with a start that she was crying, something she hadn't done in a year. Swallowing her sobs, Patty wiped her cheeks with the back of her hand.

Liberty turned luminous brown eyes on her and nickered softly. It took all her willpower to resist the urge to fling her arms around the horse's neck and cry. An overwhelming sense of misery dominated her senses and Patty didn't notice that she wasn't alone.

"There you are, Skinny." A low, edgy voice spoke from the doorway of the stall. "Thought I might find you here. Having a pity party for one?"

After a start of surprise, cold anger held her motionless. Only one person called her Skinny.

"I don't know what you're talking about, Morgan Kincaid." Patty glared at him. "And I don't particularly care, so why don't you just get out of here?"

"Maybe I was mistaken," he drawled lazily. His tall, husky, broad-shouldered frame blocked the light.

"But it seemed to me that you turned as white as your horses when you saw Lije in the stands."

Patty held his blue gaze for an instant but had to turn away. "You were mistaken," she snapped. "Definitely." She began moving the pitchfork in the straw again.

"Glad to hear it." His strong mouth curved into a smile. "Thinking the way I was that you were all tore up at seeing Lije again, I would've sworn that there were tears on your cheeks."

"Hell, no." She kept her face averted. "That was sweat. It was hot out there. And I don't know where you got the idea that it would bother me to see Lije. He and I are good friends."

"Listen, Skinny." His tone was patiently indulgent. "Nearly everyone on the circuit knows that you thought you were in love with the guy."

"I can't control what people think." Any more than she could control the shakiness in her voice.

"No, that's true." Morgan casually hooked a thumb in his belt as he watched her move the straw around the horse's hooves.

Patty turned on him suddenly, sick of his unsubtle comments. "Shouldn't you be at the chutes making sure your precious rodeo stock is all right?"

"Sam is the chute boss. That's his job," he answered smoothly. "Aren't you curious why Lije came all this way to see a rodeo?"

"Why don't you tell me?" Her tone seethed with irritation.

"He wants to sell Blake Williams a young bull-dogging horse he trained. Seems he needs the money."

"What's so unusual about that?" Patty shrugged. "Name me a rancher who doesn't need cash money."

"It isn't about the ranch." There was a watchful stillness in Morgan's blue eyes. "His wife is going to have a baby."

Nothing unusual about that either, Patty thought wildly. But to hear it now—without any warning— and from Morgan Kincaid, a man she despised, was more than she could handle. Her brown eyes widened in shock and she gasped with pain.

Morgan's gaze seemed to glitter. "Now why should that bother you? You and Lije are only friends." His mocking statement held the fine edge of cutting steel. "You certainly don't look happy. You know, a stranger might even think you were jealous."

Her fingers tightened on the pitchfork handle. "Shut up, Morgan. I don't have to listen to this. Just get out!"

Morgan didn't move as he stared at her thoughtfully. "You still think you love the guy?"

"I never thought! I knew I loved Lije!" Unwillingly Patty raised her voice, no longer trying to pretend that she didn't care. She lifted the pitchfork to a threatening angle. "And if you don't get out of here *now,* I'll run this through you!"

The sudden movement and the angry voices unsettled the white horse tied in the stall. It whinnied frantically and pulled against the lead rope, twisting and turning his head, his hooves beating an in-place cadence on the stall floor.

"Easy, boy," Morgan murmured soothingly, ignoring the pitchfork Patty had aimed at him to move to the horse's head. The animal bobbed nervously, eyes rolling, but Liberty responded to the reassuring voice and the gentle touch of Morgan's big hand. "That isn't any way for a lady to talk, is it, feller?"

The instantaneous regret that Patty felt for up-setting the sensitive and spirited horse was replaced by a flash of self-pity. "I'm not a 'lady,' " she said with scorn. "Not that you would even know one if you met one, Morgan."

Letting her remark slide by without comment, he ducked under the horse's neck and stood on the opposite side of the animal a few feet from Patty. His quiet murmurs to the horse eased her own raw nerves as well as Liberty's. At last the horse snorted and began nuzzling the hay in the manger. With his large, tanned hand trailing along the horse's withers and over its back, Morgan moved slowly toward Patty.

His almost complete indifference to her put her instantly on guard. The slightly lowered pitchfork raised a fraction of an inch. Cautiously she watched him turn to face her, her gaze centering on the movement of his right hand.

"You remind me of a bantam hen my mother used to have." His eyes insolently inspected her slender form.

Then his right hand touched the brim of his sweat-stained Stetson, lifting it off to reveal his thick black hair. Distracted by the unhurried movement, Patty wasn't prepared for the lightning swiftness of his fingers closing over the pitchfork handle and wrenching it easily from her grasp. She made one futile grab to recover it before she was intimidated by his sheer size.

He tossed the pitchfork over the manger in a lazy way and grinned at her.

Patty's back was against the stall partition. "What do you mean, a bantam hen?" she demanded, fighting back the sudden leap of fear in her heart.

He spread one hand against the wall near her head as he leaned slightly forward with an odd look in his vivid blue eyes that she couldn't quite name.

"Puny but proud," he said. Tilting his head to the side, he studied her angry expression. "Yeah, that fits. Puny, proud Patricia."

Level with his massive chest, and looking up at the strength etched in the rugged planes of his face, Patty felt at a decided disadvantage. Without thinking twice, she raised a hand to slap the mocking expression off his face, but her wrist was halted by a grip like steel.

Stopped in an instant, she lashed out, "Let go! I hate you!"

His long, sooty lashes couldn't veil the blazing look in his eyes. "Guess I can't take you over my knee, Patty King, unless I want the law after me. I'll just have to kiss you instead. Are you going to say no?"

"Ah . . ." She let out a gasp as he let go.

"Are you?"

She said nothing, furious with him and wildly attracted at the same time. Her face turned up to his as he moved closer, and her lips parted when his brushed lightly against them. And she didn't say no when he kissed her for real.

His mouth was warmly persuasive. Patty responded with every female instinct she possessed, stirred by his unexpected tenderness and his strength. She felt no need to fight back by the time Morgan raised his head.

"Okay, I understand a couple of things better now," he drawled.

"Such as?"

He grinned. "Didn't I overhear Jack Evans say you needed more practice just before you rode in?"

Furious with him all over again, she stamped her foot. "Why, you—"

Morgan waved away her rage. "And I know why Lije found himself somebody else, too. You're a novice, for all your tough talk. But hey, I would've taught you how to make love. Guess he didn't want to bother."

The underlying sensuality in his words sent a shiver down her spine, but she still wanted to smack him. "Who asked you to? Who do you think you are, Morgan Kincaid?"

He shrugged. "Not anywhere near as good a man as Lije in your eyes. Too bad. He didn't want what you were offering."

"If you had been in Lije's place, I never would've offered anything," she taunted him.

The set line of his mouth curved into a smile. "Is that right? So what are you going to do now that you've saved your kisses for a man who belongs to someone else?"

"Lije belongs to no one but himself."

"Believe it if you want to." Patty didn't reply. Morgan studied her for a long moment before he spoke again. "Does that mean you're going to break up his happy home?"

She scuffed the toe of her boot in the straw, wishing passionately that she could dodge past Morgan and escape. Lije didn't love her. He never had. To try and come between him and his beautiful wife would only make her look like a bigger fool.

"No." Patty tried to edge past without touching

him but there wasn't room. "You're in my way, Morgan. Move."

He didn't. "You going to try and hit me again? Or are you going to run in a corner and hide? Guess you just can't forget Lije's kisses."

"He was a hell of a lot better at kissing than you!" she blurted out.

He only laughed. The throaty sound was more infuriating than anything he could have said.

"What's the matter? Don't you think I can judge?" she demanded angrily. "He kissed me lots of times."

In a brotherly kind of way, if she was going to be honest about it, which she wasn't.

"Oh. I didn't know that."

"Like it was—or is—any of your business. I don't know why I told you."

Morgan leaned against the stall partition. "I appreciate it. Guess I have a lot to learn about love. Besides that it hurts."

"Right. There are ninety-six songs on the jukebox at Kelly's Bar that say just that. Go play them all."

He jingled the few coins in his pocket. "Nope. Only got two quarters. But keep talking, Patty. You seem to know everything about the subject, even if you are only—what—twenty-two?"

If looks could kill, they would have been carving the date of his death on a gravestone as Patty glared her hatred of him.

"That's right. But I'm not a kid!"

He looked her up and down with undisguised masculine appreciation. "Nope, you're not. Have to agree with that."

"Shut up!" It was hardly the most mature response, but it was the best she could do. His intense gaze flustered her.

"Don't scare the horse again, Patty," he said patiently, giving the animal a pat.

She seized the opportunity to push past him, realizing that he was deliberately provoking her for his own amusement. Well, she wasn't going to take the bait again.

"I have work to do and I'm wasting my time arguing with you." She stalked out through the stall door toward the tack room.

Morgan followed. "Need any help?"

Patty shook out Liberty's blanket, black with a white rose on the corner. "Not from you," she said sarcastically.

"Suit yourself." He gave an indifferent shrug as he turned away, then paused. "Are you going to Kelly's tonight?"

"No."

"Good. I just won a hundred dollars."

"What are you talking about?" Patty frowned, forgetting the blanket in her hands for the moment and giving Morgan her undivided attention.

"I bet your gramps a hundred dollars that you wouldn't show up because Lije and his wife are going to be there," he answered in a complacent drawl.

"Gramps? You mean—my grandpa?"

"Who else? I tried to tell him you were too grief-stricken over meeting Lije again to go, but he kept insisting you were smiling on the outside and crying on the inside. Hey, I think there's a song on the jukebox about that, too. I'll play it for you, Patty."

She threw the blanket at him, but he caught it

easily in one big hand and draped it over the tack room door. "I think you like being miserable."

Patty's mouth opened and closed. No words came to mind that would express her wrath. She was still searching for something to say as he walked away, heading toward the pens where the rodeo stock was held.

CHAPTER TWO

Everett King was seated at the small table in the travel trailer, studying a road map when Patty entered. The jacket of his light blue suit was lying on the back of a chair. His string tie was hanging loose and the top buttons of his shirt were opened. Running his gnarled fingers through his pepper-gray hair, he glanced up and smiled.

"Got the horses all settled for the night?" he asked.

"Grandpa, did you make a bet with Morgan Kincaid?" She stopped beside the table, her hands on her hips, her head tilted to the side.

"Whatever gave you that idea?" He gave her a disbelieving look before he returned to the study of the road map.

"Morgan was the 'whatever' that gave me that idea," Patty answered grimly.

"You talked to him, did you?" Her grandfather breathed in deeply at her answering nod and folded up the map. "Are you going to Kelly's?" He didn't glance up as he asked the question.

"I shouldn't go, just to teach you a lesson." She sighed.

"But you are going," he said, a definite twinkle in the brown eyes that met her equally dark ones.

"You did it deliberately, didn't you, Grandpa?" Her mouth curved in a smile of affectionate exasperation. "I'll bet you even told Morgan where I was just to make sure that I found out about it. You knew he wouldn't be able to resist the temptation of telling me."

"That sounds like I tricked you into going," he said.

"You did and you know it!" Patty shook her head and stepped into the small kitchen area. "We can't afford to lose a hundred dollars on a silly bet like that and I couldn't stand a week of Morgan's gloating. I suppose he's the stock contractor at our next rodeo?"

"Well, yes, actually, he is," her grandfather admitted reluctantly.

"Your little maneuver was successful," she sighed. "I am going to Kelly's, but you're going with me. I'll need some moral support, so don't you go off in a corner with Lefty."

"Go get gorgeous, girl. There's a clean towel and washcloth in the shower," he told her. He darted her a twinkling glance and added, "I set out some pretty clothes on the bed just in case you decided to go."

"Just in case, huh? Sometimes, Gramps, you are positively exasperating!" Patty declared as she walked into the miniature bathroom of the trailer.

"I take after my granddaughter," he called after her.

Twenty minutes later, she was tucking a flowered blouse into the waistband of tight jeans that did something for her curves. Her dark brown hair was brushed free of its braid to hang loose and tickle her shoulder blades. She didn't look like a tomboy anymore, but her light makeup wasn't exactly glamorous either.

With a resigned shrug, Patty turned away from the mirror. She couldn't compete with the sophisticated perfection of the blond model who was Lije's wife. Although she did have a grandfather who was good at getting her into interesting situations, she still lacked a fairy godmother who could suddenly transform her into a raving beauty with the wave of a wand.

Besides, hadn't she learned the hard way that Lije didn't see her as anything more than the little girl next door? She wished she could despise him for the way she had wasted all those years waiting for him. It might make it easier to get over him. But she couldn't and didn't. She just kept right on loving him as though nothing had changed.

"All right, Grandpa," she said as she walked through the tiny kitchen to the equally tiny living room of the trailer. "I'm ready. We'd better go before I change my mind."

His shirt was buttoned and his jacket back on, the Western string tie secured in its longhorn clasp. He set his tan Stetson at a jaunty angle on his pepper-colored hair.

"There aren't any quitters in the King family." He smiled at her and opened the door.

"I wish I were as sure about that as you are," Patty murmured. She followed him into the starlit night.

Her nerves were on edge, worse than any pre-performance jitters she'd ever experienced, as they approached the entrance of Kelly's bar. Because it was only a few blocks from the arena grounds, most of the rodeo cowboys went there—those who weren't flying elsewhere to compete in another rodeo. They were out in force tonight, Patty decided when she and her grandfather stepped through the doors.

The room was hazy with smoke, a gauzy cloud that hung near the ceiling. The billiard tables in one corner were the scene of good-natured competition, the loud voices mixing with the laughter and chatter coming from the tables in the rest of the bar. Overriding the din was a country dance band playing a Garth Brooks song.

"Do you see him here?" Patty whispered nervously.

"He's sitting over by the dance floor. There's an empty table beside him. Come on," Everett King ordered.

Her searching eyes found Lije easily. He was facing the door with his arm resting on the back of his wife's chair. Blake Williams, one of the leading professional steer wrestlers, was seated at the table with him, commanding Lije's attention for the moment.

But Patty wasn't interested in Blake Williams. All of her attention was centered on Lije, catching the loving glance he gave his wife. Patty felt a stab of jealousy pierce her heart. She thought dejectedly that they made a great-looking couple, but that didn't stop her from wishing that she had been the recipient of that glance.

Her grandfather's hand guided her along the edge of the dance floor. A fingertip touched her drooping chin and Patty looked up into a pair of thoughtful blue eyes. She had been so intent on

Lije that she hadn't noticed Morgan Kincaid among the dancers on the floor. But he was there, partnering Jill Van Wert, a tawny-haired barrel racer who followed the same rodeo circuit as the professional cowboys. The couple had paused directly in their path.

"I see you've changed your mind," Morgan observed dryly.

"Yes, I did," Patty said. "Looks like you just lost a hundred dollars."

His metallic gaze flickered to her grandfather. "I guess so."

"Lije is here, Patty," Jill said, sounding a little catty. "Oh, he's right over there—with his wife. Have you seen him yet?"

Patty's mouth tightened. She had never liked Jill very much. The girl was an excellent barrel racer, but Patty had always had the impression that it was not the competition that Jill enjoyed, but the cowboys—in the plural sense.

"Yes, I did notice him," she answered stiffly. "Gramps and I were on our way over to say hello."

"Okay. We won't keep you then." Morgan smiled crookedly. "See you later."

He hadn't missed her defensiveness. "What I wouldn't give to kick him right in the . . ." she muttered in a savage underbreath.

Everett King clicked his tongue reprovingly but said nothing as they watched Morgan Kincaid guide his pretty partner toward the dance floor.

Her anger at Morgan seemed to have eased some of Patty's tension and brought the color into her cheeks. Gathering her courage, she managed to put on a relatively happy face as they neared the table.

"I'm still kicking myself for not buying that red

horse of yours when you sold him two years ago," Blake Williams was grumbling to Lije. "If I had, I'd be the one raking in the dough off him instead of Tod."

"Horses, horses, horses!" Patty forced herself to laugh. "Seems like that's what you were talking about the last time I saw you, Lije."

"Hello, Patty, Everett." Lije rose to welcome them to the table. "It's good to see you again."

With a sinking heart, Patty noticed the easy warmth with which he greeted them. The cool aloofness was gone, no doubt melted by the hot glow in his wife's eyes whenever she looked at him.

"You going to introduce me to this lovely lady, Lije?" her grandfather asked after shaking hands.

"Of course." Lije smiled. "This is my wife Diana." Patty wanted to cry at the caring way he spoke her name. "Diana, I know you've met Patty King. This is her grandfather, Everett King."

A vacant table and chairs were pulled closer to include Patty and her grandfather in their small group. Patty found herself sitting next to the silvery blonde, who seemed more beautiful than Patty remembered. She felt like the ugly duckling next to the swan.

"Your horsemanship is just amazing, Patty," Diana said with obvious sincerity. "What a performance! Wish I could ride like that. I envy you."

Patty wondered what Diana's reply would be if she said that she envied Diana her husband. The fleeting look of compassion in the blonde's blue eyes gave Patty the impression that such a statement would not surprise Lije Masters's wife.

The last thing she wanted was Diana's pity. "Thank you." Patty managed a smile. "Actually my grandfather deserves a lot of the credit. He helps me with the training and perfecting the stunts."

"She's just as modest as she always was, Lije." Everett King grinned. "I may help, but you couldn't get me to stand on the backs of those two horses while I'm trying to control the four ahead of them."

"I'll bet Patty feels the same way about those bulls you used to ride." Lije laughed.

"Either way, we're a team now," Patty said.

"Talking about a pair of Kings, I saw your family before Diana and I left. They told me to be sure to give you both their love and to let you know that all of them are fine. Your mother suggested that you write if you aren't going to keep your cell phone charged. Says she's been trying to call you for a week."

"I lost the charger." Patty sighed.

"How many is that now?" her grandfather asked.

"Four. No, five. Tell her I'll get a new one soon and call her as soon as I can."

"Well, Blake," her grandfather turned to the third man at the table, "I didn't hear you say what you think of that bay horse Lije is trying to sell you."

"He's good," the man answered, turning his head to the side and smiling. "But I don't want to say how good for fear Lije will raise the price. We haven't started dickering yet."

With the focus safely on rodeo and horses, Patty was able to sit back and pretend to be interested in the conversation. But the longer she sat, the more it hurt to see Lije's hand touching his wife's shoulder, lightly but possessively. Patty wondered if the ache in her heart would ever go away.

"Is this a private party or can anyone join?" Morgan Kincaid's low, drawling voice made Patty feel tense all over.

"Pull up a chair and sit down, Morgan," Lije said.

Patty heard the sound of chair legs scraping on the barroom floor, then felt a hand at the back of her chair.

"Move over, Skinny," Morgan ordered with mock gruffness.

Flashing him a fiery look of indignation, Patty slid her chair away from Diana's. Every time he used that stupid nickname—and he was the only one who did—she felt like a bag of bones covered with a sack. Not that she was voluptuous, but she did have the basic curves. So why did he have to call her that?

His muscular shoulders and upper arms rubbed against her as he settled into the chair he had placed between the two women. Patty leaned forward a little to avoid making contact, annoyed to feel Morgan settle an arm along the back of her chair, as if she had made room for him to do just that.

"Quite a contrast," Morgan said, glancing from Patty to the silvery blonde. "On one side I have the goddess Diana and on the other, a reincarnation of Annie Oakley."

Spare me, Patty thought. His attempt at humor was even more annoying than his arm, which made it impossible for her to lean back. "And I thought you were going to say something about Beauty and the Beast. You're really believable as a beast, Morgan." Patty smiled with poisonous sweetness.

"Careful, Skinny." He winked. "Your sarcasm is showing."

Lije leaned back in his chair, surveying the two of them with that indulgent look that had always charmed Patty.

"Nothing's changed much, has it?" Lije commented. "You two are still trading insults."

"I guess it's just a case of New Mexico water not mixing with Oklahoma oil," Morgan suggested lazily, sliding Patty a meaningful look.

"I don't think I would've compared Patty with water," Diana said hesitantly. "Maybe air—like a warm summer day."

"No, it's water," Morgan assured her. "Placid and serene on the surface with treacherous undercurrents below. Besides, she's still wet behind the ears."

"Well, you're just like oil—slimy!" Patty retorted.

"Which makes me hard to catch. That's how I've managed to stay a bachelor for so many seasons." Her jab seemed not to have bothered him.

"Fortunately for womankind," Patty said.

Lije took one look at her cross expression and changed the subject. "I thought you said this was going to be your last season on the rodeo circuit, Morgan," he said. "Your brother Alex was going to take over the stock contracting part of your operations, wasn't he?"

"I considered quitting," Morgan said indifferently, "but as you can see, I changed my mind."

What a pity. Patty decided not to say that out loud.

As if reading her thoughts, Morgan darted her a knowing glance that showed his amusement at her dislike of him.

A callused brown hand clamped itself on Lije's shoulder. "Ya sold Blake that hoss yet?" Lefty Robbins asked gruffly.

"I'm trying," replied Lije.

"Hello, Lefty." Diana smiled, looking up at the short, wiry cowboy standing behind her husband. Her blue gaze moved to the cast on his arm. "How did you break your arm this time?"

"Ah, one of Morgan's buckin' horses squeezed my arm in the chute. My bones are gettin' so brittle, they break if ya look at them cross-eyed." His leathery face was cracked by a smile. "Hey, let's talk about happier things. I hear you're going to have an addition to your family, Lije."

An incredibly proud light gleamed in Lije's gray eyes as he exchanged a look with his wife. "That's right," he admitted.

"Congratulations." Patty had to force the word past the lump in her throat. "I-I think that's great."

"Thank you," Diana said warmly. She took Lije's hand and held it. "We're very happy about it, aren't we, honey?"

Her husband nodded and kissed her on the cheek. Patty winced.

"Instead of congratulatin' someone else," Lefty spoke up, "you should be gettin' married and havin' one of your own, Patty. Don't you think so?"

The corners of her mouth trembled as she tried to make them curve into a smile. "I'm afraid I'm not the marrying kind, Lefty." With Patty it was all or nothing, and if she couldn't have Lije, nothing was what she wanted.

"Well, Skinny, if you're not the marrying kind, are you the dancing kind?" Morgan Kincaid didn't give her a chance to reply as he pried her fingers free of the knot she had twisted them into and spun her out of her chair. Before she could plant her feet, he was pushing her onto the dance floor.

"If you call me Skinny one more time, I'll break

a beer bottle over your head," she threatened in a hissing undertone. She tried to pull her arm free of his iron grip. "And I don't want to dance with you!"

"I never asked whether you wanted to or not," he replied calmly, winding an arm around her slim waist. "You should be thanking me for saving you from some considerable embarrassment."

"What are you talking about?" Patty demanded.

Still holding her hand, he raised it with his. He freed one fingertip to touch the tear that trembled on the edge of her lashes.

"Right now you're so busy hating me that you've forgotten you were about to cry." He gave her a smug smile.

"I was not," Patty said. "And you would've laughed if I had."

"You can't see me as a knight in shining armor, is that it?" The hand on her back made her follow his steps.

"No, I can't." She kept her palm spread against his chest, trying to keep as much distance between them as possible.

"The truth is, I wouldn't have cared if you'd embarrassed yourself or not." His dark head was tilted to one side, a faint arch to one of his eyebrows. The cold steel of his eyes contradicted the smile on his mouth. "I like your granddad, though. Since I'd already lost my bet, I was more concerned that your quivering upper lip would collapse and he would be left with the red face. Are you satisfied, Skinny? You were partially right."

She believed what he said was true, but she had had enough of that damned nickname. Gritting her teeth, she replied, "Don't call me Skinny! I've outgrown my training bra."

"Have you?"

The taunting edge of laughter was in his voice. He moved her slightly away from him as if to see.

Unbelievably obnoxious. Patty scarcely knew what to say but she had given him the opening, unfortunately. She found her voice at last. "Stop looking at me like that. It's insulting," she hissed.

"Sorry." He grinned. Obviously, he wasn't.

"As if, Morgan!"

The grooves around his mouth deepened. "You'd better keep your voice down."

Self-consciously Patty glanced around the small dance floor, finally noticing the amused looks directed their way. She felt as trapped as a butterfly on a pin, but she wouldn't give Morgan the satisfaction of knowing that.

"You're insufferable," she murmured quietly. "You actually like making me look like a fool."

"You dig your own hole," Morgan responded dryly. "I just watch."

Long ago she had stopped hearing the music, letting her body automatically follow his lead. When the song ended, her feet kept moving until she bumped into the broad wall of his chest. Before Patty could regain her balance and step back, his arm had tightened around her waist.

"The song is over. Remove your paws," she demanded.

"Yes, ma'am. The beast hears and obeys. But where will you go? Back to our table?"

The band began playing another slow tune. The hand on her back firmly guided her to follow his steps, turning her at a slight angle so she could see the table where Lije was seated. Only he, Diana, and Blake Williams were there.

"Where's my grandpa?" she asked, tearing her

gaze from the sight of Lije's and Diana's clasped hands upon the tabletop.

"He's playing a thrilling game of checkers with Lefty," Morgan informed her. "But you could go back alone. Lije and Blake can talk about the horse and you can help Diana pick out baby names."

"Stop it!" She issued the desperate command under her breath as he moved her in the opposite direction. With a start, Patty realized that her fingers had been digging into the solid muscle of Morgan's shoulder. She tried to relax and let some of the fight drain out of her.

"Staying with me? Good choice," he said.

"I didn't make it," she whispered. "But thanks anyway."

He raised an eyebrow. "You're welcome."

They danced a few measures more without speaking until Morgan looked down into her eyes. "So do you really like following the rodeo that much? Doesn't it get sorta old after a while?"

"No," she said quickly. "I like the excitement. What are you getting at?"

"Well, at the table, you said you weren't the marrying kind," he reminded her. "But we both know that it's more a case of 'if you can't be Mrs. Masters, you don't want to marry anyone.' That leaves you the circuit."

"I was thinking about opening a stunt riding school in a few years," Patty replied without much enthusiasm.

"And where do you plan to locate it? In New Mexico? On your parents' ranch? Next door, so to speak, to Lije?" Morgan said softly. "Are you hoping you'll have a second chance with him?"

A weary frown creased her forehead. "I'm tired, Morgan. Will you please leave me alone?" She looked up at his face. His expression was thoughtful, which surprised her.

"Guess you'd like to go."

Patty didn't answer but looked to the side table where her grandfather and Lefty Robbins were hunched over the checkerboard. Their games were invariably grudge matches that went on for hours. Morgan followed her gaze.

"I'll take you back."

Immediately she stiffened. "No, thanks. I'll take the truck and my grandpa can find his own way back to the trailer."

"Might be the wee hours of the morning before they call it quits," Morgan pointed out. "They'll either have to walk or take a taxi back to the grounds."

"I don't want you to take me," Patty declared, moving away decisively from the big, warm hand on her back. "Besides, Jill will be furious if you leave with me."

"I can't imagine Jill being jealous of you."

"Thanks a lot! You're doing wonders for my self-esteem."

The song ended and Morgan laughed a little. "I only meant that she knows how much you despise me. She won't think that you and I are sneaking off for a passionate rendezvous. Chances are I'll be back before she realizes I left . . . unless you're in a kissing mood."

"Funny you should mention it . . ."

He looked at her hopefully. Disappointing him was going to feel really, really good, Patty thought.

"I'm not. Forget it, Morgan."

Patty broke away and made her way swiftly through the tables to the exit, only to feel Morgan's hand reach around her to open the door.

Her mouth tightened as she walked out of the

door, his long, broad shadow falling over her, blocking out the light from the bar's interior. She took one step in the direction of her pickup and stopped when he spoke.

"You're riding with me," he said.

She turned, arrested for a moment by the sight of Morgan's roughly masculine face above hers, midnight black hair curling upon his forehead. The blue of his eyes was lost in the dark of the night and his downcast lashes. The calm, determined set of his jaw irritated her.

"I have no wish to ride with you," she said frostily.

"We aren't talking about wishes here. You have three choices. We can stand here and argue. You can go with me peaceably or I can carry you. I have to see that you get home safely or your grandfather will give me hell. Now, which is it going to be?"

Their eyes locked in silent challenge.

"Gramps acts like I'm six years old."

"He's protective. What's wrong with that?"

"I don't need to be protected. I wish I were a man sometimes." Patty broke away from his gaze as tears of angry frustration filled her eyes.

"Ya know, it's not as easy as it looks," Morgan said wryly. "Anyway, let's take my truck, get you to your trailer, and my manly duty will be done."

She gave an acquiescent shrug and they walked in silence. He opened the passenger-side door for her, closed it after she clambered up, and went around to the other side, slamming the door when he turned the key in the ignition. The motor growled to life.

Patty fastened her seat belt and huddled against the door.

"Don't worry, Skinny, I'm not trying to compete with Lije or his memory for your favors."

"His memory?" Involuntarily, Patty shuddered. "You make it sound as if he's dead."

"For you, he is."

Patty stared at the profile etched against the window on his side of the truck: the strong, straight nose, the firm mouth and jutting chin. As much as she hated to admit it, Morgan Kincaid was right.

If she truly wanted to get over Lije, she had to bury the past, all her love, memories, and dreams. But they had been a part of her for so long . . .

Patty watched the road stretch away before them into the darkness as they drove, thinking about her future, a troubled light in her brown eyes. She had been living one day at a time. That had to change. A lot of things had to change.

"Cat got your tongue?"

She looked over at Morgan, just able to see the amused crinkles at the corners of his eyes. Before she could reply, she realized that the truck had swung into the rodeo grounds. They were within sight of the trailer and he had parked the truck in front of it in just a few seconds.

The hint of a smile was gone from his face. "What's the matter, Pat?"

"Nothing's the matter," she answered in a taut voice. "I was thinking, that's all."

Her hand searched for the door handle but she paused, not ready to say thank you or good night. Morgan's presence was a compelling force that kept her in her seat, waiting for something to happen. Something she wasn't sure she didn't want. A kiss.

He looked at her, studying the mutinous set of her lips. One side of his mouth quirked upward at the corner. "Make a move. Say something. Hit me. Anything. I can't stand the suspense."

"Please, Morgan. I don't know what to do or say right now."

"Taking requests? How about a kiss? If you let Jack Evans kiss you for luck, why not me?"

"Okay. Go ahead."

Morgan looked at her. "What?"

"I said, go ahead. Kiss me. But it will only bring you bad luck."

He shrugged. "Like the song says, that's better than no luck at all."

His thumb brought her chin up as Morgan accepted her challenge. His breath warmed her lips an instant before his mouth claimed hers. A flash of sensual fire raced through her veins, quickly burning out when the firm pressure lifted from her lips. Resentment smoldered in the look she gave him.

"Sweet dreams." Morgan winked good-humoredly when she slid away from him on the seat. He watched her jump down and go into the trailer without glancing back at him. He grinned again and started the motor.

CHAPTER THREE

Unwrapping the last of the protective leg cottons from the white horse's leg, Patty straightened, arching her back to relieve the fatigue of the long drive. The travel days in between rodeos always seemed a lot longer than other days, with so much preparation to be done before leaving and upon arrival at their destination.

After affectionately stroking Legend's silken neck, Patty gathered the cotton and bandages and walked to the tack compartment of the goose-necked horse trailer. The crunch of footsteps on the gravelly sand sounded behind her and she glanced over her shoulder.

"Hi, Grandpa. Are you all done or do you need some help?" she asked.

"I'm all done except for Liberty," he answered, a look of tired concern on his weathered face. "I thought the roads were smooth enough for him not to need a cold water application midway through the trip, but I guess the long haul was too long. There's a slight swelling in his legs."

"Good thing we don't have a performance tonight." Patty sighed. "Do you want me to help rub him down?"

"No." Everett King waved aside her offer. "Go put on a pot of coffee and get our trailer straightened around."

"Sounds like a plan," Patty agreed with weary enthusiasm, handing the leg wrappings to her grandfather to put away.

As Patty left the stabling area and headed toward their travel trailer, the blare of a semi horn tooted behind her. She slowed her steps to wait for the large truck to pass. The stock trailer behind the semi was emblazoned with the words Kincaid Rodeo Company. The semi shifted gears and rolled alongside her.

"Hello, Princess. Where are you off to?" The driver slowed to a stop and stuck his head out of the window, his wide-brimmed white hat tipped at a cocky angle to reveal wavy brown hair.

"Hi, Jack!" Patty called, her feet moving lightly over the ground as she walked to the semi's cab. "Just heading to the trailer to fix some coffee."

"Got your horses all settled in, huh?" Jack motioned toward the back end of the truck. "I'll be getting rid of my cargo of bulls pretty soon myself."

"When did you start driving for Morgan?" She stood on the running board to raise herself to his level.

"Since I finished out of the averages at the last four rodeos and discovered my pockets were empty." Jack Evans grinned.

"That's what you get for looking at the buckle bunnies in the stands instead of paying attention to the horse you're riding," Patty teased.

His face lit up and he turned on the practiced cowboy charm. "What I need is a sweet, steady girl to keep me in line. Why don't you volunteer for the job, Princess? We'd make a great combination."

"If I ever took your flirting seriously, you'd fly out of here as fast as a horse that's just backed into an electric fence," Patty replied easily.

"Oh, I wouldn't be too sure about that." He cocked his head to the side as his gaze roamed over her face. "Those baby brown eyes and those two pretty dimples of yours could turn me into a fool for love."

A pair of large, strong hands nearly circled Patty's waist from behind as she was lifted from the running board and set on the ground, despite her startled outcry of protest.

"Sorry to interrupt, Skinny." Morgan's tone was unapologetic. "But I have to get those bulls unloaded and settled in."

"You could've said so!" Patty retorted. "You didn't have to manhandle me!"

The smile he gave her was cold. "Calm down. I didn't manhandle you and you know it."

Jack Evans flashed Patty a guilty grin until Morgan's steely gaze turned to him. "Get that truck up to the pens, Jack."

The cowboy shifted gears. "Right away, Morgan," he said cheerfully, raising a one-fingered salute to Patty. "See you later, Princess."

"What are you princess of?" There was a mocking look in Morgan's eyes. "Ice or snow?"

Since the night at Kelly's bar more than a week ago, Patty had deliberately ignored Morgan, responding with chilly civility only if he spoke directly to her. "You'll have to ask Jack," was all she said.

"I wondered how long it would take Jack to put the moves on you. He's gotten around to nearly all the other girls on the circuit."

"Look who's talking!" There was a haughty arch to her eyebrow.

Her indignation seemed to amuse him. "Well, I'd love to stand here and argue with you, if only to keep in practice. Unfortunately, I have other things to do." He took her by the shoulders and turned her around to face her trailer.

Patty whirled right back around. "Get your hands off me!"

"What's the matter? Afraid I'll slap you on the rump?" He grinned wolfishly. "That would be fun. But I'm too much of a gentleman."

"Like hell you are!"

Her response only made him laugh. "Get along home, Skinny. You can sharpen your tongue on me another day."

Patty looked around for something to throw that wouldn't do too much damage, but there were only a few pebbles at her feet. Throwing a pebble would only make her look ridiculous and he wouldn't even notice. Besides, Morgan's long strides had already taken him several yards away in the direction of the semi.

With her target practically out of range, she pivoted sharply toward the trailer, her unvented temper making her walk fast. She cursed herself for letting Morgan Kincaid get under her skin the way she did.

It was that know-it-all attitude of his that irritated her—that, and the way he laughed at her. All she had to do was see him and the happiest song would hit a sour note.

When the old-fashioned enamel percolator was filled with water and coffee, Patty set it on the small propane stove and lit the burner with care. She began putting back the breakable items she had packed away before the morning's journey. She was in the bedroom setting a battery-powered clock on the small shelf near the bed when her grandfather came in.

"Coffee's not ready yet," she called out. "Do you want to shower and change while you wait?"

"No, I don't think so," he answered.

"I think I will," she said, speaking her thoughts aloud without actually addressing her comment to him. She ran a hand over her hair. "Gotta wash this hair sometime."

"You go ahead, girl." Her grandfather nodded as she stepped from the bedroom into the narrow hallway and opened the door to the closet containing the bath towels and bedding.

Patty paused and leaned against the wall, her expression serious. "Gramps, there's something I've been meaning to talk to you about."

"Do you want to save it for another time, honey?" He bent to peer out the window of the trailer. "Pete Barber just walked by and I wanted to talk to him about using the arena tomorrow for practice. We'll discuss whatever it is another time, okay?" With a wave of his hand, he was walking out the door.

With a shrugging sigh, Patty hung the bath towels on the rack beside the shower stall, walked into the small kitchen to turn down the fire under the bubbling coffeepot and returned to adjust the water temperature for her shower. A few minutes later she was beneath the refreshing spray, the tingling jets of water massaging her tired muscles.

She had just lathered up her hair when she heard the trailer door open and her grandfather walk in again. "The coffee is done," she called. "You can pour yourself a cup now."

Ducking her head under the spray to rinse away the shampoo, Patty called out again. "The thing I wanted to talk to you about was next year's bookings. I'd like to change our tour to another circuit."

"Why?" was his answering question.

Her hair squeaked clean and she turned off the water, stepping from the shower to wrap herself in one towel as she dried herself with the other.

"I know all the arguments for staying here," she replied. "It's closer to home. The dates are all fairly close, so we don't have very many long trips to make from one rodeo to another. And we've performed in all these places before, so they know us and it's easier to book. But I think it's time we made a change, saw a different part of the country."

She paused, staring at the wall as if she could see through it to the kitchen on the other side. Her mouth twisted wryly.

"The truth is, Gramps, I want to get away from the people who've known me since I started in the business. They all remember me as that pigtailed little girl who followed Lije around. They mean well—some of them do, anyway—but I'm sick of their sympathy."

She tossed the towel on the rack, aware of how clipped her voice sounded but unable to control it. "Especially Morgan Kincaid! I know you like him but I just can't stand him!"

Reaching for the robe that she usually kept on the bathroom hook, Patty discovered it wasn't there. The clink of a cup against a saucer sounded from the kitchen as she reached for the damp towel on the rack and wrapped it sarong-style around her body, knotting the top two corners together.

"Before you start telling me all the reasons why it's impossible to switch circuits, pour me a cup of coffee," she called out.

Her grandfather's muffled okay was followed by movements in the kitchen and another clink of a cup while Patty wiped up the scattered droplets of water that had escaped from the shower. She and her grandfather had discussed the possibility of changing their tour before, right after Lije was married. At the time she had been too miserable to argue and had simply accepted his reasons to stay with the same circuit.

But that was then and this was now. The shower had invigorated her and she was ready to do battle. He would find that she wasn't so easy to convince this time. As she stepped from the small bathroom into the narrow hallway, a cup of coffee was held out to her.

Patty froze at the sight of the large hand that held it. Her gaze moved to their visitor's face. The searing heat in her cheeks wasn't the result of the warm shower, but from the appraising look Morgan Kincaid was giving her. Taking his sweet time, he inspected her from bare head to bare toe, stopping to survey all the bareness the towel exposed in between.

"What are you doing here? Where's Grandpa?" Patty breathed, unable to meet the bright gleam in Morgan's eyes or see past the massive shoulders to the living area of the trailer.

"Outside, talking to Pete." The hand holding the cup moved forward. "Don't you want your coffee now?"

With fumbling fingers, she took the cup from him, her knees quivering at the intimate way he kept looking at her. The warmth from the cup was comforting and she wrapped her fingers around it to give herself some strength.

"Was that you I heard come into the trailer? Grandpa didn't . . ." Her voice began to tremble, too.

"Gramps didn't hear a word you said. You'll have to repeat your carefully rehearsed speech again." Morgan smiled at her with infuriating complacency.

"You knew I thought my grandpa was out here. You could have told me," she said accusingly.

"I didn't find out anything that I didn't already know, so what's the harm?" He lifted one shoulder in a mocking shrug.

"None!" Patty retorted. "I mean, I can't stand you and I'd say it to your face! But that was supposed to be a private conversation. If you had any manners, you would have let me know you were here." She set a hand on her hip in challenge. "Exactly why are you here?"

"I wanted to talk to you and your grandfather together," Morgan replied easily. "He was busy with Pete, so he suggested that I come in here and wait. The coffee was your idea. Incidentally, you make very good coffee."

"Oh, choke on it!" Patty snapped, turning to go to her bedroom in the rear of the trailer.

"So you've decided to run, have you?"

"Yeah," she said, throwing him a furious look over her shoulder. "All the way down this ten-foot hallway. Big, dramatic exit, isn't it?"

"I was talking about you leaving this circuit."

She stopped and turned to face him. "That isn't running. That's a new start."

He just stood there and she didn't feel like listening to his answer.

Patty entered her bedroom and took the few remaining steps to her bed. "Why am I explaining my reasons to him?" she said aloud. Whether it had been the blood pounding in her ears or a subconscious belief that Morgan wouldn't follow her, Patty didn't hear his footsteps. Not until his voice came from inside the doorway did she realize he was behind her.

"Get out of my bedroom!"

The knots she'd made in the towel almost slipped loose when she whirled around, but he wasn't looking at her. Good thing, too, because she was still holding the cup of hot coffee.

His gaze swung with casual interest around the cramped space. "Is this yours or does your grandfather sleep here?"

"Grandpa sleeps on the couch, not that it's any of your business. And he doesn't collect stuffed animals." She picked up a tattered teddy bear with her free hand and shook it threateningly at him.

"Ooh. I'm scared now."

"Leave, Morgan!"

He didn't move.

"I want to get dressed. So get out. Is there any part of those two short sentences that you don't understand or didn't hear?"

He shook his head. "No, I heard you clearly."

Her teeth were grinding together as her nerves reached overload. His powerful body seemed to fill the room, and the force of his masculinity was overpoweringly apparent.

"I'm going to kill you. I mean it!"

He took the teddy bear from her hand and tossed it on the bed. "Not with this."

"I'll find something—"

"Too bad you wear jeans all the time," he said, continuing to ignore her fury. "You have great legs. Really great." His gaze moved from her bare thighs to the shadowy cleft between her breasts, just visible above the towel wrapped around her body. "Along with other things," Morgan added suggestively.

A crimson flush tinted her cheeks as she hitched the towel higher. Her protective gesture made him smile in a very male way.

"I have to get dressed," Patty repeated. Nothing was going to happen—her grandfather was right outside—so why was she nervous?

"Don't mind me."

The casual step he took farther into the room prompted Patty to take an immediate step backward. Her complete concentration on his presence blocked out her awareness of how close she was to the bed. She backed into it, lost her balance, and started to fall onto its softness.

Morgan's reflexes were swifter. With lithe coordination, a saving arm circled around her waist while his hand removed the spilling cup of hot coffee from hers.

The next breath she took, she found herself held closely against his chest, the towel around her wet hair brushing his tanned cheek. The rough denim of his Levi's was rubbing against her thighs while one of her hands clutched his shirt and the other kept a death grip on the towel.

Drawing a shaky breath, Patty tilted her head back to see the amused glitter in his eyes through the smoky veil of his half-closed lashes. The pressure of his hand against her arching back increased slightly, bringing her closer. Her coffee cup was now sitting on the shelf near her bed and his free hand moved slowly up her arm to caress her smooth shoulder.

Her heart gave a leap as she noticed the deliberately slow descent of his mouth. Twisting her head away, she gasped at the provocative touch of his lips along her neck. Flames of sensuous delight licked her skin, emanating from the sensitive area he was exploring.

"Let me go." She breathed erratically, not really wanting him to stop but afraid she would lose the towel. If she did, they'd be going from zero to sixty in about five seconds flat and she knew she wouldn't say no.

"Kissing you could become a habit," he murmured against her neck.

"A bad one," Patty answered, fighting the shivery sensation that was running up and down her spine.

Morgan kept right on tenderly kissing her neck, his searching mouth moving higher every second. She tried half-heartedly to elude him by turning her face to the opposite side, an action he seemed to anticipate. His hand was there to halt her chin so the sensual warmth of his mouth could find hers.

The awkwardness of hanging onto the towel faded away. She gave in to the moment . . . but Morgan chose to end the kiss.

She gasped, stood up straight, and took a hasty step toward the hallway door. At least she could escape if he tried to kiss her again—not that she was sure she wanted to escape. Her jerky, uncoordinated move was her downfall. The knotted towel came loose at last and she grabbed at it.

"Want me to tie that for you?" Morgan grinned.

"Don't you come near me!" she warned in a husky voice, clutching the towel with both hands.

But he took a step toward her anyway, catching her by the waist by the second step when she turned to run down the hallway. She twisted and wriggled to be free, kicking at him with her bare feet and encountering only the hard leather of his cowboy boots.

"If you don't stop it,"—a gleam of amused indulgence lit his eyes despite the firmness in his voice—"I'm going to throw you on that bed. Now stand still."

Patty started to ignore his command and continue her struggles, until she felt his hands on her waist and her feet lift from the floor.

"All right!" she said, gasping out her agreement in a panicked voice.

Morgan set her on the floor. "You're the hardest person in the world to help." His large hands kept their grip on her waist as if he expected her to start fighting him again.

"Nobody likes to accept help from someone they don't like," Patty snapped. "Especially if nobody—I mean me—is wearing only a towel and someone—I mean you—shouldn't be in my bedroom in the first place."

He nodded. "Got it. I think."

She took a deep breath and summoned up whatever dignity she could. "If you really want to help me and not embarrass me, you would leave this room and give me privacy to get dressed."

He only shrugged. "You may be right. I'll try to remember that next time I see you in a towel."

"Hey, you walked in on me. Not like I could help it."

He pulled the edges of the towel from her fingers with a movement that was swift and sure. Before she could recover from her surprise, the towel was firmly in place. The tingling warmth in the breast he had accidentally touched sent hot flames of embarrassment up her neck.

"You're all cinched up again." Morgan laughed sensuously. "Do you feel better?"

"I won't feel better or safe until you're out of my sight!" she retorted.

The grooves remained around his mouth as his gaze narrowed on her face. The hand that had been negligently hooked in his belt loop moved to capture her chin.

"I'd hate to have you find out you're wrong about thinking that way," he murmured.

Her fingers closed over the steel sinews in his wrist, trying to push his hand away from her chin. But she stopped when the firm pressure of his mouth was on hers, lingering and warm. She decided to enjoy it—and then . . . oh, hell.

"Well, well, well. What's going on here?" Her grandfather's curious, laughing question made Morgan release her instantly. Patty stiffened, feeling like a teenager caught doing something she shouldn't. *You are over twenty-one*, she reminded herself. *And you never did say no*.

There was nothing hurried or guilty in Morgan's actions as he turned toward her grandfather. "You should have come in sooner. A minute ago, Patty was in danger of losing her towel."

Her eyes widened with righteous indignation. "Gramps, tell him to get out of my bedroom!"

"That sounds like her grandmother's rolling-pin voice." Everett King chuckled. "You'd better retreat while you're still in one piece, Morgan."

Before turning to go, Morgan touched a finger to the tip of her slightly tilted nose. "Get some clothes on," he said with mock authority. "You shouldn't walk around like that. You might catch cold."

"Oh, get out of here, Morgan Kincaid!" Patty said through clenched teeth.

He met her glare and winked. "It's all right, Skinny. I'm going right now, but you really don't have to put on an act for your grandfather's benefit."

Everett King seemed to be trying not to laugh. So much for being treated with respect, Patty thought angrily. Wasn't he supposed to say something grandfatherly and stern?

As the two men walked away, Patty reminded herself that Everett often said his grown-up granddaughter was entitled to lead her own life so long as she made safe choices about it. He just wasn't judgmental by nature, even if he was a little overprotective sometimes.

But not this time. She was embarrassed by his evident assumption that she had enjoyed her, uh, time alone with Morgan. But she hadn't. Well, that wasn't entirely true. Parts of it were great. The man could really kiss.

She just stared at them a moment longer, then Patty slammed the bedroom door as best she could—there were definite disadvantages to living in a trailer and today, not being able to slam a door when she wanted to was a big one. She stamped to the small closet to yank out some clothes to wear.

As she dressed, she heard their quiet voices filtering into her room from the opposite end of the trailer. With her clothes on and the towel removed from her wet hair, the voices faded, and the outside door opened and closed three times. Once the snarls were combed out of her hair, Patty walked to the door, listened silently and heard nothing. Morgan was gone.

Or so she thought until she walked into the hallway and saw the ebony blackness of his hair against the ivory curtains at the window behind the couch. The roughly carved face was turned toward her, his knowing blue eyes inescapable. When he let himself look lower, at her jeans and checkered blouse, Patty turned back toward her bedroom, determined not to endure any further teasing.

"Patty, come in here," her grandfather called out loudly.

"What for?" Her hand remained on the doorknob to her room. She didn't turn around, knowing that Morgan was still looking at her.

"Do you remember where I put your resume? I've looked everywhere and can't find it." The sound of papers being shuffled muffled the rest of what he was saying.

"It's in the folder with those publicity photographs," she answered.

"I can't find that either." Everett King sighed. "I don't know where you hide things in this damn trailer!"

"Can't I look for it later?"

The faintly desperate tone of her voice prompted a deep chuckle from Morgan. "What she means, Everett, is after I leave."

Patty turned around at last, annoyance flashing in her eyes. "You read my mind. That's exactly what I mean."

"This is business, Patty," her grandfather said

calmly. "So skip the temper tantrum. Morgan wants to take your resume with him when he leaves."

His quiet reprimand brought her back to the living room. "Why does he need it?" she asked defiantly.

It was Morgan who replied instead of her grandfather. "A feature writer for the local newspaper wants to do an in-depth article on rodeo life—the people, the animals—everything. Since your specialty act follows the circuit, I thought I'd get some background material on you. Your experience, age, future plans, et cetera."

"Morgan plans to meet the reporter tonight," her grandfather added, "and I've arranged it so he can interview you tomorrow after you've practiced."

"Thanks for telling me," she said, looking from one man to the other.

"I didn't know a thing about it until Morgan told me just now," Everett replied. "Now don't be so cantankerous. Publicity sells tickets—and this here is free publicity. Can't turn that down. We got horses to feed and a show to put on."

It was difficult to dispute that, as much as Patty wanted to, if only to thwart Morgan. The corners of her mouth turned down in resignation as she walked to the compact bureau against the wall near her grandfather. Flipping through papers stacked on the shelf, she quickly found the folder containing the information Morgan wanted. Without a word, she handed it to her grandfather and retreated to the kitchen.

"That should do it," Morgan said crisply, and Patty knew her grandfather had given him the resume.

She kept her back to the two men as she heard

Morgan get to his feet and walk to the outside door. The tingling along the back of her neck said that he was looking at her.

"Okay, I'll be going now," he said casually, though there was a mocking undertone to his words. "I know how anxious Patty is to talk to you about her decision, Everett."

Stiffening with anger, she heard her grandfather's curious voice ask, "Her decision?"

"She's decided that this circuit isn't big enough for the two of us. Next year she wants you to book her on a different one," Morgan explained with open amusement.

Gritting her teeth, Patty glared at him from the kitchen. "Just you wait, Morgan . . . I'll get you for that. You overheard what I meant to tell him."

"It's all right, Patty," Everett said patiently. "You said as much once or twice."

Morgan's mouth curved into a mirthless smile.

"I have half a notion to stay, just to make your life as miserable as you make mine," Patty fumed.

"Then stay. Just so long as you get your way, right?"

"What?"

Morgan waved a hand in farewell. "It's been hell knowing you, too, Skinny." He flicked a look at her grandfather. "I'll see you later, Everett."

Her fingers dug into the edge of the kitchen counter, an unaccountable tightness in her throat at the sound of the door closing behind Morgan.

Patty liked to be liked by others. Although at the moment she thoroughly disliked Morgan Kincaid, she felt an odd little hurt that he should dislike her with equal fervor all of a sudden. That being so, she couldn't figure out why he had kissed her.

Just to prove who was boss, she supposed. She sighed, totally confused.

"What's this all about, Patty?" her grandfather asked gently.

"I just can't stand it anymore!" She shook her head vigorously. "Everywhere we go, he shows up and drives me crazy. Making fun of me, ordering me around—I hate it!"

"You don't exactly turn the other cheek." He lifted one brow in affectionate reproof.

"No, I don't." Patty sighed. "I don't mind so much being called Skinny and Annie Oakley and kid. I know I'm not a raving beauty, not like Lije's wife—"

"That's enough," her grandfather said warmly. "Did I tell you how proud I was of the way you handled things at Kelly's bar? I know seeing her wasn't easy for you."

"Morgan doesn't make it easier with his tactless comments about me and Lije. I want those wounds to heal."

"Maybe he's just trying to make sure all the poison is out so they'll heal without leaving a scar," her grandfather suggested.

She gave him a narrow look. "Have you two been talking about me?"

"Not really. I mean, no." Everett tried to appear nonchalant.

Patty shook her head. "I don't believe you. Grandpa, I've made up my mind. Next year I want to be on an entirely different circuit, as far from him and everyone else as we can get."

"Well, if you've decided and you feel that strongly about it, you can consider it done." He gave her shoulders a gentle squeeze. "Now, I'll take that cup of coffee."

She hadn't expected his capitulation to be that easy. Smiling, she realized that she had forgotten how very understanding her grandfather was. "You don't mind, do you, Grandpa?" She blinked away the tears gathering in her eyes. "I know you have a lot of friends on this circuit."

"I'll make more on another circuit," he said, winking at her. "Should I toss a coin to see whether we'll go north, east, or west?"

She brushed an affectionate kiss on his leathery cheek. "I love you, Grandpa. I don't care which way we go. You choose."

CHAPTER FOUR

"How's Liberty?" Patty asked, tying her hair back with a scarf as she studied the six white horses lined up in pairs.

"The swelling's gone down," Everett King answered. "I couldn't feel any heat in his legs, but I'd take it easy. Get them accustomed to the new arena and loosen them up some, then we'll see."

"Right." She nodded.

Wiping the sweat from her palms onto her faded jeans, Patty walked to the right rear horse and vaulted onto his bare back. Stroking Loyalty's neck, she waited patiently while her grandfather made certain none of the reins were tangled before he handed them to her. With her grandfather walking at Liberty's head, they made their way to the arena.

The horses snorted and bobbed their heads at the newness of their surroundings as Patty guided them around the arena at a walk. As their interest reverted back to her, she stood on Liberty's back, shifting one foot to Landmark when she had achieved her balance. Taking a wrap of the reins, she urged them into a canter, weaving them snake-like through the center of the arena, their friskiness diminishing as they settled down to work.

Only once during the practice session did Patty take the horses through the routine she used for the performance. Constant repetition tended to make the horses anticipate each move before she gave them the signal. That anticipation would lessen her control in the event of a problem, minor or major. She slowed them to a halt at the arena gate where her grandfather stood.

"What do you think?" she asked, glancing from their tossing heads to him. The expectant look on her face faded as she saw she had acquired an audience.

Standing beside her grandfather were Morgan Kincaid, a pretty blonde in a fitted, cranberry red jacket, and a thin man wearing glasses with camera equipment hanging around his neck. Hiding her resentment at their intrusion on her private practice session, Patty nodded politely to the two strangers who were obviously from the local newspaper.

"Liberty doesn't seem to be favoring one leg over another. Should we try a jump, Grandpa?"

He didn't immediately reply as he climbed over the fence and walked over to run an examining hand down Liberty's legs. After an affectionate slap on the horse's rump, Everett made his way to his granddaughter.

"We'll make it a small one, two and a half feet. I don't want to put any strain on him, not with the performance tonight," he said. Patty nodded agreement. Looking past her, her grandfather called out, "Morgan, will you give me a hand setting up the jump?"

When Morgan excused himself to help, Patty noticed the way the blonde watched him swing effortlessly over the fence into the arena. She had seen that animated look before—most women responded like that to the aura of virility that surrounded Morgan.

As Patty moved the horses out at a walk, she wondered why so many women found his male charm so totally exciting when she could take it or leave it. In fact, she found it obnoxious more often than not.

Maybe obnoxious was not the right word, she decided. Perhaps her love for Lije made her immune to Morgan's attraction, or perhaps it was that they just got on each other's nerves without even trying.

The jump was set. Instead of walking to the gate, her grandfather and Morgan moved to the center of the arena. There must be something about Morgan to like, Patty thought as the trotting horses approached the two men, otherwise her grandfather wouldn't regard him as highly as he did.

Liberty stumbled slightly and Everett King immediately waved her to the center of the ring. Again he ran an experimental hand down the horse's leg while the other horses moved restlessly.

"Maybe you should shift him to the wheel position," Morgan suggested quietly. "He's been about a step behind his partner all the time."

"Liberty has always been slower." Patty was quick to defend the horse. "That's one of the reasons why we put him in the lead pair, to steady the others."

Except for a thoughtful look, Morgan ignored her comment. Her grandfather moved away from the white horse, nodding his approval without glancing at Patty.

"Take 'em over," he ordered.

Moving them away from the center, she urged them into a canter, narrowing the circle to avoid the jump for three times around the arena. Each time the horses went by the small jump, their ears pricked toward it, waiting for the signal that would take them over it. Only when Patty was satisfied with the even rhythm of their gait did she widen their circle to put them in the path of the jump.

Checking Landmark's increase in stride as they neared the white rails, Patty noticed the high arch to Liberty's head. While his lead partner gathered himself for the jump, Liberty hesitated for an instant, on the point of refusal before he hurdled the jump. That hesitation threw the others off their stride.

Patty's heart was in her throat, waiting any second for the fall of one or more of the horses. She had to shift both her feet onto Loyalty's back when Landmark fell a neck behind. The low height of the jump saved the day. All the horses went over it cleanly with the exception of Liberty, who clipped the top.

Her knees were trembling badly as she continued the six horses on their circle around the track, ignoring her grandfather's voice when he called her in. Twice around she went, settling the horses into a steady canter and waiting for her legs to stop shaking beneath her. Then she widened their circle to include the jump again, certain in her own mind that Liberty's easy stride indicated he was not hurt.

The pricked ears signaled the nearness of the jump. Her voice urged the last two horses over. This time Liberty did not hold back, but leaped into the air in perfect precision with his teammate Lodestar. Not until they had made an almost complete circle of the track after the jump did Patty draw a breath of relief and turn the horses toward the stern countenance of her grandfather.

"I nearly found out what the arena tasted like on that first one!" Her laugh was shaky. She knew she'd had a close call.

"That was a damned foolish stunt!" Morgan snapped. Eyes the color of blue diamonds glared at her from the harsh ruggedness of his face.

"If Liberty had hung back the second time, I would have turned them away from the jump," Patty retorted sharply. "If I'd let him get by with it this morning, he might have tried to refuse tonight. On a bigger jump. You know he wouldn't have been able to clear it at the last second like he did this one."

"Your grandfather didn't think so. He called you in—or didn't you hear him?" Morgan already knew she had, but he was deliberately baiting her.

Patty glanced at her grandfather, who was virtually ignoring the sharp exchange as he examined Liberty again. She slipped astride Landmark an instant after Morgan had walked to his head, a steadying hand closing over the bridle.

"Yes, I heard him." Seething temper made her voice tremble. "But my judgment of the situation told me to take them over the jump again."

"Yeah? Someone ought to take you over a knee!" Morgan lashed back, fury in his face.

She planted her hands on her hips. "I bet you'd like to be that someone, wouldn't you? Well, you just try it, Morgan Kincaid!"

Without warning, he reached up and grabbed her arm, yanking her off the horse's back. Patty fell against his hard chest, but he made no attempt to check her, letting her momentum take her where it would.

"Watch out, brat!" he growled as she recovered and pulled away from their contact. "Don't tempt me!"

"Why don't you take care of your stupid bucking horses and quit sticking your nose into my business?"

The muscles working in his jaw warned Patty of the tight curb he had on his temper. "I don't know whether it matters to you or not, but the chance you just took added ten years to your grandfather's age. The next time you decide to play Annie Oakley,"— his lip curled with sarcasm—"give a thought to him."

The heat of her anger cooled quickly. He had a point. Her stance softened ever so slightly. Squaring her shoulders, she returned his steel-hard gaze. "Grandpa knows I don't take unnecessary chances."

"But you do put my heart in my throat once in a while," her grandfather interjected, walking to Lodestar's head. "Now, if you two don't mind, I'd like to get these horses back to the stables. And that reporter you brought along might be getting impatient, Morgan."

The broad chest rose and fell as Morgan took a deep, calming breath. "Carla wants to interview you," he told Patty, "and get some pictures of you with the horses."

"Yes, sir. Anything to please you, Mr. Kincaid." She spoke a little too softly for her grandfather to pick up on her sarcastic tone.

Morgan's gaze narrowed on her for a split second before focusing on the two spectators at the arena gate. He waved at them to enter while Patty walked to Landmark's head, using the time to calm herself down. She managed to smile quite naturally when Morgan introduced her to Carla Nicholson, the feature writer, and the photographer, Fred Kowalski.

"What beautiful animals," Carla murmured.

"Wow. Pure white, aren't they? They're so graceful and spirited." She flashed Patty a professional smile, making Patty feel awkward and unsophisticated. "I hope their names match their beauty."

"The front pair are Liberty and Lodestar," Patty recited. "The middle ones are Legend and Legacy, and the wheel horses are Landmark and Loyalty."

"Alliterative and imaginative names. That's a nice touch. Fred, get some good shots of Ms. King with the horses."

When the photo session was over, her grandfather led the horses from the arena. Patty remained, patiently answering all the questions that had been put to her before at one time or another. Despite the way Carla focused her attention on Patty, she had the feeling that the reporter was determined to impress Morgan more than anything else.

"Considering how well trained your horses are, how do you feel about the other horses in the rodeo—specifically, the bucking horses?" Carla asked.

Patty had never fielded that question before, but she replied quickly. "If you're asking if I have any favorites, the answer is yes." She smiled. "Red River."

The blonde leafed back through the pages of her notebook. "I believe Morgan mentioned that horse, didn't you?" She glanced quickly at him.

"Yes." He nodded. "He's been bucking horse of the year a few times. This will be his last season on the circuit."

"I remember." A smile warmer than any Carla had given Patty spread across the reporter's face as she looked at Morgan. "You told me you were going to retire him this year. I wanted to look at some of your stock. Would you mind, Patty, if we walked to the pens now?"

"Of course not," Patty answered.

She half expected the woman to fall into step beside Morgan, but he and the photographer led the way while Carla Nicholson continued her questions.

"Why is this particular horse your favorite, Patty?"

"He's something of a ladies' man, I guess," Patty explained. "He's very affectionate when there's a woman around, although he still won't let one ride him."

"Do you know how he got his name?"

Morgan answered, "My father kept hearing about this Texas rancher in the Red River Valley, who had a horse nobody had been able to ride. He went to see him, got bucked off, and bought the horse. Originally he was named Star. After the first year on the rodeo circuit, he was referred to so often as the horse from Red River that my father changed his name."

When they arrived at the enclosure containing the bareback stock, Morgan whistled. A golden chestnut separated itself from the other horses, trotting close to the rails and stopping to toss his head at the man who had summoned him. Not until Patty climbed onto the rail did the chestnut horse with the white star on his forehead come closer to butt his head affectionately against her leg, muscular and sleek, moving lightly on his hooves. The gray-white hairs around his nose were the single clue to his age: twenty-one years.

The blond reporter remained on the ground on the opposite side of the fence from the horse, admiring him through the slatted rails.

"He's really friendly," Morgan said, a warm smile softening his face. "Come on, I'll give you a hand up onto the fence so you can get a good look at him."

Patty found that warm smile a little grating, not to mention unnecessary. Carla Nicholson was clearly already under his spell. Although she pretended an interest in the horse, she saw the provocative look the reporter gave Morgan when she was perched on the fence beside him.

Neither the fitted jacket nor the strappy high heels were what Patty would have chosen to tiptoe through the rodeo grounds. She wondered in passing if she disliked Carla because the reporter reminded her more than a little of Lije's wife.

The mocking glint in the look Morgan gave Patty made her face hot. She had the uncomfortable feeling that he was reading her mind again.

"He's a gorgeous horse," Carla was saying. "It's a pity an animal like that has to earn his keep by bucking in a rodeo. It must be a tough life for him."

Morgan chuckled. "If there is such a thing as reincarnation, I'd like to come back as a bucking horse! So far this year, Red has come out of the chute fifteen times. Five of those times he was ridden to the eight-second limit. This year he'll actually work only four minutes total. In return, he's fed, watered, sheltered and cared for as if he were a thoroughbred racehorse. If that's a rough life, I'll take it."

"But surely those four minutes are painful. Isn't that strap around his middle cinched tight to make him buck?" the photographer asked.

Morgan exchanged an amused smile with Patty before he turned slightly on the rail to call to one of the cowboys standing not too far away.

"Kirby, bring me a flank strap." He turned back to Carla and Fred. "The hue and cry that's raised every so often at the apparent cruelty of the rodeo isn't based on fact. Yes, we do have a few tricks to get animals to perform in a certain way. And horses have a few tricks of their own."

He looked down at the horse docilely nuzzling Patty's hand.

"If you put an ordinary saddle on Red," he continued, "or any horse in the string, he would buck the average rider off every time. It's his nature. He's discovered he can get rid of the rider and be his own boss, so he'll do it every time he can for the sheer fun of it."

The flank strap was handed to Morgan by the cowboy who had fetched it. Morgan handed it on to Carla and the photographer for their inspection.

"In rodeos, the flank strap is used to get the best performance out of the horse. It's fastened around his belly, back by the horse's hindquarters. Just like a saddle cinch, it can't be fastened too tight or it will interfere with a horse's movement. If that happens, chances are he'll simply stand in one spot and wait until you loosen it."

Morgan turned the strap up so they could examine the area that actually touched the horse's belly. "This wool padding on the underside is partially for the horse's protection. But its main function is to tickle the horse's belly. Essentially what happens is that a horse will kick out with his hind feet, trying to stretch away from the object that's tickling him, exactly as a human would do. The result is that he becomes harder to ride, even for a professional rodeo rider."

"You mentioned that Red River came from a

ranch. Is that where you find the majority of the rodeo stock?" Carla asked.

"For the most part," Morgan said. "Dependable bucking horses are a rare commodity and a good one is expensive. That wild, stubborn streak is generally being bred out of today's horses to make more tractable mounts."

"Do the people contact you and tell you that they have a horse that bucks?"

"Either that, or when a rodeo is in town, the owner brings the horse in for the stock contractor to try out."

"Have you ever competed?"

"When I was younger and more foolish," he replied with a wide grin.

"What about you, Patty? You're a phenomenal rider. Have you ever thought about getting on a bucking horse?"

"Thought about it? Sure. Lots of times." She shrugged. "I mean, as a lark, just to see if I could, I guess I would. But I don't think I would ever do it professionally. I get plenty of thrills and risk in my own act."

"Are those the bulls in the far pen?" Fred asked. "Let me just get a few of Red River before we move on." He took several shots of the chestnut horse and pressed the button to close the lens of his digital camera.

"That's right. Would you like to see them now?" Carla nodded eagerly.

"I'd better go help Gramps with the horses," Patty said, sliding easily from the top rail to the ground.

The photographer kept a protective hand on his camera as he swung down. A vaguely helpless look crossed Carla's face as she stayed on top of the fence rail. In the next instant, Morgan, who had been the first to climb down, was reaching up, his large hands closing around her waist and lifting her safely down.

Patty wanted to gag. It wasn't as if the ground was a million miles away. Even in those dumb high heels, Carla could have managed to get down herself. Patty turned away to hide her scowl.

"I want to thank you for your time, Patty."

Carla offered her hand, and good manners dictated that Patty take it. Besides, Morgan was watching her a little too closely.

"You have a very interesting and exciting life," Carla continued.

Patty knew it might seem that way to a stranger, but those weren't the adjectives she would have used. The grind of constant travel, practice and almost nightly performances had become monotonous. Perhaps the magic had worn off—or maybe it was just that nothing seemed like much fun since Lije had married.

"My pleasure." Patty nodded politely. "I know you'll find the rest of the tour just as interesting. Well . . . gotta go. Nice to have met both of you."

Fred, who was fiddling with his photographic gear, didn't even look up. Patty took a first step but not a second one.

"Wait!"

The clipped command was emphasized by a halting hand on her wrist, the hold seemingly casual, but Patty knew she could not escape Morgan's grip if she tried. Without a word of explanation, his gaze swiveled to the grizzled cowboy walking by with his arm in a cast.

"Lefty, would you step over here, please?"

The battered-looking cowboy complied while

Patty made a furtive—and futile—attempt to break free. "I'd like you to meet Carla Nicholson and Fred Kowalski from the local paper. This is Lefty Robbins, a permanent fixture on the rodeo circuit." When the introductions were out of the way, Morgan turned to the blonde. "Would you mind, Carla, if Lefty took you on to the bull pens? I want to have a few words with Patty before I join you."

"Of course not." Carla slid a curious glance to Patty's less than pleased countenance.

As soon as the group was several yards away, Patty no longer tried to conceal her efforts to twist free of his hand.

"I don't know what you have to say to me," she told him in a low voice, "but you don't have to cut off the circulation in my hand to say it!"

He slackened his grip slightly but didn't release her. "I'll get right to the point, Patty."

"How unusual. You're always so reserved."

He ignored her jab. "Listen up. You're not going to ride any bucking stock and that's that."

"Says who?" Patty snapped.

"I do. Just put that ridiculous notion out of your head right now."

"Don't give me orders, Morgan Kincaid," she warned. "You're not my keeper."

"I'll give you any damned orders I please!" He towered above her, but Patty wasn't in the least intimidated.

"Save your breath. I don't have to obey them. I don't work for you, remember? If I decide that I want to ride a bucking horse, you're not going to be able to stop me from doing it, Morgan!"

"Okay, Annie Oakley, but I have a surprise for you." Morgan breathed in deeply to control his temper, blue eyes glittering with complacent triumph. "That rodeo stock in those pens belongs to the Kincaid Rodeo Company. No amateur is going to mount any of them. They're restricted to card-carrying professional riders."

"I'm hardly an amateur!" Patty protested, refusing to give in though his point had been made. "I can ride as well as any man on this circuit!"

"Maybe you can, but you're not going to break your foolish neck while I'm around."

"Maybe?" Her voice squeaked with indignation. "Did you say 'maybe I can'?"

Her free hand clapped onto her hip, a defiant gesture that Morgan knew only too well. "Listen, you pint-sized little witch," he growled. "I'm not going to argue over every word with you! I don't care if you think you can ride every animal in the string. I am not going to give you permission to try! Have you got that?"

"You've made your point. Now let me go." She glowered at him.

"Not until I have your word."

"Let me go!"

He released her at last, but the expression on his face was still unrelenting. His gaze focused on her trembling mouth. "I swear there's only one way to keep you quiet, Patty King. And you and I both know what it is." He brought his face close to hers.

Patty's brown eyes widened. She knew his very masculine mouth was about to capture her lips and she realized, deep down inside, that she wanted him to do just that.

But she didn't want him to know that she wanted him to kiss her—oh, no. She wasn't about to give him that much power over her. She backed up a little. Morgan stepped forward.

"Hey, Morgan!" A couple of passing rodeo hands

stopped to look at them and laugh. "Didn't know you could two-step like that. But you better grab your dance partner. Looks like she's about to cut and run."

Their guffaws stopped him cold, but only for a second. Following an impulse he couldn't resist, Morgan suddenly picked Patty up and threw her over his shoulder. To hell with being protective—she didn't want to be protected—and damn the consequences. He'd had enough of her sass.

She beat at his back with her fists. "Put me down! Do you hear! Put me down!" Her face was flaming with embarrassment. She didn't know what was worse: him ignoring her or the unwanted attention from the rodeo hands.

"You'd better shut up," he said softly. "No telling what I might do next." His long strides began eating up the distance to the stable area. He was carrying her effortlessly.

"What in the world—!" came her grandfather's exclamation.

Patty's somewhat limited view prevented her from seeing Everett's face. She could see the ground beneath Morgan's feet and his boot heels and that was about it. Gasping in outrage, she found herself being unceremoniously dumped into a bale of hay.

"Here's your granddaughter, Everett," Morgan said calmly. He watched her efforts to sit upright and brush scratchy bits of broken hay out of her hair and off her jeans. "Maybe you can talk some sense into her."

Her grandfather's mouth opened, the question silently written in his curious and confused eyes about to be spoken, but Morgan abruptly turned and walked away, leaving Patty to supply the answer.

"What was that all about?" Everett King inquired.

"Oh, Morgan was being his usual obnoxious self, throwing his weight around—or my weight, in this case," Patty answered grimly, brushing hay from her jeans.

"And what set him off this time?"

She looked from her grandfather's face and back down at her clothes. "I just happened to tell that reporter that I'd thought about riding a bucking horse—she asked, so I answered. But I never said I planned to do it, only that I'd thought about it. Anyway, Morgan had to play the dictator and tell me I couldn't do it."

"Well, I certainly hope you don't." He shook his head.

"Don't you start in on me, Grandpa!" Patty warned, and started toward the tack room to soap the leather.

CHAPTER FIVE

The black rein was not lying very smoothly on Loyalty's neck. Patty slid from his neck to adjust it, her trembling fingers nearly competing with her quaking knees. She had given two performances at this particular rodeo and neither had been up to her usual high standards.

A pair of hands closed over her shoulders and she jumped in surprise.

"Hello, Princess, I'm back," Jack Evans greeted her in a soft voice.

The kiss he attempted to brush along her neck misfired as Patty turned around to face him, striving for nonchalance that she was far from feeling. Her glance took in the calf roper still working in the arena, the last event before her performance.

"Hi, Jack. How did you do tonight?" she asked, trying to sound lighthearted.

"I'm gonna be taking the average." He winked with a boastful gleam in his eyes. "And all because of my good-luck princess. We'll have to go out tonight to celebrate."

"I don't know, Jack," Patty hedged, liking the cocky cowboy without really trusting him.

"Sure you do." He curled a finger under her chin. "We're a team. I'll meet you at the stables when the rodeo is over. In the meantime, let me give you back some of the luck you've given me."

The warmth of his lips was comforting, almost reassuring, and Patty responded with gratitude. Not that she was about to admit it, but she had a feeling that she would need all the luck she could get before the night was over.

"Say," Jack said, raising his head and studying her through narrowed eyes with interest, "I'd better keep an eye on you. You've been getting in a little more practice on the side, haven't you? I'm the one who's supposed to be teaching you about kissing."

"Don't be silly. Who would I practice with?" Her gaze sought the arena again as the announcer introduced the last contestant in the calf-roping event.

For the first time she noticed Morgan Kincaid leaning against the inside rails of the arena near the gate. He wasn't looking in her direction, but Patty flushed anyway.

"I'm in next," she said, checking the rein again to be sure it was lying straight, and swung herself onto Loyalty's back.

"I'll be rooting for you from the chutes," Jack promised, and patted her knee lightly before heading off in that direction.

Her mouth began to get dry as she watched the arena being cleared of horses and riders. She glanced at her grandfather standing at Liberty's head. He gave her a thumbs-up and she nodded with a weak smile.

The leader of the small four-piece band looked

at her from the announcer's stand, nodding as he raised his baton. Standing up on Loyalty's back and shifting a foot to Landmark, Patty nodded to Lefty to open the gate. As it swung open, the rousing first notes of "She'll Be Comin' Round the Mountain" were sounded by the band.

The six white horses pranced through the gate, breaking into a spirited, rolling canter while Patty waved to the crowd, who applauded her entrance. Then every sight and sound was blocked out as she concentrated on the routine.

The weaves, the figure eights, all were executed without error. Patty breathed easier as she saw her grandfather supervising the setting up of the jumps, and paid little attention to the process until, after nearly a full turn around the arena, she sensed that something was different.

Her lips tightened when she saw the tall, dark man standing next to her grandfather. Morgan just had to interfere and make the jumps lower than usual.

She reined the horses to a stop beside them. "What's going on here?" she demanded. "Those are supposed to be three-foot jumps."

"We thought it would be safer to lower them," Morgan answered.

"We?" Patty asked. "You mean *you* thought it would be safer. Well, you can just raise them. I take my horses over three-foot jumps, not kindergarten hurdles!"

"Liberty refused the jump this morning," her grandfather reminded her. "You barely avoided disaster, Patty."

"But he took the jump the second time," she said stubbornly.

"Be reasonable," Morgan said in a quiet voice. "Take the horses over the jumps and we'll argue about it when the performance is over."

"Yes, sir. Of course. Not." She turned to him, placing her feet on Landmark's back to get closer. "Why don't you tell me about your plans before the performance instead of now? Changing the height of the jumps could throw my timing off, you know. Did that occur to you?"

Morgan was silent.

"This is just another one of your attempts to trick me into a position where I have to do what you want. It's not going to work this time."

Morgan sighed and shook his head. "Look, Patty, all indications are that Liberty is sound. But he could still be sore. Whatever the cause he seems to have lost his confidence. What does it matter if you have to take smaller jumps for a few nights as long as you don't injure yourself or the horses? He's one of the leaders. He has to have confidence."

Her pride wouldn't allow her to acknowledge that he was essentially right. But if the horse was sound, as he had said, then she regarded the decision as hers and her grandfather's to make—not Morgan's. She jumped to the ground.

"Either you raise those jumps or I will," she declared.

She watched her grandfather and Morgan exchange glances. Everett King gave a resigned shrug and said nothing more. Tight-lipped, Morgan turned away and walked to the jumps. He raised the bars to their customary notches with a few swift jerks that showed how angry he was.

She remounted Landmark and heard the rodeo announcer explain the delay to the audience. "Ladies and gentlemen, there seems to have been an error in the height of the jumps. Patty King is having them raised."

Scattered applause followed his statement but Patty ignored it, setting the horses at a canter and waiting for that moment when their strides settled to a rhythmic pace. Then she turned them to the jumps, talking to them in a soft voice, calming and urging, as the six approached the first hurdle.

Liberty's ears swiveled to the jump, his neck arching a fraction in protest. The momentum of the other horses and the guiding rein carried him to it. Patty held back a silent scream as she heard the solid whack of Liberty's leg against the bar, but he cleared it without mishap, stumbling only slightly as he landed and matched his stride with Lodestar's.

Around the arena curve, the six horses galloped slowly, the double set of jumps coming into their path. Moistening her dry lips, Patty clicked to the rhythmically bobbing heads. The bars suddenly seemed much higher and the stunt more formidable than ever before.

Would they make it over? A dreadful doubt assailed her. As well as she knew her team, as often as she had put them through practice sessions and performances, perhaps she had misjudged the situation just this once.

She had taken her grandfather's silence to mean that he agreed with her and not Morgan. But if she had been wrong—and Morgan in the right after all—she didn't want to think about it. Couldn't think about it now.

Patty knew with grim certainty that it was too late to stop. Closer and closer they came to the first of the obstacles until they were almost directly upon it. As Lodestar gathered himself for the jump, Liberty tossed his head in the air and tried to turn away from the rails. His refusal came too late. There was no room to swing away from the jump.

While Lodestar leaped into the air, Legend crowded the white horse from the rear. Then, valiantly, Liberty tried to take the jump. His front legs cleared it, but his hindquarters caught it squarely, tumbling him to the ground.

In agonizing slow motion, Patty saw the second pair attempt and fail to avoid the fallen horse. Lodestar, unable to continue without his partner, was nearly pushed to the ground by the momentum of the next two tumbling clumsily over the jump.

The bars came down as Landmark and Loyalty joined them, their hooves ripping on the wooden rails. Patty had already shifted her weight to Landmark's back as Loyalty lurched forward and fell into the two horses struggling to regain their footing.

In the next instant she was flying through the air as Landmark went to his knees. Instinct had not allowed her to act swiftly enough to push herself to the outside. Instead she fell between the horses. Pain screamed through her at the impact of her body on the arena floor.

With tightly closed eyes, she waited for the moment when a flailing leg would strike her or a horse's heavy body would roll over her and crush her.

By some miracle neither happened. Except for a few punishing blows, she lay on the sand-clay arena unscathed. Human voices wavered through the chaos of her mind, the searing pain in her chest nearly separating her from reality. The oppressive heat of the horses' bodies was no longer pressing around her. The touch of someone's strong hands forced her lashes to flutter open.

"Don't move!" The order was issued through clenched teeth.

The blazing fire in Morgan's eyes halted her hysterical impulse to laugh. Movement seemed beyond impossible, but at least the order had the reverse effect, encouraging her to move, if only to make sure that she was in one piece.

Her lungs burned in an attempt to fill with air. But she sucked in a breath somehow. Despite her hard fall—or because of it?—she still wanted to show Morgan Kincaid that she couldn't be ordered around, even if she had a woozy idea that her response was totally irrational.

When she tried to push herself into a sitting position, he held her down, running a free hand along her arms and legs to look for obvious injuries.

"I'm . . . a-all right." She gasped and took painful swallows of the dust her fall had raised. "Just got the w-wind knocked . . . out of m-me. Need to . . . sit up."

"You lie down or I'll break your neck, if you haven't already!"

"G-good idea." She lay down again, trying to focus on his furious face.

"I told you not to take the jumps at that height!"

The last thing Patty wanted to hear was a bunch of I-told-you-so's. Acid tears burned in her eyes as she averted her head from Morgan's accusing gaze. Her grandfather kneeled down beside her, his weathered face etched with concern, fear in his eyes.

"For the love of Jesus, shut up, Morgan! She could be hurt bad! Patty, gal, are you really all right?"

Choked, she could only nod that she was, as a tear spilled from one eye to race across a dirt-smeared cheek.

"Says she got the wind knocked out of her." Morgan kept his voice under tight control. "She was damn lucky if that's all it is. And she'll have to be evaluated later for internal injuries and head trauma no matter what she says."

"Help me up, Grandpa," Patty murmured, hating Morgan at that moment for the coldness in his tone.

But it was Morgan's arm that curved around her back, his hands that supported her carefully and gently as he lifted her onto her feet. Her mind had reconfirmed the fact that she wasn't seriously injured, but Patty felt like one big, throbbing ache. Her legs were trembling and as much as she wanted to shake away Morgan's supporting arm, she needed it. The arena thundered with applause.

"Put me back on the horses," she said between gulping breaths as strength began flowing to her legs and arms again.

"Skip the heroics," Morgan snapped. "Besides, which injured horse would you ride?"

With a jerk of her head, Patty focused her gaze on the six white horses. She winced at the sight of the blood-red gash on Liberty's flank and Landmark, who was favoring his right front leg. There were cowboys at each horse's head, soothing the frightened, nervous animals while others worked swiftly to untangle the mess of harness and reins.

"How bad—" Patty could get out no more than that before an enormous lump blocked her throat.

"Nothing looks broken," her grandfather answered, touching her shoulder in reassurance.

"Oh, Grandpa, I'm sorry . . . so sorry," Patty

gulped, tears running more freely down her face now.

"I know, honey," he replied.

"You can skip the tears, too. The damage is done." Compassion was noticeably absent in Morgan's rough tone. "Wave to the crowd so we can get out of here."

Squaring her shoulders, Patty shrugged away from his arm, stepping free to lift an arm in salute to the cheering audience. The horses were already being led to the gate as she turned toward it. With the same determination, she pushed her guilty feelings to the side as she attempted to assess from a distance how extensive the horses' injuries were.

Lodestar was walking easily, as were Legend and Legacy. Patty tried desperately to ignore the eyes that were boring holes in her back.

"Where do you think you're going?" Morgan demanded when Patty turned with her grandfather to follow the horses to the stable area.

"Morgan Kincaid, don't you talk to her like that," her grandfather said forcefully. "Turned out that you were right, but at the moment I don't give a damn. Patty needs to rest."

Morgan drew in a sharp breath and nodded, letting the older man have the last word but flashing Patty a look she couldn't quite interpret.

"I promise you that I'll have the doc check her out thoroughly. You're right about that, too." Everett's voice was weary. "You'd better go to the trailer, Patty. Change your clothes. Maybe fix a cup of tea to calm your nerves."

"Okay, Grandpa." Patty turned and commanded her shaky legs to take her to the trailer. She knew she probably deserved at least some of Morgan's scorn—yet her grandfather's kindness was almost

worse. She was still too groggy to think clearly but
the thought that her own stubbornness might have
contributed to the horses' fall was deeply upsetting.

When she stepped out of the shower a half hour
later, the teakettle was whistling on the stove. She
tossed a teabag into a cup and poured the boiling
water over it, toying absentmindedly with the paper
tag while she waited for the tea to steep. She had
dressed quickly in soft sweats, not wanting to be
chilled after her shower.

The beginning of a headache pounded at her
temples. After the first tentative sip, Patty set the
cup down, her elbows on either side of it, her face
buried in her hands. She couldn't just sit in the
trailer. She had to go to the stables and help.

Her grandfather would simply shoulder the burden, just to let her rest. That wasn't right, especially since it was pretty much her fault that the
accident had occurred in the first place. As much
as she wanted to blame Morgan for riling her to
the point where her good judgment was compro-
mised by her pride, she couldn't.

Patty rose from the table, ignoring the bruises
and stiffness that were just beginning to set in.
Once outside, she traveled the distance from the
trailer to the stables with hurried steps, not stopping until she was at Liberty's stall. The top half of
the stall door was open and her fingers closed over
the edge of the lower door.

A local vet was examining the gash on the white
flank, obviously caused by one of the other horses
as it fell. Patty's heart constricted painfully at the
unsightly wound on the shimmering white coat.

"Is it serious?" Her question came out in a taut

whisper, not carrying to the vet or her grandfather, standing at Liberty's head, preoccupied with the injured animal.

"Not as serious as it looks," Morgan's low voice sounded beside her and Patty turned her head quickly in surprise.

An overwhelming feeling of guilt widened her brown eyes. "I . . . I couldn't stay at the trailer."

His diamond-hard eyes returned her look, his rugged face self-contained and implacable. An odd tension took hold of Patty, making her pulse race.

"So you came here," Morgan observed. "To help?"

"Yes." She nodded weakly.

He glanced at her hands clutching the stall door and he didn't miss their faint tremor. "With those shaking hands? We just got the horses settled down. The last thing they need is anyone that nervous around."

Her knuckles turned whiter as she tightened her hold, the quiet edge in his voice somehow worse than his open anger before.

"It was my fault," she said softly, feeling too ashamed to look directly at him. "I should be here doing something about it."

"Everything is being handled. Your grandfather would rest easier in his mind if he knows you're at the trailer. The shock of the fall hasn't worn off, whether you want to admit it or not."

"I'm all right!" A note of desperation crept into her reply.

"So you keep saying," Morgan agreed. "But you still haven't seen a doctor. And your stiff upper lip is quivering again."

He opened the half door and came out, moving her away from Liberty's stall and into the corridor.

It didn't matter. Busy with the horse, her grandfather and the vet seemed not to have noticed that she was even there. Patty felt her chin tremble and bit into her lower lip, the pain of it almost a relief from thinking. Why did he have to be so perceptive?

"I . . . I can clean the tack or something," she argued.

"If you're trying to assuage your guilt, you'll have plenty to do taking care of the horses over the next few weeks while they recover. In the meantime, you can spend the rest of the night thanking God that the injuries weren't any more serious than they are, and reminding yourself that if you hadn't been so damn stubborn—"

"You don't have to say 'I told you so' again!" Patty broke in sharply. "I don't need you to tell me it was my fault! If you hadn't taken that tone or tried to manipulate me into doing things your way—oh, what's the use!" She ended with a raw sob.

She started to turn her back to him, planning to walk to the tack room and soap down the leather tack but before she could take a single step, Morgan was swinging her off her feet into his arms.

"You're going back to the trailer." As Patty started to struggle, he directed a glare at her. "I wouldn't argue if I were you," he warned her softly. "You haven't been winning too many arguments lately."

Patty held herself rigidly, although a quaking weakness was shuddering through her body. If it had been anyone but Morgan who held her, she would have willingly rested her head against that muscular chest, so broad and so strong. But to seek his comfort and support was something her stubborn pride still would not allow her to do, no matter how miserable she felt.

So, while she stared at the inviting expanse of his denim shirt-clad chest, she kept in view the powerful line of his jaw and the firm male mouth. He had already noticed her quivering chin. She wasn't about to cry on his shoulder.

"I don't want to argue with you. It won't fix anything."

"No, it won't." He adjusted her weight in his arms and strode outside the stable.

"I can walk."

"I know." But he showed absolutely no sign that he was willing to put her down. "But you wouldn't go. This seemed like the quickest way to get you out of the stable."

Her eyes suddenly smarted with tears, self-pity and guilt warring with her dislike for Morgan Kincaid.

"Don't you think I feel guilty?"

"Hey, I do, too," he said coldly. "I knew something would happen. I never should've raised those jumps." They had reached the steps of the trailer when he finally set her on her feet. His intent gaze roamed over her upturned face.

No wonder he was studying her. She was startled by his unexpected admission and it undoubtedly showed.

"I have to take the blame for giving in to that stubborn streak of yours. Not to mention bowing to your damn pride."

In the few seconds it took for him to say this— and it was *not* exactly what she would call taking responsibility for his actions—he opened the trailer door and put her inside.

"If you feel that way"—she turned on him roundly, her brown eyes flashing as he closed the door—"then I understand why you were so mean.

You never even asked if I was all right, just said you would break my neck!"

He sighed. "I don't remember that. But seeing you struggling to get up—and then trying to hold you down—Patty, let me explain. Sometimes talking tough seems like the only way to handle you. Otherwise you're so intent on proving that you're some kind of superhuman female that you'd end up killing yourself. 'Put me back on the horses,' " he mimicked. "The minute your grandfather arrived, you started acting like the heroine of an old Western."

"That's what you're supposed to do when you've been thrown or have fallen," she insisted.

"Not when you're too dazed to know if you're hurt or not."

"Well, I wasn't hurt!"

"I'll believe it when I hear a doctor say it. You could have broken your stupid neck. You could still have a concussion or some other damn thing."

She put her hands on her hips in challenge. "Brilliant diagnosis. Your bedside manner could use some work, but thank you, Dr. Kincaid."

"You're welcome." His tone was gruff.

"Just so you know, I've fallen off horses and hit my head before."

"I believe it."

She ignored that. "Here's what happens: the doctor looks in your eyes with a flashlight to check your pupils, and asks you who the president is."

"Doesn't sound too hard. Even Jack could get that right."

Patty flashed him an oh-shut-up glare. "Then you get the trick question: who is the vice-president? For some reason, I never remember. Then you have to count backwards from twenty. If you can do that, the receptionist gives you the bill. And it's usually a lot, even with the co-pay."

He waited a moment before replying. "If it's a question of money . . ." he began.

She cut him off. "It's not. And it's none of your business. Grandpa will get me to the doctor, not you."

"Somebody had better," he responded curtly.

"Just stay out of it, Morgan."

He shrugged. "I guess you can take care of yourself."

"Don't guess. I can."

Morgan couldn't resist one final jab. "Seems like you have an armadillo hide to go with your stiff upper lip."

"Well, I don't!" Patty's hair danced around her shoulders at the vigorous shake of her head. "And I hate the way you keep making fun of me!"

"I didn't know you listened to anything I said."

She wanted to smack him but lacked the strength. He looked at her without saying anything more.

"Maybe if we . . ." She didn't finish the sentence, unsure of what she wanted to say. "We could be friends, I guess. Grandpa likes you so much I feel like I should." She gave him a level glance. "Sometimes, I mean."

"Don't do me any favors, Patty."

"Okay, whatever! I won't!" she cried, a despairing tremor in her voice.

"You act like you can't stand me, and now all of a sudden you're ready to be my friend. What do you want, girl?"

"I don't know." Her weary sigh was full of emotions she couldn't even name, except for a sense of deep frustration. "But I'm sure as hell tired of all this baiting. I'm tired of trying to defend myself. I'm tired of everything!"

At that last feverish exclamation, Morgan stepped forward, his hands closing over her shoulders.

"You're getting hysterical," he said gently. "The reaction to your accident is beginning to set in."

She tried to twist her shoulders free of his grip, a betraying shine of tears filling her eyes. "Hey, I don't need your shoulder to cry on."

Her attempt to resist was ignored as he pulled her against the hard wall of his chest. "There isn't any other shoulder around," Morgan said softly. "You might as well use mine."

The reluctance she heard in his voice diminished what little consolation he seemed to be offering. Patty tried to push away from him, but his strong, muscular arms had already encircled her.

"I don't want your pity," she insisted. "I don't want anything from you."

"I got that," Morgan answered dryly.

His hand curled around the nape of her neck, bringing her head to his chest and keeping it there. The steady beat of his heart and the warm hardness of his embrace made her feel weak. There was so much comfort in just being held in someone's arms. A surrendering sigh tumbled from her lips as Patty relaxed against him, waves of fatigue sweeping over her. As if she were a child, he gently rocked her from side to side and all her animosity slowly evaporated.

"I was so frightened, Morgan," Patty finally said, a few tears slipping from her lashes to slide down her cheeks.

"I know, kid." There was a husky softness to his voice.

His fingers wiped the tears from one cheek and brushed the hair from her face. The soothing caress was like the rough lick of a cat's tongue.

"The best thing for you to do is climb into bed and get some rest," Morgan said quietly.

Unconsciously Patty wanted to agree, but said nothing for a moment, not prepared to leave the security of his embrace just yet. It was so strangely right.

"Every time I close my eyes," she murmured, "I keep seeing Liberty fall. It's like watching instant replay over and over—I can't turn it off."

Her eyes were closed. As the image flashed through her mind once more, a tiny shudder of terror quaked through her shoulders. A finger raised her unresisting chin. In the next instant, the warmth of Morgan's mouth was covering hers with lazy thoroughness. The cold fear that had gripped her heart slowly melted away.

When he raised his head, she was still clinging to him. Her head was tilted back against his hand, her lips trembling slightly from the satisfying pressure of his mouth. Slowly her eyes opened and she gazed into his face.

The blue of his eyes contrasted sharply with the thick, sooty lashes and the blackness of his wavy hair. There was an obstinate but very attractive power in the hard lines of his features, the straight nose and strong jaw and chin. The virility, the maleness was still there. Yet Patty felt that something had changed. Maybe it was the openness in his gaze—or maybe it was because the usual cynical twist to his sensual mouth wasn't there.

Maybe it was her.

She had an uneasy feeling that she had just given in to something—something she should have guarded against. Whatever it was, her heart skipped a beat. She felt compelled to say something, anything, to break the tension.

"What was that?" There was an edge in her voice. "A kiss to make it all better?"

"Something like that." The arms around her slowly relaxed until she was standing loosely within their circle, no longer molded against his broad chest. "Okay, go to bed. Get some rest." It was an order but one that didn't seem abrasive for a change. "I'll send your grandfather up so you won't be alone."

All she could do was nod in agreement. Morgan had released her a little abruptly and was walking to the outside door. It was true. She didn't want to be alone. But it wasn't her grandfather that she wanted to be with her.

CHAPTER SIX

"I'm not surprised." Patty sighed wearily. She stroked the neck of her black horse as he tugged at the hay in his stall. "But I am sorry it had to be this way. The rodeo producers were paying for a complete equestrian act, not just a solo trick rider. Were they able to find someone to replace us?"

"They didn't say," her grandfather answered with a shrug. "But there are plenty of quality acts around. I'm sure they'll find someone."

"Two months without any income." She sighed again.

"We can't accept any other gigs," Everett King told her with a rueful smile. "Liberty is going to take some time healing and even when he does, I'm not sure he'll be in top form. We might have to start looking for a replacement."

Her brown eyes widened. "A replacement? That means breaking in a new horse."

"That's why I figured we need at least three months. We've been talking about getting a spare horse anyway. This is the time to do it."

"But what about our finances?"

Everett didn't answer.

"How bad is it, Grandpa?"

"Vet bills, feed bills, boarding—it never ends, honey. You know that." It was his turn to sigh. "Liberty's fall put a big dent in our emergency fund and his troubles ain't over yet. And I won't let you max out your credit cards on our expenses. That's no way to live."

"We'll have to go back to New Mexico, won't we?" She scuffed the toe of her boot in the hay scattered along the concrete walkway in front of the stables.

He shrugged. "That's more than seven hundred miles, Patty. Texas is just too damn big. It would be foolish to try to trailer the horses that distance in their condition. Foolish and risky. Besides, the doc said you oughta take it a little easy for a while. And so did your mother."

"You listened in on that phone call?"

"Of course."

"Well, we can't afford to stay here either," Patty pointed out. "Not without any money coming in. It's all going for stalls and feed."

"And the vet. Guess I mentioned that already," her grandfather said.

"We have to go back," she said forcefully. "We can make the trip in stages, resting the horses for a couple of days in between."

"Do you think it's a good idea?"

"Well, yeah." Patty glanced at him in confusion. "It's the only thing we can do. What do you mean?"

"I was thinking about Lije. Back at your parents' ranch, you're bound to run into him and his wife."

For a freezing second Patty couldn't reply. Was it possible that she hadn't given Lije Masters a single thought? Her longing for the man had filled her heart and mind for as long as she could remember. Now, suddenly, the feeling just wasn't there. She couldn't believe it, and had no idea where it had gone.

"Patty?" Her grandfather's weathered hand touched her arm, his voice echoing the concern in his eyes as he gazed into her nearly colorless face. "You just about turned white. What's wrong?"

"I . . . I . . ." Patty stumbled, unable to put into words something she couldn't understand herself.

"Is it your shoulder again?"

"Yes." She seized on that almost with relief. It wasn't exactly a lie—she had strained her shoulder in the fall. "I've been favoring it, I guess," she murmured.

"You're as tense as a bucking horse waiting for the chute to open." He shook his head as his experienced fingers touched the tight muscles in her neck. "Turn around, girl."

Patty did as he asked, turning her back to her grandfather while he began gently kneading the taut cords until she relaxed a little.

"Ooh. That feels great. Right there. Mmm." His touch was expert. "We really can't stay here, Grandpa," she said after a few minutes more, her eyes closed as she enjoyed the soothing massage.

"I don't think we should go back to the New Mexico ranch."

"There isn't anyplace else we can go. Besides, it doesn't matter."

"I still don't think it's a good thing to go stirring up the ashes of a dead fire."

The determination in his tone was obvious. *A dead fire*—the words lingered in Patty's mind. Perhaps that was it. Perhaps she had finally gotten over her heartbreak. She could even visualize Lije's face without feeling much of anything.

"What's the alternative, Grandpa?"

His hands left her neck and shoulders for a moment. She started to turn around and they were replaced. Their touch was firmer than before, a hard strength that demanded her muscles to surrender under its pressure. A sudden tingle raced down her spine and her lashes flew open.

"I've already offered you the alternative."

She hadn't really needed to hear Morgan Kincaid's voice to realize why the hands had felt so different. She pulled free and turned to face him.

"Which is?"

Her grandfather answered for him. "Morgan's ranch is less than two hundred miles from here."

"So?"

"He's offered to let us keep the horses there as long as we take care of them, until they're ready to go back on tour."

"That's your parents' ranch, isn't it?" She had the inescapable feeling that she was being maneuvered again. "Is this your idea or theirs?"

Morgan shrugged. "Does it matter that much, Patty?"

She nodded a little defiantly. "I wouldn't ask if it didn't matter."

"The ranch is a family holding," he said in a slow drawl, amusement flickering in his blue eyes. "There's plenty of room in the stables. I discussed it with my dad. He seconded the invitation."

"Thanks but no, thanks. We don't need your charity."

"It isn't charity. That's just how we do things in Oklahoma." Morgan's broad shoulders moved in an expressive shrug as if he had plainly expected her to take this stand. "I wouldn't be much of a friend if I didn't offer your granddad a helping hand when he needed it. I already warned him that I thought you would refuse."

"You're right. I do!" Patty declared. More than anything, the thought of owing Morgan Kincaid for any reason scared her half to death. Besides, he'd put her on the spot. She had no choice but to make her decision now and think about the reasons why later.

"Well, for my part, I accept," Everett King stated firmly.

"Grandpa!" She turned on him with a look of surprised outrage.

"I've made up my mind." He held up his hand for silence. "Patty, you can argue, shout, throw all the tantrums you want, but you aren't going to change my decision. We can't afford to stay here, and we're not driving back to New Mexico. So I'm taking the horses to Morgan's ranch and you can come or stay as you please."

"What?" Patty looked from him to Morgan, but both men had put on matching tough-cowboy expressions. Were they in league against her? It wasn't right. In the past, she and her grandfather had arrived at major decisions together. Even when she was a teenager, Everett King had treated her as an equal partner and a professional. "Grandpa . . . you don't mean it."

"The way I see it, Patty, we have no choice." There was a look of apology in his eyes, but his determination didn't seem to waver. "Morgan's leaving in a couple of hours with the rodeo stock. The decision has to be made now so he can let them know at the ranch."

With a hopeless sense of frustration, Patty darted

a glance at Morgan, silently accusing him of waiting until the last moment to extend his invitation.

"Guess I should've suggested it earlier," he said calmly. "But yesterday didn't seem like the right time—you were having a rough day."

"Thoughtful of you."

"I try to be thoughtful, Patty."

"That explains why you went behind my back."

He grinned. "I guess I did. You seemed to enjoy the shoulder rub even more when I took over."

"Funny, Morgan. That's not what I meant and you know it."

His dark eyes shot her a despairing look. "I've said it before. You are the hardest person in the world to help. That pride of yours makes you look for an ulterior motive every damn time. Well, I don't have one. It's a straightforward offer to let you stay on the ranch until your horses recuperate and you can get back on tour."

He held her gaze for a long moment, transmitting some silent message that there was nothing for her to worry about. Yet Patty couldn't shake off the feeling that there was. She broke free of the compelling blue eyes and glanced helplessly at her grandfather.

"Will you let them know I'll be there, Morgan?" Everett King asked, not reacting to the unspoken plea in his granddaughter's eyes. "The horses should be able to travel a week from Tuesday."

"I'll tell them to look for you." Morgan nodded, his gaze sliding again to her. "What about you, Patty? Going along?"

Taking a deep breath, she tried to stall for time, hoping that she could come up with a better solution in three seconds or less. Of course she couldn't. There didn't seem to be any other.

"Yes," she agreed, exhaling tiredly and turning away.

"All right," Morgan said. "By the way, you have nothing to worry about. I won't be seeing you for a couple of months or more." He gave her a particularly annoying grin. "So it'll be a well-earned vacation for both of us."

Staring at his hard, strong face, Patty realized she had forgotten that. As much as she disliked him a lot of the time, she wouldn't know what to do without him around to drive her crazy.

"Guess so," she said.

"Who knows?" he drawled. "I might even discover that I miss arguing with you."

Before she could retort that she wouldn't miss him at all, he was turning to shake hands with Everett King and saying good-bye. She felt a vague tightness in her throat as she watched him walk away. The peace and quiet would be wonderful, she told herself.

"I'm sorry, Patty," her grandfather spoke at last.

For an instant, she couldn't think why he was apologizing. "It's all right, Gramps," she answered quietly. "I just wish there was some other way we could've worked it out without accepting Morgan's offer."

"You still can't abide him, can you?"

"You noticed," Patty said wryly.

"He's a good man all the same," Everett King pointed out, then turned toward the stalls. "I'm going to check on Landmark."

Most of the rodeo cowboys had left the day before, but when Morgan pulled out with his men and the rodeo stock a few hours later, the arena grounds seemed like a deserted ghost town.

Patty and her grandfather were busy caring for the injured horses but the loneliness crept in. It wasn't the hustle and bustle that she missed so much as . . . well, at least she didn't miss Morgan, Patty reminded herself. Several times.

Tuesday morning, the day they were to leave, her spirits lightened considerably. She still didn't like the idea of going to Morgan's ranch. Considering her ambivalence about him, she felt guilty accepting his parents' hospitality.

Watching her grandfather load the last horse into the trailer, Patty stood back, trying to understand the conflicting emotions that had her looking forward to the journey and feeling guilty at the same time. The only answer that came to mind was that she was glad to escape the emptiness of the grounds, although being alone and separated from other people had never bothered her when she was growing up on her parents' ranch.

"All loaded up and ready to go," her grandfather announced as he locked the trailer gate in place.

"Do you want me to lead the way or follow?" she asked.

"You'd better follow me for a while until we see for sure how the horses are going to do. When we get to the Oklahoma border, you can take the lead."

"Okay. You go ahead and start out. I'll catch up," Patty said.

"You aren't still mad at me, are you?"

"I'm not mad at you." She frowned.

"You've been so quiet all week, I thought you were upset because I'd accepted Morgan's offer. I only did what I thought was best."

"I know that, Grandpa." She smiled, flashing her

dimples. "And I can't hold a grudge or I wouldn't be going along. But you knew that all the time."

"Still, it makes me feel better to hear you say it." He smiled in return. "Now, we'd better get on the road or we'll be traveling all day."

After a jaunty salute in her direction, Everett King clambered into the pickup's cab and started the motor. Waving her own good-bye, Patty set out for her pickup and the travel trailer parked some distance away. Her grandfather was pulling out of the rodeo grounds gate as she neared her vehicle.

Blinking uncertainly, Patty looked again toward the passenger side of her truck. The crown of an ivory Stetson was level with the window. Someone had evidently decided to hitch a ride. Her mouth tightened into a firm line as her long legs carried her swiftly to the passenger door.

"Get out of there!" she ordered, and yanked the door open at the same time.

The man who had been leaning against the door gave a startled curse when he nearly fell out. But he caught himself with one hand and straightened back into an upright position in the seat, clapping the Stetson back on his head.

"For God's sake, you could be more careful!" Morgan Kincaid growled. "Are you trying to break my neck?"

Patty gaped in surprise as she stared into his blazing blue eyes and then noticed the stern frown on his sensual mouth.

"What are you doing here?" she demanded when she got her breath.

"I could ask you the same thing," he retorted. "I thought your grandfather always drove the truck pulling the travel trailer."

"He changed this time so he could keep a closer watch on the horses," she answered instinctively, forgetting for a moment that Morgan had not answered her question.

He turned in the seat to face her with painstaking slowness. "You could have checked to see who was in here before nearly killing them," he muttered. "Ouch."

It was only when he had completed the turn that Patty saw his left arm was in a sling. Her anger and surprise became curiosity and concern.

"What happened to you?"

"I dislocated my shoulder. And damned near did it again when you tried to send me sprawling."

"Just how the hell was I supposed to know it was you? You could have been a carjacker or a rapist. I was by myself."

He tipped the brim of his ivory Stetson at her. "Nah. The bad guys always wear black hats."

"Oh, shut up, Morgan. Come to think of it, you are lucky I didn't kill you."

"I'll keep that in mind, little lady."

Her eyes narrowed suspiciously. "Don't call me little lady. Hey, did Grandpa know you were going to be here?"

"Of course he didn't," Morgan snapped. "If he had, I would've known which truck he was pulling, right?"

"Then why are you here?"

His mouth curved into a cold, exasperated smile. "A friend dropped me off here; I wanted a ride home and I knew that was where you were going." With his good hand, he lifted his slinged arm slightly. "I can't drive very well with this."

"You never did say how it happened."

"Snowball went through the fence. I didn't get out of his way fast enough," Morgan replied tautly.

Snowball sounded like a name for a kitten, but Patty knew he was one of the rodeo bulls, renowned for his complete lack of respect for any fence when he chose to be on the opposite side of it. He was a Brahman cross and an extremely mild-tempered beast unless he got a notion in his mind to wander.

"So what happened to Snowball?"

There was a hint of amusement in Morgan's blue eyes. "He's a good draw for the cowboys and always gives them a high score when they ride him. So I sold him to Jim Byers's outfit. I figured they could borrow trouble for a while."

"Okay, that still doesn't explain why you're here or how you got here."

"Bob Andrews gave me a lift. Listen, if you keep on asking all these questions, your grandfather is going to be thirty miles down the road. Let's get going."

"Right." Morgan slammed his door shut while Patty walked around to the driver's side. Not until she was out on the highway did she speak to him again.

"Who's taking care of the rodeo stock while you're gone?"

"My brother Alex and his wife drove down on Sunday. He's taking over while I give my shoulder a couple of weeks to heal."

"A couple of weeks?" she repeated uncertainly. She had understood that he would be on the road during her stay at the Kincaid ranch—safely far away and out of sight.

The sideways glance she gave him was met with

a grin. "What's the matter, Skinny? Don't want me around?"

"I didn't say that." She slid a country music CD into the player and turned it up loud. He winced, reached out, and turned it down to a barely audible level.

"I was beginning to enjoy the peace and quiet."

"Have it your way," Patty retorted. "I could use a little noise myself." She would never admit that having him right next to her made her nervous—any more than she would admit that the rodeo grounds had seemed awfully empty without him. In fact, she had listened to this particular CD over and over every day just to shatter the silence.

"Turn it back up then." He settled down in the seat and tipped his hat forward to cover his face. "That way you won't have to entertain me."

"Hey, I'm driving. You'll have to entertain yourself, pal."

He cradled the sling in his good arm. "Okay, I'll take a nap. And drive carefully. I'm in enough pain as it is without getting my teeth jolted out of my head."

"I always drive carefully," she said. "And I'm aware that you're hurt."

At that particular moment, a railroad crossing loomed in front of them. Patty's concentration had been more on her passenger than on the road and she was unable to slow down much before they bumped over the crossing, drawing a muffled exclamation of pain from Morgan.

"Call that careful?" he began.

"I just didn't see it! Sorry!" She reached over and turned up the volume on the CD player again. "Maybe if you didn't talk to me—"

"Maybe if you weren't so irritable—"

"I am not irritable!"

"You're yelling."

"Shut up! Please shut up!" A semi that she hadn't seen either passed them on the left, blaring its horn as it barreled down the highway. She felt a little guilty for losing her temper at Morgan instead of the semi's driver, but only a little.

"Sorry. Maybe I should have said you were talking loudly and not yelling. Does that description sound more flattering?"

Patty gritted her teeth. "Yes, Morgan. It does. Now go to sleep and be a good cowboy. I'll let you know when we get to Oklahoma so you can lean out the window and shout yee-haw."

"Thanks." He tipped the brim of his hat over his eyes.

She pressed her lips tightly together when the player skipped to a catchy tune about worthless men. Morgan wasn't worth the breath it took to insult him by singing along. Several miles farther on, she caught sight of the horse van her grandfather was pulling and accelerated until she was a hundred feet or so behind him.

Morgan was asleep, if the even rise and fall of his chest was anything to go by. Even so, his mere presence made her edgy and—he had been right about that much—irritable. Forgetting how tedious the peace of last week had seemed, she found herself wishing for it now.

After an hour's drive, the horse trailer in front of her flashed its turn signal and pulled off the highway into a rest area. Patty eased her foot off the accelerator and followed. The change in speed did not go unnoticed. Morgan pushed back his hat and looked around, his eyes bright.

"What's the problem?"

"I don't know. Maybe nothing," she answered shortly.

He asked Everett King the same thing the instant the older man stepped from the cab of his truck. The genuine surprise on her grandfather's face removed Patty's last doubt—he hadn't arranged for Morgan to ride with her to Oklahoma.

"No problems that I know of," her grandfather responded. "Just taking a breather for the horses. What are you doing here?"

Morgan told him more or less what he'd told her, but Patty wasn't listening. She walked to the horse trailer, using her own key to unlock the access door. They had lined the van's stalls with extra padding to make sure that the horses didn't accidentally do further injury to themselves. Before she actually began the individual inspections, her grandfather was entering the van.

"I'll check the horses," he said. "Why don't you get some cups from the trailer and pour us all some coffee? And bring that bag of cookies, too."

Patty checked the impulse to remind her grandfather that the rest was for the horses and not them. He meant well, after all. "Okay."

She walked back through the door, hopping to the ground before Morgan could take the few steps necessary to offer her a hand.

With only a glance in his direction, she walked around the horse van, feeling inside the pocket of her tight jeans for the key to the trailer door. She was just taking the enameled tin cups out of the cupboard when Morgan stepped in.

"Want some help?" he offered.

Patty shook her head. "Believe it or not, I can manage it myself." She regretted the flip remark when she saw him adjust the sling and wince. She did have to give him points for trying.

"I see you're still in the same sweet mood," he commented dryly.

She searched impatiently through the shelves for the bag of cookies. "Your nap doesn't seem to have improved yours any."

"Then I guess I should say I'm sorry."

"Huh?" She stopped and stared at him. Apologizing was so not like him. She told herself that some men would do anything for a cookie and went back to her search.

"Why so quiet? Don't tell me you're still holding a grudge because your grandfather accepted my invitation."

She banged the cupboard door shut and began looking in the next one. "No. I'm not that childish, Morgan. I'm just looking for the damn cookies, okay?"

He reached up to the highest shelf with his good arm and pulled out the bag she couldn't see. "This what you're looking for?" He thrust it at her.

She took the bag and glared at him. "Yes. Thanks."

"You're welcome. Gee, I can't wait to introduce you to my parents. They're very warm, friendly people."

His sarcasm wasn't lost on her. "Pity you don't take after them." She didn't quite meet his eye as she turned away from the cupboards.

"You've never bothered to get to know me well enough to know whether I do or not," Morgan pointed out, his tall frame blocking the path to the door. "Let me carry that."

"You only have the use of one arm." Patty ignored

his outstretched hand, setting the bag on the counter to slip the cup handles on her fingers.

"That doesn't make me an invalid." To prove his point, his fingers closed over her wrist, drawing her to him, the cups clanging against each other at the sudden movement. Her free hand came up to push him away and touched the sling. She didn't follow through.

His rugged face was only inches from her own, the tantalizing curve of his mouth close enough to kiss.

No. She wasn't going to give in to temptation.

His grip tightened slightly and he brought her nearer, molding her against his length and quickening her pulse at the hard imprint of his male outline.

"Are you going to accept my apology?" he asked softly. "You never did say."

"Um . . . yes. I guess so." There was a breathy catch to her voice that Patty couldn't control.

"Do you forgive me?" he prompted.

She darted an angry glare into his mocking blue eyes. "Yes."

Lightly he brushed his lips against hers, teasing her for a provocative second before drawing away. She felt a flash of dismay and it must have shown on her face.

"Cheer up, kid." He laughed softly. "I'll only be around for a couple of weeks. You've endured my company for a lot longer than that and managed to survive."

"I'm not a kid," Patty retorted.

"No, you're a stubborn baby goat. Someday you're going to get tired of butting your head against me," he said complacently.

"Excuse me? I don't think I was doing that just

now, Morgan. I wish you'd stop teasing me, that's all."

He grinned wolfishly. "Your wish is granted. Now quit dawdling and get those cups out to your grandfather. He probably really wants that coffee."

"When we start back out, you can ride with him," she said through clenched teeth.

"And deprive myself of your charming company? I don't think so." A satisfied smile deepened the grooves around his mouth and nose as he walked out of the trailer door ahead of Patty.

CHAPTER SEVEN

Red clay soil churned in the water, changing its color to a murky red shade. The same red soil lined the banks of the river and surfaced to form tiny island bars in the river itself. The Red River, part of the borderline between Texas and Oklahoma.

"Welcome to Oklahoma, the Sooner State," Morgan said as the pickup traversed the bridge over the Red River and moved onto the highway stretching northward.

"Why the Sooner State?" Patty asked with a wry curve to her mouth. "The sooner you get here, the sooner you can leave?"

"Do I talk like that about your home state?" he asked with a hint of reproving sharpness.

"If you haven't, you will." Her sliding gaze encountered his uncompromising profile. Morgan shifted his position with a slight grimace of pain. Patty guessed that his shoulder was bothering him. "But I actually am curious," she added, leaving the sarcasm out of her voice. "Why is it called the Sooner State?"

He didn't reply right away. She could sense his measured look studying her, but she kept her eyes on the road ahead.

"The word dates back to the land rush days. Some settlers jumped the gun and staked their claims for homestead land sooner rather than later, before it was actually open for homesteading. So they were called Sooners. And some who were lucky enough to get good land were called Sooners by the ones who didn't. Sore losers, I guess," Morgan explained. "Now it's just a nickname for an Oklahoman."

Patty nodded. "How much farther to your ranch?"

"Not far now," he answered, his gaze turning out the side window of the pickup. "We're north and west of Ardmore, near the foot of the Arbuckle Mountains. The river peninsula we're on right now used to be a refuge for outlaws. Some of them are buried near Thackerville. Have you been in Oklahoma before?"

"I've been through it," Patty answered noncommittally.

"Maybe you'll have a chance to see some of it while you're here." But Patty noticed he didn't offer his services as a guide. "The pine forests of the Ouachita to the east are beautiful, especially the drive through the Winding Stair Mountains. And don't miss Turner Falls in the Arbuckle Mountains. Have you been to the National Cowboy Hall of Fame in Oklahoma City?"

"No."

"You and your grandfather should check it out."

"If you say so." She stifled a disappointed sigh that had come from nowhere.

A half an hour later they were turning west of Ardmore onto a state road. After another fifteen minutes of driving, Morgan pointed out the ranch road, marked simply by a sign on a post carved with the name Kincaid. Slowing down the pickup, Patty eased it over the open rails of the cattle guard and followed the graveled clay road into the rolling hills, trailed by her grandfather with the horse van.

They traveled several miles into the open country before Patty sighted the main building of the ranch protected from the cold blast of winter storms by a small hill to the northwest. The tall, rambling house with its clay red brick and cream trim was off to the side. The white stables and barns were to the northeast of the house, next to interconnected corrals and a small rodeo arena complete with bucking chutes and a judging stand.

As she followed the lane that made a wide circle to encompass both the house and the ranch buildings, Patty saw a tall man striding effortlessly from the nearest white barn to meet them. His height made him appear deceptively lean and well muscled, but Patty wasn't taken in. The resemblance of the man to Morgan was too strong for her not to guess that it must be his father.

When the distance lessened and his features became clear, Patty knew she was right. His face was strong, but not nearly as unrelenting as Morgan's, and lines crinkled the corners of his eyes in a friendly way. His sideburns were snow white, but the rest of his hair was ebony black with an occasional strand of white.

"You can park by the stock trucks near the barn," Morgan said, and Patty complied.

Morgan was out of the pickup within seconds after it had stopped, waving to her grandfather to park beside Patty. Then she watched the warm handclasp between father and son, pleased at the way Morgan's face lit up with a broad smile. She wanted to wait for her grandfather, but as the two men turned their attention to her, she knew she couldn't.

As she slid from the cab of the truck, a screen door slammed at the house and a woman hurried gracefully toward Morgan. Her dark auburn hair was touched with gray, but the multitude of freckles on her face made her seem young. Patty waited discreetly near the door of the truck while Morgan greeted his mother.

"It's so good to see you again!" Mrs. Kincaid said enthusiastically as he lowered his head to receive the affectionate kiss she placed on his cheek. "It seems like ages. How's your shoulder?"

"Don't fuss over him, Molly. The boy just got here, didn't he?" Her husband's voice was low and teasing.

"Patty, come over here." Morgan motioned her over to their group. "I want you to meet my parents."

Unwillingly she obeyed, wishing he had ignored her for a few more minutes until her grandfather had positioned his trailer. Despite her initial nervousness, she found herself responding to their warm smiles of welcome.

"So this is your harum-scarum Annie Oakley, huh, Morgan?" Lucas Kincaid laughed.

"This is the one and only," Morgan agreed, a mysterious smile flitting across his face as he met Patty's defiant look. "I don't think she can shoot as well as she rides. Fortunately, or I'd be dead by now."

"Morgan, I'm sure you're exaggerating," his mother said.

"Am I exaggerating, Skinny?"

The knowing look of amusement in his eyes was thoroughly annoying but there was nothing Patty could do but smile politely at him.

"Okay, she won't say. But she sure has a go-to-hell gleam in her big brown eyes, wouldn't you say, Momma?" He chucked Patty under the chin.

"Can you blame her?" Molly Kincaid retorted. She took Lucas's arm and the older couple turned to walk to where Everett King was parking.

"Feel better now, Patty?" Morgan asked quietly.

"What do you mean?" she asked, feeling decidedly on the defensive.

"You now have an ally in the enemy camp—namely my mother."

Patty colored furiously, glancing in embarrassment at the older couple, wishing they were farther away so she could tell Morgan off.

"No need to be polite on their account. Momma and Daddy are aware of the state of war between us."

"The state of—what have you been telling them?"

Molly Kincaid looked back over her shoulder at her unrepentant son. "Don't tease Patty so." She frowned at him.

"Don't worry, Momma." He chuckled. "She fights back."

Having maneuvered the trailer to one side, her grandfather got out and was striding over. Morgan introduced Everett King to his parents, who welcomed him to the ranch in a warmly hospitable way.

Patty was pleased. Her independent-minded grandfather hated to impose on people, but the Kincaids made it seem like the arrival of a trick riding team of six horses and two total strangers was no trouble at all.

"I'd like to get the horses unloaded and settled in right away, if you don't mind," he asked finally.

"Of course," Lucas Kincaid said. "I'll show you the stalls we've got ready."

As Patty started to follow the two older men, Molly Kincaid put a detaining hand on her arm. "Come up to the house with me and I'll show you your rooms."

"Rooms?" Patty repeated blankly, turning toward their travel trailer to explain that she and her grandfather would be staying in it. "We—"

Morgan's hand curled under her hair to circle the back of her neck. The pressure of his touch turned her automatically toward him. His gaze locked on to hers, refusing to release her.

"Mind if I speak privately to Patty for a few minutes?"

His mother looked uncertainly at Patty before sending a slightly warning glance at her son. "Come up to the house when you're through."

"We will," he answered her firmly as she walked away.

"You know very well that Grandpa and I are staying in our trailer," Patty declared before Morgan had a chance.

"Listen very carefully, Patricia King." His gaze narrowed on her. "I am not going to repeat myself. When we go up to the house, you are going to very politely accept the rooms my mother has fixed for you and your grandfather. Forget about your pride. Forget that anybody's doing you a favor. My parents don't see the situation that way and you shouldn't either. Do you understand?"

Patty stared into his set features, longing to tell him to go take a flying leap off a cliff, but she realized there was no use in arguing.

He smiled. "Good. I'm glad we agree."

"I wouldn't go that far, Morgan."

"Whatever. Just so you don't insult them."

She wanted to smack him for what seemed like the millionth time in this whole unlucky month, but she folded her arms across her chest instead. "I would never do that and you know it."

"Maybe not, but you can be stubborn."

"I never should've given in to Grandpa on this. I knew it from the git-go," she muttered, and turned away.

"Don't try to change the subject."

"I'm not! And stop ordering me around!" Hot tears were building in the back of her eyes. The fatigue of the long drive was getting to her, that was obvious.

"Where else would you have gone? Back to New Mexico?" Morgan scoffed. "Planning to do a little reconnaissance and see if Lije is happy with his wife?"

Pivoting sharply back, she swung her hand in a swift arc and connected with his cheek. His dark stubble scraped the palm of her hand just before Morgan caught her wrist on the downswing to keep her from slapping him again.

"What's the matter? Did I get too near the truth?"

"You couldn't have been farther from it!" Her voice trembled. "And whether or not you believe it, Lije Masters means nothing to me."

He studied her for a long moment. "Are you really over him?"

"Why do you care?"

He shrugged and didn't answer.

"Guess I hit a nerve this time," Patty said slowly.

"No. You didn't. But somebody has to talk some sense into you every now and then."

"Does it have to be you?" It was a strange question, but one that she spoke before she had a chance to think about it.

There was a faintly inquiring tilt to his head, a lightning change from self-righteousness to curious amusement. "Are you tired of fighting me, Patty?"

"Yes," was her clipped admission.

"I never thought the day would come when I'd hear you say that," Morgan replied, a vaguely satisfied expression on his strong face.

"Well, you have. Don't look so smug."

"Was I? I'm sorry." A warm smile creased his face.

Her heart thudded against her rib cage as she felt his virile charm working its spell on her. An irrational desire to have him hold her within the circle of his arms again nearly overpowered her. The reaction of her senses struck her as being slightly crazy. She must be hearing things, at the very least. He couldn't possibly have apologized to her twice in one day.

But he had.

She looked away from the captivating gleam in his eyes. "May we go to the house now?"

"First I want to get one thing straight. Hear me out," Morgan insisted. "I didn't know myself until a few minutes ago that my mother intended you and your grandfather to stay at the house. I know you two are used to bunking down in your own space, but she really wants to make you feel welcome here. I hope you'll go along."

The softness in his tone calmed her down. God,

he was good at it sometimes, considering how incredibly annoying he could be the rest of the time. "I will," she agreed.

And the undeclared truce began.

During the following five days, not one harsh word was exchanged between the two of them. Patty had to admit that they didn't see each other that often, mainly at mealtimes or at the stables, and then generally in the company of others. Morgan still teased her, called her Skinny, but there were no disguised insults in his remarks.

As for his parents, Patty knew she could get awfully fond of them. His mother, vivacious and warm, made her feel like a member of the family. When Patty wasn't at the barns helping her grandfather take care of the horses, she was at the house helping Molly Kincaid prepare meals and clear away the dishes of the last one.

Lucas Kincaid was a big, vital man, embracing life and those he loved with an invisible bear hug. A great storyteller, he livened up the dinner table with his tales, invariably laced with salty Western humor. In appearance, he and Morgan were similar, but they were independent individuals in terms of personality. It was obvious that they cared deeply for each other.

The Kincaid home was Molly's pride and joy, and it showed. Western touches were everywhere in the rustic furnishings, but Patty's discerning eye hadn't missed the signs of unpretentious wealth: bronze sculptures by Frederick Remington as well as his paintings depicting life on the frontier, and other works of art by equally famous Western artists.

scattered here and there. But it was a place that was lived in with love and happiness, an atmosphere that could not be bought with any amount of money. It was a gift from the hearts of its occupants.

Even the guest bedroom, where she was now, had a theme that she loved: retro cowgirl. Patty had already memorized every detail of the decor. She wanted a real room like this someday.

Burying her head deeper in her pillow, Patty tried to block out whatever sound it was that had awakened her. Then it came again—a whinnying neigh from the stables.

She recognized it as one of her own horses . . . probably Landmark. Lifting her head from the pillow, she glanced at the luminous face of the bedside clock. Nearly midnight. Right about the time her grandfather made his last check on the horses.

He never turned in early, declaring now that he was old, he didn't need as much sleep. Patty waited, trying to decide if the whinny had been one of welcome or a call for help. Her grandfather could be at the stables or he might have checked on the team already and left. She waited, all thought of sleep gone.

After several minutes of continued silence, Patty threw back the covers and slipped out of bed, padding in her bare feet to the window. From this angle with the branches of the large oak in the way, she couldn't tell if there was a light on in the stables. She walked to the door of her downstairs bedroom and listened for the sounds of anyone stirring in the house. There was only the ticking of the large grandfather clock.

Retrieving the light cotton robe from the end of

her bed, Patty slipped her arms into it to cover the bare skin exposed by her shortie pajamas. She tiptoed from the room. Moonlight streamed in through the windows, making it unnecessary to turn on a lamp as she hurried to the less obstructed view from the living room window.

The stable was dark. There were no lights shining in its small windows. With the house so quiet, her grandfather must have already looked in on the horses and retired for the night.

But another whinny came from the stable, muffled this time because there were no windows open here as there had been in Patty's bedroom. Still, she was sure she'd heard a plaintive note in the whinny. Something was the matter.

She hesitated near the window, not sure whether to check on the horses herself or get her grandfather. She figured the last would be best. Chances were he wasn't asleep yet and if there were a problem, she would have to seek him out anyway. Under expert guidance, she could care for most routine injuries, but she didn't have the depth of experience to diagnose every problem.

The closed stairwell to the upper floor was dark. The moonlight didn't reach this far. Her fingers touched the light switch and hesitated. Her grandfather's bedroom was the second door on the right at the top of the stairs. Patty had no wish to waken the rest of the household for what might be no more than a false alarm.

With a hand on the banister, she climbed the stairs, a board creaking occasionally as it took her weight. Her hand searched the darkness at the top of the stairs for the wall. Several tentative steps later, her fingertips touched it. Tracing them along the wall, Patty encountered the first door, tiptoed by it and paused beside the second door.

Silence and the even sound of someone breathing greeted her as she opened the door and quietly closed it behind her. Just inside the room, she hesitated, unwilling to wake her grandfather if he was truly asleep. The leafy branches of an oak outside the window admitted only enough light for her to discern the shadowy human form in the bed.

She edged closer to the bed until she was bending over it. When the dark figure stirred her mouth opened to call out softly to him. Only a startled gasp of surprise came out as her wrist was seized and she was pulled onto the bed. The rest of her cry was smothered by the large hand that gently covered her mouth. Wide-eyed, she gazed horror-struck at Morgan Kincaid's face, only inches above her own.

"I wonder what my mother would think if she found you creeping into my bedroom in the middle of the night." He laughed softly, his warm breath dancing over her skin.

The shock receded as his words provoked a spurt of anger. Not only was his hand over her mouth, his body was pushing hers into the mattress. She managed to push his hand away, at least as far as the side of her neck.

"What are you doing in Grandpa's room?" she demanded in an accusing whisper. "This better be a mistake."

"I don't think my momma would buy a case of mistaken rooms," Morgan said softly, "since this has been my bedroom since the day I was born."

The hand she raised to push him off encountered the searing bareness of his chest, muscles rippling beneath her touch, igniting all sorts of fiery sensations that left her slightly breathless.

"This isn't Grandpa's room?" Her voice sounded weak ever to her own ears. "But . . . but this is the second room on the right."

"The second room, yes,"—a half smile curved the inflexibly male mouth—"but the third door. You forgot about the linen closet."

A tiny "oh" slipped from her parted lips. She licked them nervously and saw his gaze center on her mouth. Her pulse hammered in her temples as his lazy, half-closed look slid back to hold her gaze. Never in her whole existence had she been so sensually aware of a man as she was at this moment, with the smoothness of the sheets beneath her and the heat of his body burning through the material of her thin pajamas and robe.

She wanted nothing more than to run her fingers through his thick, tousled black hair, but she held back. It was not the only temptation that presented itself: his broad chest and shoulders were beneath her hand to explore. Morgan had kissed her before but always she had struggled either physically or mentally. Now Patty found herself wondering what it would be like to give herself up to the burning mastery of his caresses, to glory in the fiery responses she had involuntarily felt before.

In the past, Patty had only imagined Lije making love to her. Hot color swept her cheeks as she realized it was Morgan who filled her imagination now. Not only filled it, but dominated it with his virility.

Shifting beneath his pressing weight, she pushed her palm against his shoulder in an effort to free herself.

There was a sharp intake of breath and a quick

"Careful!" as Morgan winced. Until that second, Patty had forgotten all about his shoulder.

"I'm sorry," she said, swiftly and breathlessly.

The fleeting moment of pain was gone. The fire in his gaze ran over her face. His voice took on a low, seductive quality.

"Do you think you can manage a gentle resistance?"

"Morgan—"

Whatever else Patty had intended to say was lost as his mouth tantalized the corners of her sensitive, trembling lips, playing with them until they ached for the light teasing to stop. Instinctively her hand slid up his chest to curl around the back of his neck, the fingers edging into his black, wavy hair. When her hand tightened around his neck, his sensual kisses hardened into possession.

Sanity was abandoned in the chaotic whirl of her emotions. Parting her lips, Morgan explored her mouth, sending fresh waves of desire exploding deep within her. His intimate caresses awakened her to a level of sensuality she hadn't dreamed of reaching. She could only gasp at the wonder of it when he pushed the collar of her robe away to bury his head in the hollow of her throat.

"Your heart is racing," Morgan muttered huskily as he dropped kisses around her ear, nibbling at the lobe.

"So . . . so is yours," Patty whispered, surprised and frightened at the way her arms were clinging to his strong, naked back. Self-consciously she lowered them to a safer position near his waist, only to make another discovery. "You . . . you don't have any clothes on." Her cheeks flamed as she realized how thin the sheet was that separated them.

"You don't have much on yourself," he said with a soft chuckle. "If we keep this up, we'll ruin your reputation."

What's left of it, Patty thought.

"Do you want me to stop?" he whispered.

"No," she whispered back. "But what about your parents? I mean, you're a grown man but this is their house and—"

He nuzzled her neck. "My parents would insist that I do the right thing and marry you pronto."

"But you don't love me," she protested as he continued to kiss her tenderly around her cheek and ear.

"*You* don't love me." An invisible shrug accompanied his reply.

Yes, I do, Patty answered silently, qualifying it quickly in her mind. She *thought* she loved him. That was all. But at this moment, she seemed dependent on his touch in order to keep her heart beating.

"Well, your parents don't know I'm here," was what she said out loud.

"And if they found out we had been making love, what would you do?" He was nuzzling her neck again.

"I'd . . . I'd be too ashamed to face them."

She felt his muscles tense as he held himself motionless for an instant. Then he raised his head to study her face in the dim light.

"Is that how my kisses make you feel? Ashamed?" A note of harshness crept into his low voice.

Her heart stopped for an instant and Patty had to close her eyes to keep herself from drawing him back into the closeness of her arms.

"What self-respecting woman would want a man who doesn't like her making love to her?" she argued quietly.

Morgan rolled away, lying back on the mattress beside her. "I suppose there is some twisted logic in that," he agreed dryly.

She turned her head sideways on the pillow to look at him.

"Morgan, why did you kiss me?"

His face was in the shadow so she could only see a dim outline of his rough features.

"I wanted to," he answered calmly. "And I sensed that you wanted me to. You did, didn't you?"

It wasn't exactly a question, but Patty answered it anyway. "Yes, I did." She struggled to sit upright before she revealed the strange sensation that she had fallen in love with him. She had disliked him for so long it seemed crazy that she could reverse her emotions in the space of a few minutes.

"Tell me," Morgan commanded. "Did you enjoy it?"

"I wasn't taking notes." Patty tried to shrug away his question.

"I certainly hope not." He chuckled, a pleasant sound that moved caressingly over her skin.

"Uh . . . I have to see Grandpa." She slipped from the bed before Morgan could try to stop her.

Her haste was unnecessary. He didn't move. Quickly she clasped the robe around her neck, heat rising in her face at the intensity of his gaze.

"What the hell is so urgent at this hour?" he asked with a trace of amusement at her hurried and fumbling movements.

"Landmark was fussing. I thought Grandpa should check—I mean, I was going to go myself—" If she had, none of this would have happened, Patty realized with chagrin. "I should have," she finished grimly.

"Oh, lighten up, Patty," Morgan said quietly.

"Nothing happened, right? Don't answer that." He inhaled deeply as if to control a growing impatience. "There's no need to waken Everett. I'll check on the horses for you."

Patty was about to make some silly protest that she didn't want to bother him, then she changed her mind. The dim light played over his naked chest as he sat up in the bed.

"Would you like me to go with you?" she asked nervously.

She turned away as the sheets rustled. Next she heard him get up, reach around for something to wear and then slide a pair of jeans up over his bare legs.

"I don't think that's a good idea, Patty."

He didn't explain but then he didn't have to. Patty was aware of the kindled passion inside of her that required only the spark of his touch to be ignited into flame again. For all Morgan's self-control, his eyes showed a dangerous fire very close to the surface.

"Thank you," she murmured.

"For what?" he mocked. Cat-quiet footsteps had brought him to her side.

"F-for checking on the horses," Patty stumbled.

A brilliant light burned in his eyes as he looked down on her with a knowing smile. "I need the fresh air anyway."

Patty knew her guarded silence as she felt her way back down the stairs amused Morgan, but at this point she couldn't handle the embarrassment of being discovered.

"Go back to bed," he murmured near her hair when they reached the ground-floor hallway. "And don't stick your nose outside the door again tonight."

"The horses—" she began.

"If there's any trouble, I'm capable of taking care of it. Now, good night," Morgan said firmly.

"Good night." Patty moved reluctantly toward her room.

CHAPTER EIGHT

Patty didn't go immediately to bed when she reached her room. For a long while she stood at the window gazing at the stables and the light that flickered with the movement of the night breeze through the leaves of the tree outside. The absurd sensation that she had fallen in love with the tall, dark-haired man out there in the stables persisted.

You couldn't simply dislike a man for years and then have it all change in one night, she argued with herself. It wasn't logical.

With the dawning of the new day, Patty still refused to accept the possibility that she had fallen in love with Morgan Kincaid. It was physical desire, she told herself firmly. Her body had simply reacted to his expert caresses. There was no need to try to justify her response with the ridiculous notion that she loved the man. Morgan's amazing virility attracted her. That had to be all it was . . .

The tightening of her stomach at the sight of him sitting at the breakfast table, dark and sexy, made her doubt her own judgment. She avoided the glittering blue of his eyes as she took her chair.

"Good morning. Did you sleep well?" Molly Kincaid greeted Patty, as she set a glass of orange juice in front of her.

"Yes, thank you, I did." The immediate clamoring of her senses at Morgan's presence made her voice unnaturally tense.

"When she finally got to sleep," Morgan added. The half-angry look she gave him was an unspoken plea for his silence that he ignored. "Patty came to my room last night," he explained, his eyes dancing with laughter at the sudden flames in her cheeks. "She heard one of the horses whinnying and mistook my room for her grandfather's."

"I thought I heard voices around midnight coming from your room," Everett King declared. "I couldn't make up my mind if I was hearing things or if you were talking in your sleep."

"Was there any problem with the horses?" Lucas Kincaid glanced at his son.

"No, I checked." Morgan shook his head. "A case of lonesomeness, I guess."

"I'm sorry I woke you unnecessarily," Patty offered stiffly.

"Oh, you made up for it," he murmured, the edges of his mouth twitching in mockery.

Lucas Kincaid gave Patty a look of amusement before exchanging a knowing smile with his wife. Patty stared at Morgan in helpless frustration. Why couldn't he have just shut up about last night? He didn't have to make her accidental visit to his bedroom into headline news at the breakfast table.

Molly Kincaid came to her rescue. "Morgan, stop embarrassing Patty."

"Am I?" He studied Patty's downcast gaze and the high color in her face that she couldn't control. "You have to admit, Momma, that she looks guilty. Anyone would think by looking at her that she'd crawled in bed with me."

Her fingers closed around the orange juice glass, fighting the urge to throw it into his face. The gleam in his eyes told her that Morgan had read her mind. He was plainly daring her to do it and let everyone see how close his remark had come to the truth.

With quivering control, she picked up the glass and drank the juice. It had no taste. In fact, it barely made it past the knot in her throat. How could he make fun of what had happened last night? He probably thought the whole business was funny.

"I'm not very hungry, Molly." She addressed his mother with forced evenness. The two women had called each other by their first names almost from the first day of her arrival. "I think I'll check on Liberty."

"I've finished," her grandfather announced as she rose from her chair. "I'll walk with you, Patty."

Pausing near the table, she waited for her grandfather. She could hardly run from the room. Unwillingly her gaze swept over Morgan. He was leaning back in his chair, regarding her indolently through half-closed eyes. There was something piercingly thoughtful about the way he looked at her. She guessed he was trying to make up his mind about something, but what that might be, she didn't know.

Then her grandfather's hand touched her elbow, his lean frame at her side. Patty broke free of Morgan's compelling gaze at last.

* * *

"It was a mistake to come here, Gramps," Patty said, her steps slowing dispiritedly.

"Morgan?" he questioned softly.

Darting a startled look at his impassive face, she thought for a minute that he had guessed, with his usual astuteness, that she was on the brink of falling in love with Morgan, if she hadn't already crossed it. She took a deep breath and looked at her grandfather again. No, he hadn't guessed, she could tell.

"His shoulder can't heal soon enough," she remarked, breathing easier that her secret was still safe.

It was true. Patty did want Morgan to leave, and the sooner the better. If she wasn't in love with him, only attracted to him, then she could consider herself lucky. If it was love that she felt—and she was beginning to suspect the worst—then it was vital for him to get back on the circuit and out of her life.

An inner voice told her that the pain she'd felt when her infatuation with Lije had ended was nothing compared to what she might feel for Morgan. Patty was determined not to be so foolish again and fall in love with a man who didn't care for her.

"I'm not going to be able to remain in the same house with him much longer," she murmured.

"He's only teasing." Her grandfather smiled without amusement.

Was he trying to ease the frustration that seethed beneath her controlled calm? Patty couldn't quite tell. "Then let's just say that I don't appreciate his brand of humor, Grandpa."

"I can't very well ask him when he intends to leave," Everett pointed out. "This is his home and we're guests of his family."

"Then keep him out of my way!" Patty bit out desperately.

A moment of awkward silence followed as they resumed their course to the stables. Preoccupied, Patty didn't notice it at first. Then she glanced over at Everett King's solemn face.

"Grandpa, what have you maneuvered me into this time?" she asked warily.

He shot a look at her out of the corner of his eye. "Well, you have to understand, girl, I thought you and Morgan were getting along pretty good. The last few days you've seemed to take his joking in stride."

"What did you do?"

His tanned and wrinkled hand adjusted the Stetson on his peppery gray head. "Morgan offered to take us into Oklahoma City the day after tomorrow. I'd mentioned how often you and I had talked about going to the Cowboy Hall of Fame. I meant to say something to you about it last night, but I forgot."

"I'm not going!" she declared forcefully.

"Patty—"

"I'm not going!" she repeated.

"Don't be stubborn now. Listen to me," her grandfather said in his most persuasive voice.

"Every time I listen to you I find myself getting talked into something. No." Patty shook her head vigorously.

"Have I ever convinced you to do anything that wasn't for the best in the end?"

"In the end," she admitted tightly, tossing him an angry look. "But not at the beginning or the middle."

"It's the way a thing ends up that counts."

Sighing heavily, Patty gave in. "All right. I'll listen, but that doesn't mean I'm going to agree."

There was a decided twinkle of triumph in his brown eyes and Patty knew she shouldn't have allowed her grandfather the smallest foothold. He was like Morgan in that respect. The minute she gave an inch, he took a mile. *But that's what happens when you love someone,* she thought. Her lips compressed at that admission.

"You see," her grandfather began, "Morgan isn't making the trip into Oklahoma City specially for us. He's going there on business. While he's taking care of that, he suggested that we could go to the Hall of Fame. It's not as if you would have to spend the entire morning in his company, just the ride there and back. That's no more time than you would spend at the dinner table. And I'll be there to act as a buffer."

"I'm still not going."

In her mind, she was visualizing the journey, sitting in silence in the backseat of the car, mesmerized by Morgan's broad shoulders and the black hair that curled around his muscular neck. Not to mention the blue eyes that would catch her studying him in the rearview mirror and glitter with knowing mockery.

"You're being stubborn," her grandfather said with a sigh.

"So are you. After all, it's not imperative that we see the Hall of Fame now," Patty argued. "You and I can drive to Oklahoma City anytime by ourselves. It's not that far. When Morgan leaves, we can make a day of it."

She considered her arguments to be based on sound logic, but she had forgotten her grandfather was just as stubborn as she was, especially if he believed he was right.

For the next day and a half, he kept up a subtle pressure, chiseling patiently away at her adamant stand until Patty toppled and agreed.

On Thursday morning she was at the breakfast table, dressed in a summery cotton dress of sunny yellow, trying to convince herself that she had worn it because she was going into the city and not because she wanted to impress Morgan with the feminine curves that the dress showed off so well.

Patty made sure to avoid his glance, in case he commented on her appearance, a decided change from her usual jeans and T-shirt. But Morgan was uncharacteristically silent, barely speaking at all during the morning meal.

Not until they were walking from the house to the ranch's SUV did he say anything directly to her. "I didn't think you were going to come."

Patty glared at her grandfather, several steps in front of them, guessing that he had mentioned her initial refusal.

"Neither did I," she retorted.

"You grandfather made me promise to be on my best behavior."

Flushing self-consciously, she kept her gaze downcast. She didn't want to make any reply, but she knew she had to, for pride's sake. "And are you?"

"Going to be on my best behavior?" he finished the question, turning his dark head to look at her. Shrugging, he answered, "It's going to be difficult."

"It's not so difficult," Patty said, refusing to look at the compelling man at her side. "We can simply ignore each other."

"It's not easy to ignore you."

His softly spoken reply drew her gaze like a magnet. Something in his voice insisted that she look at him. A slow, lazy smile was spreading across his face, crinkling the corners of his eyes. Patty's breath caught. She was tempted to run back to the house before the pull of his charm became irresistible.

She wished her grandfather had never extracted that promise from him. She would rather have endured Morgan's careless teasing than be exposed to this potent friendliness.

"I don't find it difficult to ignore you," she declared, sharply averting her gaze.

"I've noticed that—at times," Morgan said dryly, placing obvious emphasis on the "at times."

Patty winced. Yes, there had been times when his touch and kiss obliterated all thought of anyone or anything else. The silent acknowledgment was accompanied by a betraying warmth rising in her neck. She quickened her steps to give herself time to summon up some self-control.

Her grandfather was holding the door to the backseat of the SUV open for her and Patty slipped in as fast as she could. She made a big deal of adjusting the flared skirt of her dress as the driver's door opened.

"There's plenty of room in the front, Patty." Silent laughter ran through Morgan's voice. "Bench seat, custom made. My father can't stand bucket seats. He likes to have Momma right next to him. Just so you know, you don't have to sit back there by yourself."

But Patty knew that she would be in the middle in the front seat, between the two men and in constant physical contact with Morgan for the whole of the ride to Oklahoma City.

"I'm perfectly comfortable here, thank you,"

she insisted, putting a chill in her voice that Morgan couldn't miss.

"Suit yourself." He shrugged, and slid behind the wheel.

Her heart sank as the SUV started and Morgan drove away from the house around the circular drive and down the lane to the highway. She was miserable. The last thing she wanted to do was be snappish and standoffish, but it was the only way she knew to keep Morgan at a distance. Not that he wanted to be any closer; she was the one who wanted that.

Forcing her attention away from the dark, curly head in front of her, she tried to concentrate on the undulating hills with their green dots of trees. In some ways, the landscape reminded her of her own home in New Mexico. Patty would have liked to explore it on horseback, but it was better if she wan't too familiar with Morgan's home. Better for her peace of mind, at least.

How long would it be before Morgan returned to the rodeo circuit, she wondered. He had said initially that he was going to take a two-week rest. That was more than half gone. He had removed the sling three days ago, although his shoulder still wasn't capable of heavy work.

When he was gone, then what? She and her grandfather were supposed to stay another two months, more or less. Patty didn't want to take advantage of his parents' kindness, though they treated her like part of the family.

Thus far, she hadn't had to hear too many stories about his childhood days or be treated to an evening with the Kincaid photograph albums. But it was bound to happen. He was their son, they were proud of him, and it was natural for them to talk about him.

What a mistake it had been to come here. Patty nibbled her lower lip dejectedly. She caught the movement of Morgan's head as he half turned it toward her, revealing his strong profile, powerfully carved and rugged. His blue gaze left the road in front of them long enough to flick briefly at her.

"What do you know about Oklahoma?" he asked.

"The usual." Patty shrugged, watching the traffic zooming along the expressway.

"There are quite a few interesting places to visit around here. You and Everett should do some exploring."

"We might do that," she said tautly.

"To the east of Ardmore is a small town called Tishomingo. It's the site of a big wildlife refuge and the headquarters of one of the Five Civilized Nations," Morgan said.

"Indian tribes?" she asked, biting her lip the instant the question was out, wishing she had let the conversation die its own death.

"Yes, Indian tribes," he replied in the bland tone of a tour guide. He grinned at her, as if he knew that she would find it annoying. "The Cherokee, Chickasaw, Choctaw, Creek, and Seminole Indians are known as the Five Civilized Nations. I'm sure you're aware that Oklahoma was originally the Indian Territory. Sixty-seven tribes were transported to reservations here. But a lot of the credit for the developemnt of the Indian Territory into the state of Oklahoma belongs to the Five Civilized Nations. When they arrived, they brought with them an advanced system of education and a complex tribal organization and government, as well as Christianity.

It was their leadership that truly organized the Indian Territory."

"I didn't know that," Patty murmured, her tone self-conscious.

"The first newspaper in Oklahoma was the *Cherokee Advocate,* published in Tahlequah, Oklahoma, the capital of the Cherokee Nation."

The expressway on which they were traveling began to climb into the Arbuckle Mountains, monoliths that were weathered and rounded by time, sand-colored rocks thrust out here and there or exposed in sheer cliffs where the road carved its way through.

Morgan pointed out the exit to Turner Falls, explaining that there were two large swimming areas near the base of the famous waterfall as well as a campground and picnic facilities. On the north side of the Arbuckles were the rolling flatlands.

"Pauls Valley." Morgan identified the town they were approaching. "On the last Saturday in June the World Championship Watermelon Seed Spitting Contest is held here."

In spite of herself, Patty smiled. Morgan caught the brief look she darted at his reflection in the rearview mirror, a suggestion of an encouraging smile around his mouth. He was arousing her interest and he knew it. She had the distinct feeling that he was determined she enjoy the trip, although she didn't know why she should care.

"I'm not boring you with all this trivia, am I?" he asked.

She shook her head ever so slightly. "No."

"I know your gramps coaxed you into this trip." Morgan shot a look at the older man, who was trying to be as unobtrusive as possible. "Since you're sweet enough to tolerate my company, I thought the least I could do was be informative."

He had read her thoughts again and was letting her know that he had. As long as he didn't read any more than that, Patty didn't mind.

"I'm learning a lot," she replied. "Thanks for the history lesson."

"If you want to go back in history," he said, checking for traffic before edging into the passing lane to go by a slow-moving truck, "then you should visit the Heavener Runestone Park in eastern Oklahoma."

"What's that?" her grandfather asked, Morgan's glance ending his self-imposed silence.

"More than four hundred years before Columbus supposedly discovered America, some Norse explorers traveled through that section of the state and marked their passage by carving runes, characters from their runic alphabet, onto a stone."

"And what did it say?" Patty asked. "This way to IKEA?"

"Very funny." But Morgan did laugh. "I don't remember what the stone said, come to think of it."

During the rest of the trip into Oklahoma City, Morgan told them about the cattle trails that had crossed the state, the Chisholm and the Western Trails, and Butterfield Overland Southern Mail. He talked about the government land rushes that opened the Indian lands to homesteaders.

Then they crossed the bridge over the Canadian River, skirted Norman, Oklahoma, and entered the city limits of Oklahoma City. Leaving the expressway, Morgan took a route through the city streets to the state capital grounds. As the domeless capital building came into view, he glanced in the mirror at Patty's reflection.

"The only state capital in the world with an oil well underneath it." He smiled.

His statement was unnecessary. There was a steel derrick almost directly in front of the columned portico entrance to the gray stone building.

More derricks dotted the capital grounds, straddling pumps that bobbed monotonously up and down to extract the precious oil from beneath the surface.

At the north edge of the city, Morgan drew their attention to a hill looking over the downtown section. He turned onto the street that lay at its base. The white peaks of a roofed structure were visible on the top of the hill, along with flags snapping in the wind.

"That is Persimmon Hill and the National Cowboy Hall of Fame on top of it. One of the branches of the Chisholm Trail used to run along the foot of the hill," Morgan explained. From the street at the base, he turned onto a side street and onto another that climbed the mountain. "The flag esplanade on the side displays the flags of the seventeen Western states that built and sponsored this national memorial to the cowboy, as well as the United States flag."

Bypassing the parking area, he drove closer to the walk leading to the entrance and stopped. Patty was halfway out of the SUV when the hand she placed on the open door for balance was taken by Morgan. She found herself trapped in a triangle: the SUV, the door, and a set of broad shoulders.

For an instant, she stood immobile, her head tilted back, her brown eyes staring into his impassive face. Morgan made no move to let her pass, while her heart hammered like a trapped bird.

"Well?" He arched a brow complacently.

"Well, what?" Patty frowned.

"Did I keep my promise or not?"

"What promise?" She was too disturbed by his nearness to think straight.

"That I'd be on my best behavior." He looked her up and down.

Her tongue moved nervously over her suddenly dry lips. She regretted the action immediately as Morgan's attention shifted to her lips. Her senses quivered in response, but the deliciously pleasant reaction was not one that she wanted to feel.

"Yes, I suppose you were," she murmured, wondering if he noticed the slight breathiness in her voice.

"You don't sound sure."

"The day isn't over yet." Her response wasn't exactly as strong as she wanted it to be.

"What are you afraid of, Skinny?" he asked thoughtfully.

She regained her composure somehow. "Nothing. Don't be ridiculous."

"Hm. Something is bothering you. I can see it in your eyes." His gaze narrowed. "Feeling homesick? Or just blue?"

"Maybe it's none of your business." She yanked her hand free of his.

"I do make you angry, don't I?" Morgan smiled.

"Yes, you do!" Patty glared at him. "I think you enjoy making me lose my temper."

"It's better than seeing you wasting your time mooning over Lije Masters." He shrugged and stepped to one side.

"Where did that come from? I haven't even mentioned his name once—and I don't want to hear you say his name again!"

"Guess I hit a nerve," he said complacently. "So, when are you going to get over that guy?"

I am over him, Patty wanted to shout. But of course she couldn't. He might ask how and why. And the answers to those two questions were all tied up with her feelings for Morgan.

"I think I told you," she said instead, "that I wish Lije all the happiness in the world. What more do you want?"

"It's not what I want that counts. It's what *you* want," said Morgan.

"At the moment all I want is to tour the Cowboy Hall of Fame," Patty snapped.

"Nothing's stopping you." He glanced at the open passageway between himself and the SUV and Patty walked hurriedly past him. "My business is going to take me a couple of hours, so the two of you can take your time."

"We intend to," Patty shot back, darting an angry glance at her grandfather for leaving her to deal with Morgan and not attempting to rescue her.

CHAPTER NINE

Despite her parting shot at Morgan, Patty didn't take her time. She raced through the first part of the exhibit and had to retrace her steps to see it again.

It seemed impossible that her emotions could be in such a turmoil, so contradictory. While she had been quivering with desire to know Morgan's love, she had felt mostly anger. Or had it been frustration?

The art on display distracted her from her confusion eventually. The sculpture exhibit featured renowned works of the great masters of Western art, including Russell and Remington. She toured the National Rodeo Hall of Fame section with her grandfather, enjoying his accounts of some of the rodeo contestants he had known and sharing his appreciation of the lifesize replica of Russell's "Bronc Twister."

He sat down to rest for a few minutes and Patty went alone to the last exhibit, the pure, gleaming white statue called "End of the Trail," symbolizing the end of the frontier and the traditional ways of Native Americans. No matter which angle she viewed the massive work from, it dominated and awed her. The statue stood out against its background of glass walls and steeply sloping white ceilings.

"Impressive, isn't it?"

Patty had not paid any attention to the footsteps behind her, thinking it was another visitor like herself. A startled look over her shoulder caught Morgan's bland gaze before he looked back at the statue. His hands were slipped casually in his pockets, his stand relaxed. Patty felt as taut as a high tension wire.

"Is it that late already?" She glanced at her watch. More than two hours had passed, closer to three.

"I haven't been here but a few minutes," he assured her calmly. "My business took longer than I anticipated. I was afraid you were waiting for me."

"Grandpa—"

"I've already seen him," Morgan interrupted. "He told me where you were."

"If you'd like to leave now—" Patty began. She couldn't summon any coldness. He had caught her by surprise and her responses were stilted and nervous.

"No hurry." He brought his gaze from the statue to her face. "Have you seen the fountains?"

"Only from the windows."

"Let's go outside then."

His fingers lightly closed around her elbow and guided her toward a glass exit door. Strolling around the grounds, they followed the bridge walk that meandered over the fountain pools. The water shimmered a pale blue, reflecting the color of the milky sky. Here and there jets of water sprayed into the air. Once by the pools, Morgan directed her along a path to the top of the wooded hill. There they stopped and gazed back at the modern structure.

"The building was designed to symbolize the tents used by the early settlers. At night, with the light radiating from the center, it looks like a tent encampment around a fire," Morgan explained. "The fountains and pools are reminders of how vital water was to the pioneers. The glass walls give you a sense of the vast sky of the West."

"It's beautiful," Patty murmured.

Morgan nodded and guided her toward the graves on the overlooking knob of Persimmon Hill where some of the famous bucking horses were buried—Midnight, Five Minutes to Midnight, and others. There Patty paused, resting a hand against a tree and looking out over the valley below.

"It's quite a view."

"Nothing like what the Eighty-Niners saw," he agreed.

His voice came from directly behind her, and Patty could sense how near he was. She moved closer to the tree, leaning slightly against it for support. "Shouldn't we be leaving?" she asked.

"Everett is going to join us out here when he's finished." Morgan braced an arm against the tree trunk, his hand inches from her head, but his gaze on the city below.

She didn't exactly know what kept her from moving away, but the feeling was dangerous. Patty shifted away from the tree trunk and Morgan.

"I'd better see what's keeping Grandpa."

"I said he'll be along." His blue gaze swerved back to lock on hers.

"I know, but—"

"But you can't stand to be in my company another minute, isn't that right?" Morgan asked smoothly.

His lack of anger or mockery was unexpected. The expression on his face revealed only a calm acceptance of his statement.

"Not really," Patty contradicted him, even though what he said was true.

"I have some news that should bring a smile to your face," he continued without acknowledging her reply. "I'll be joining up with my brother on Sunday. He's going to help me with the rodeo stock for a week, then come back."

"But I thought—" Frowning with surprise, she began to remind him that the two weeks weren't up yet.

Again Morgan ignored her words. "That calls for a celebration, doesn't it?" He smiled, a casual, easy smile without a trace of taunting.

"That's unfair," Patty said softly.

"Face it, Skinny, we're just making each other's lives miserable," he said. "We're a little too good at ticking each other off. You're not going to change and I won't."

Her hands clenched into fists at her sides, her fingers digging into the palms to keep tears from filling her eyes.

"If you wouldn't make fun of me all the time," she began.

"And if you weren't so stubborn and proud," he replied with a flash of humor. "There isn't anything we can agree on. Just about all our conversations end in an argument of some sort."

"That's because you—"

"See what I mean?" Morgan said lightly. "You're starting another one. Never takes long. Well, we can never be friends." He shook his dark head. "I couldn't, anyway."

His compelling look was asking her a question. "Neither could I." Patty realized at that moment that she loved him, fully and completely. To be just his friend would be impossible.

"I have to admit, I'm tired of the fighting." He looked away but not for long. "But I also admit that I can't ignore you. Whenever you're around, the sparks just seem to fly. So . . . I'm leaving ahead of schedule."

"Big decision. Didn't take you long to make it." She felt an unhappy coldness in her heart.

"Hey, I kept thinking something would change or you would lighten up, if only for your grandfather's sake. I tried today to be impersonal and friendly."

"You pulled it off. You could be the world's greatest tour guide," she said bitterly.

"Thanks. Anyway, being friendly doesn't work with you. So I'm getting out of the picture."

"I'm sorry, Morgan."

"Be sorry for yourself." He refused her faint apology. "You're the one who wants to live with memories for the rest of your life. And you're too stubborn to open your eyes and see what else the world might have to offer."

"I do not—" Pain flickered in her brown eyes as she instinctively raised her voice.

"Whoa. I take it back." His hand came up to stop the rest of her denial. "I take back what I said. Our last private conversation is not going to end in an argument."

White teeth bit into her trembling lower lip before Patty exhaled a shaky sigh. "Yes," she agreed. "We should be capable of that."

"Here comes Everett." Morgan pushed his hands into his pockets and turned toward the lean older man walking their way.

A strange, brooding silence hung over the Kincaid ranch on their return, one that had begun on their journey and remained to throw a dark cloud over Morgan's last two days. It was an atmosphere that everyone noticed and no one commented on.

For those same two days, Patty had carefully rehearsed the good-bye speech she was going to give to Morgan, a hopeful attempt to keep the door between them from closing permanently. When she came down to breakfast Sunday morning, she discovered that Morgan had left two hours earlier.

"But he didn't even say good-bye," she murmured, not really aware that she was speaking aloud.

"He told us," Molly Kincaid replied, "that you two had already said all there was to say." She hesitated and then added quietly, "I'm sorry, Patty."

Patty's fingers clasped the edge of the table as she stared at the coffee cup in front of her. "It doesn't matter," she replied tightly.

But it did matter. It mattered very much. The backs of her eyes felt scorched with hot tears. Any second now they would brim over and roll down her face. She pushed away from the table, mumbling a polite request to be excused as she rose to her feet and hurried to the door.

In the solitude of the stables, the burning tears refused to flow. Her heart ached nonetheless and her hand unconsciously caressed the head of a white horse, not even aware of which horse it was stroking.

"I think Lodestar could do with some exercise." Her grandfather's voice spoke quietly at her side.

She didn't look at him but stared into the luminous brown eyes of the white horse. "You know why he left, don't you, Grandpa? It was because of me."

There was no need to identify Morgan. Everett King knew whom she was talking about.

"I guessed that," he said.

"His parents?"

"I think they knew the reason, too."

She forced herself to swallow over the knot in her throat. "I feel awful." She closed her eyes and rested her head against the horse's forelock. "How do you put up with me, Gramps?"

"I love you," he replied simply.

"I'm sorry," she murmured.

"Why? Grandfathers are supposed to love their granddaughters," he teased, a sympathetic twinkle lighting his brown eyes.

"You must be so ashamed of me." Patty sighed.

"You can't help the way you feel toward Morgan any more than he can," he said quietly. "But I have to say that I hoped you two would bury the hatchet."

She started to explain her sudden realization that she loved Morgan, then stopped. Her grandfather had understood her pain when Lije married. It wasn't fair to ask him to listen to more of her misery. She was an adult, a woman. It was time she stopped crying on the nearest available shoulder, especially since it always seemed to be his.

"I . . . I think I'll take Lodestar out." Her voice faltered and she said nothing more.

"That's a good idea."

* * *

The days trickled by with the slowness of grains of sand in an hourglass. Patty worked with the horses to the point of exhaustion, collapsing in bed at nights to cry herself to sleep. Her appetite was nonexistent and she lost weight.

Hell, heartbreak was good for something, she thought miserably. The thought made her want to laugh but she knew how hollow it would sound.

Her grandfather made his concern for her clear, but Patty merely shrugged and said that she was fine. He didn't seem to believe her. The worry lines etched on his forehead didn't go away.

One day he asked pointedly, "Is it still Lije? Don't tell me you're still carrying a torch for him."

The rhythmic stroke of the currycomb didn't pause as Patty thought a minute. She kept her reply deliberately ambiguous. "You don't stop caring for someone simply because they don't care for you."

Her grandfather sighed and walked away, his peppered gray head shaking sadly. From that day on, she truly tried to regain her former high spirits to ease his mind. But she knew he couldn't be fooled.

Two months later, she was driving the pickup that pulled their travel trailer through the entrance gate of the rodeo grounds. Until the moment she saw the stock truck and the bold letters Kincaid Rodeo Company, Patty hadn't realized how much she had been anticipating the moment when she would see Morgan again. Out of sight had never made him out of mind.

Her eyes searched the throng of men in well-worn denim for a glimpse of his black hair and broad shoulders. But he was nowhere to be seen. There were plenty of welcoming shouts and waves as their van and trailer were recognized but no sign of Morgan.

He had known they would be coming. Her grandfather had phoned last week to confirm that they would be keeping the engagement.

As disappointment and depression set in, Patty realized that secretly she had been praying that Morgan would be there to welcome them back—if not her, then at least her grandfather. Hope was a difficult emotion to ignore.

All the while they were unloading the horses and settling them into their stalls, she kept watching for him, trying to convince herself that the minute word reached him of their arrival he would come to greet them. News traveled fast around the rodeo grounds.

A lot of people—too many—stopped by especially to welcome her and her grandfather back to the circuit. Finally she could pretend no longer that Morgan didn't know they were there. He knew, but he just didn't care.

Her sense of rejection was nearly unbearable. She wanted to do nothing more than throw herself onto her bed and howl, but she forced herself to go through the motions of putting the trailer in order.

Sitting at the small table, her cheeks cupped in her hands, Patty saw her grandfather making his way toward the trailer. She breathed in deeply, ordering the self-pity to leave. For his sake, she would smile and be happy.

The pot was on the stove, fresh coffee warming on the low flame. She rose from the small couch to pour him a cup. Through the window, she saw him stop in midstride and turn around. Wild joy leaped into her heart as Morgan came into view, a broad smile of welcome flashing across his rugged face.

She saw without really noticing the warm handshake between the two men and the friendly clasping of shoulders. She was drinking in the sight of him, her heart filling with the fullness of her love.

Then the smile vanished from his face, his expression hardening as he glanced at the trailer. He shook his head in curt refusal. An invisible knife plunged into Patty's stomach. It didn't take longer than a few seconds to guess that her grandfather had invited him to the trailer—and told him that she was there.

So Morgan had no desire to see her.

For an instant Patty submitted to the pride that kept her rooted to the floor, the pride that insisted if he didn't want to speak to her, she didn't want to speak to him. Then she told herself that she was stronger than that—she had to be. She loved him.

Ignoring the jelly sensation in her legs, Patty walked to the door and opened it, fixing a smile of greeting on her face as she stepped outside. The metallic glint in the gaze that met hers nearly sent her back inside, but she gathered her courage and walked forward.

"Hello, Morgan." Her voice was deliberately controlled.

"Hello, Patty," he responded in a clipped tone.

For the first time in her life, she would have welcomed Skinny, or kid, or any of the other nicknames he had used. His impersonal tone of voice felt like a bucket of cold water. He looked at her as if she were a nodding acquaintance.

"Excuse me a minute." Everett King touched her arm, seeming oblivious to the coolness in the air. "I want to go and say hello to Lefty."

Her eyes left Morgan's face long enough to see the grizzled man hobbling alongside one of the pens. Then her grandfather was walking away, lifting a hand in greeting and calling to his friend. Her gaze slid apprehensively back to Morgan.

"You're looking well, Morgan." Trite words, but that was all she could come up with.

The line of his mouth thinned. "Thank you."

Her nerve was slowly beginning to shatter. "Um, your mother sent her love—and this." Patty had barely touched her fingers on his chest, starting to rise on tiptoe to plant a kiss on his cheek when he stepped away from her.

"Just tell me," he snapped. "You don't need to act it out."

What had she hoped? That at the touch of her lips Morgan would fold her into his arms and sweep away the barriers with the mastery of his kiss? Why had she so foolishly exposed herself to his rejection? She looked down at her feet, feeling like an idiot.

"I thought . . . I hoped things had changed," she murmured.

"We aren't friends, Patty." There was an edge in his tone. "Let's not pretend that we are."

"I wasn't," she said defensively.

"Of course. You were only delivering a message from my mother. I'd forgotten how, uh, reliable you can be sometimes," he said. "You're like a bulldog. Once you get hold of an idea, you won't let go even when you know it's wrong."

"You don't know everything, Morgan Kincaid." Patty's voice was weary.

"At least I don't keep hoping for something that isn't ever going to happen."

"I don't need you to preach to me!"

"Well, you need somebody!" Then he clamped his mouth tightly shut and banked the blazing fire in his gaze. "Nothing has changed," he said in a quieter voice. "Five minutes and we're yelling."

Her urge to give him what he gave vanished. "Morgan—" She was on the verge of an apology.

"Tell your grandfather I'll talk to him later," he cut in with a heavy sigh and turned away.

Dejectedly Patty returned to the trailer. Another standoff. Not exactly a grown-up resolution to their pointless squabble. Before, their arguments had only angered her more. Now . . . it was hard to say how she felt. But as Morgan had said, the sparks seemed inevitable. If she wanted to avoid further conflict, she would have to avoid him.

Love had a way of making things worse, she reflected. Anyway, how could she avoid someone that she was likely to run into around any corner of the rodeo grounds?

The next morning's practice rehearsal was flawless. The horses were in peak form; their injuries had healed, and they were back in top condition. The only lasting effect had been the lessening of Liberty's speed, but her grandfather had compensated for that by switching his lead position to Landmark's wheel spot.

"They're ready for tonight, Gramps!" Patty declared with a satisfied smile as she halted them at the arena gate and vaulted to the ground.

"They're eager, too," Everett King agreed, patting Landmark's snorting nose. "Hard to believe the accident ever happened."

"Hey, Princess!"

Patty recognized *that* cowboy's voice and sighed.

"I heard you were back." Jack Evans winked as he put an arm around her shoulders and squeezed her tightly. "I missed you."

"I bet there was some pretty blonde around to console you." Patty laughed.

"She never takes me seriously." The comment was addressed to her grandfather with a fake frown.

"I wonder why," Everett murmured dryly.

"Are you going with me to the big doings Sunday night?" Jack ignored her grandfather's remark and grinned at Patty.

"What big doings?" She smiled a little. Might as well stall him.

"For Morgan, of course."

She stiffened and the faint smile vanished completely.

"Yeah. Morgan." Jack nodded. "Haven't you heard the news?"

"I g-guess not." She glanced uncertainly at her grandfather.

"He's sold out lock, stock, and barrel to a rodeo outfit based in Dallas," Jack explained.

"You . . . you must be mistaken." Patty frowned.

"No, it's a fact. The new owner is taking over on Monday. Morgan's not even going to finish out the season. So we're throwing him a farewell party Sunday night."

Her grandfather didn't meet her questioning look. "I'd heard talk," Everett King hedged.

Patty shook her head. "I don't believe it."

"Well, there's the man." Jack shrugged. "You can ask him yourself."

Morgan was standing at the far end of the corridor that led to the arena gates, talking to one of the local rodeo promoters. As Patty followed Jack's look, she saw Morgan touch a hand to his hat and turn away from the man.

"I will ask him," she said determinedly.

Scrambling over the gate, she ran down the corridor after the retreating broad back. She called to him once and he stopped and turned, his hands moving to his hips in silent challenge. She halted a few feet in front of him, her eyes searching his expressionless face.

"Is it true?" she asked in a voice slightly breathless from her run.

"Is what true?" Morgan countered blandly.

"That you're selling out?"

"Yes." He turned and began walking away. His long strides almost forced her into a trot to keep up with him.

"You've sold everything? The horses, the bulls, the stock trucks?"

"Everything except Red River," Morgan said.

Patty frowned for a second or two until it came back to her. "Oh, right. The bucking horse you were going to retire."

Morgan nodded. "I'm taking him back to the ranch with me and turning him out to pasture."

"Why?" she said suddenly.

"Why what?"

"Why are you selling?" Patty asked.

"I've been thinking about quitting for quite a while. Since Alex doesn't want to travel with his wife and family and Dad is getting too old, we decided to sell," he explained in the same unemotional tone he'd used before.

"But why now? Why not finish out the season?" she persisted.

Morgan stopped and faced her, steel in his gaze.

"You once indicated that this circuit wasn't big enough for both of us. I've come to the conclusion that you're right." There was a cynical twist to his mouth. "Too bad you didn't wait another week before coming back. Then we wouldn't have had to see each other again."

Patty breathed in sharply. One dilemma had been solved: how to avoid meeting Morgan. It was confirmed. He was selling. And she was supposed to be rejoicing at the news. That was what he expected. With a defiant toss of her head, Patty confirmed his opinion.

"I'm glad I'm here," she retorted. "This way I can dance at your farewell party."

"Bring some champagne. It's going to be a night to celebrate," Morgan agreed, a muscle twitching uncontrollably in his jaw.

"Right. With all your friends in low places. I'll bring a whole case and share it with them," she vowed.

"Whatever you do," he muttered, "please don't say something nice to me. I'd hate to ruin a perfect record."

Her hand connected with his cheek in a resounding slap. Before he could say anything, she was stalking away, fighting back tears.

CHAPTER TEN

From a stranger's point of view, Morgan's farewell party was a huge success. A local tavern had been reserved exclusively for the celebration. There was music and laughter, hooraying and backslapping, and enough food and drink for an army.

Patty was one of the last to arrive. She had turned down Jack's invitation to the party, choosing to go with her grandfather instead. If she hadn't been certain that Morgan would notice her absence, she wouldn't have gone at all. At least with her grandfather, she could leave when she pleased and not be dependent on an unreliable guy to take her home.

It wasn't easy to pretend to be happy, not when her heart was sick at Morgan's leaving. Only knowing how much he wanted to be away from her enabled her to hold her head high and just get through it.

She only faltered once—when he proposed a toast to her.

"To Patty King, who always knows when to say

the wrong thing. And she usually says it twice," Morgan had proclaimed with mocking laughter and downed the drink in his glass.

She hadn't been able to lift her own glass to her lips. She hadn't been able to break away from the intensity of his gaze. Within seconds, her grandfather was at her side, gently leading her away from Morgan's table.

"He hates me, Grandpa," Patty had whispered as he led her out the door.

"No, gal," he had replied quietly, putting a comforting arm around her shoulder. "It just seems that way."

When the sun blinked into her window the next morning, it was hard to accept that Morgan was really gone, that he had left at daybreak. She and her grandfather were staying over another day before traveling to their next stop on the circuit. He wanted the horses to have one full day of rest before trailering them on a long drive.

At the stables, Patty learned from Lefty that the new owner of the rodeo stock was keeping them over one more day as well—not to rest the animals but to complete the installation of his managers and chute bosses and to test out some horses that a couple of local ranchers had brought in.

A few minutes after Lefty had gone, Jack Evans leaned over the door where Patty was currying Lodestar.

"Some bronc busters from around here think they have some rough, tough horses, and I've volunteered to top off for them. Why don't you come on down and watch?"

"I don't feel like it, Jack. Some other time, maybe." She wanted to be left alone.

But Jack wasn't the type to take no for an answer. He opened the stall door and walked in, taking the currycomb from her hand at the same time that he grasped her by the wrist.

"Those stupid old horses of yours can wait. You and I are goin' to the arena and have some fun," he announced.

"But Jack—" Patty protested as he continued to drag her along with him.

"You turned me down flat last night when I asked you to the party," he reminded her. "Now you gotta make up for it."

"I think you partied too much last night," she said with thinly disguised exasperation.

"I could be stone-drunk and still ride those mangy-tailed excuses for horses. Even you could ride one of these 'wild' horses." His eyes widened with mock fear as he emphasized the wild. "You come watch me and I'll buy you breakfast."

They were nearly at the arena. "Do I have much choice?" Patty asked, sighing as she accepted her fate.

"None at all, my princess." Jack grinned back at her, drawing a reluctant smile in return.

There were a dozen or so cowboys perched on the rails of the arena near the chutes. Half a dozen more were working behind the chutes, running the ranch horses into the partitioned runway, dropping the gates as each one was at its designated place, trapping them inside.

"Hey, Rafe!" Jack called. "Have you got my rigging with you?"

One of the men in back of the chutes waved that he had.

While Patty found herself a seat on the top rail, Jack made his way to the first chute where a horse was haltered and ready for the saddle. Working in the close quarters of a chute, the saddling and flanking of a horse was something that was never hurried. But experience made the procedure swift and sure.

A few minutes later, Jack was sitting deep in the saddle, his hat crammed tightly on his head, his blunted spurs lying along the horse's neck, one hand on the rope and the other in the air. A quick nod to the man on the chute gate and it was swung open with an accompanying, "Let 'er buck!"

The horse bucked, but even Patty's less than experienced eye could see that it was not rodeo-horse caliber. It wasn't a genuine bucker, just a rank horse that needed to be shown who was boss. Before the bell signaled the end of the ride, the horse was only buck-jumping around the arena. Jack waved off the pickup riders and jumped from the horse, landing on his feet with a flourish of his hand.

"How was that, Princess?" He ambled to the fence, a cocky grin of triumph on his face. "Told ya it would be a snap. Do you want to try one?" Before she had a chance to respond, he was turning away. "Paul, do you care if Patty here tries out one of your horses?"

The man named Paul shook his head that he didn't mind and went back to his conversation with two men who appeared to be the owners of the horses in question.

"Eddy," Jack waved to one of the men on the fence rail, "Patty's going to ride."

Then he was taking her hand and helping her down from the rail, taking it for granted that she intended to ride. In a sort of numbed shock, she followed him without protest. The thought occurred to her that if Morgan had been here, he would have hit the ceiling.

But Morgan wasn't there anymore. He couldn't order her around and dress her down for being fifty kinds of a fool.

As Patty climbed up the sides of the chute where a Roman-nosed buckskin was held, she knew she was going to ride, a symbolic gesture that Morgan's presence—or lack of it—didn't cast a shadow on her life any longer.

It was crazy. It was stupid. But she was going to do it.

She had the best in the business instructing her. And for all of Jack's wild cockiness, he was one of the top saddle bronc riders in rodeo and had been for several years. When he stood above the chutes, he was all professional. Now that he had her at the chutes, he wasn't rushing her.

"Let Sam go out first on that sorrel. We're going to take a few minutes," he ordered crisply, then turned to Patty and smiled. "Are you nervous, Princess?"

"A little," she admitted.

He winked and smiled broadly, his vague excitement contagious. "Take a few deep breaths," he ordered.

While Jack supervised the saddling, two chutes down the gate swung open for the rider named Sam. His horse stood in frozen stillness in the chute. Finally after much pushing, shoving, and hat waving, it trotted out, gave a few half-hearted jumps, and hurried to the side gate that would take it back to the pens and the rest of its companions, to the boos of the spectators.

"Okay, Princess." Jack signaled that they were ready for her. Patty stood above the horse, her feet on the inside chute rails. "You're going to ride this horse all the way. Don't you forget that." Patty knew that confidence was the key and nodded. "When you settle into that saddle, be quiet and firm. Let him know you're boss. Get your feet in the stirrups and get set. We want to swing the gate open and give you some elbowroom as soon as you're ready. Old Buck here is supposed to be a straight-out, honest bucker with no fancy tricks."

Patty nodded again, not quite capable of speech. Balance, timing, and nerve were what she needed in the arena. Two out of three wasn't bad, she thought with an inward smile.

Taking a last deep breath, she started to lower herself into the saddle, a feeling of exhilaration beginning to bring her dead senses alive as the adrenaline began to flow. She had blocked out the sound of the other men around the chutes, listening only to Jack.

Then, from behind her, came a savagely muttered, "What the hell do you think you're doing?"

Her heart leaped into her dry throat at the familiar voice. She didn't have a chance to turn her head around before an iron band was circling her stomach and lifting her out of the chute. As if she were a weightless object, she was swung over the top rail and lowered to the arena ground with Morgan a half step behind her.

He towered above her, hands on his hips, his expression unyielding in its harshness. "You can't even let me leave this place before you're trying to break your neck with another fool stunt!" he shouted.

The anger blazing in Morgan's voice and eyes

triggered Patty's own temper. Her booted foot stamped the ground as she returned his glare with defiant fury.

"It's my neck and I can break it if I want to, Morgan Kincaid!"

"I'll be damned if you will!" he snapped.

"You have no right to tell me what to do. Now get out of my way!" Tears of anger and humiliation burned her eyes as she tried to push her way past Morgan. She was too aware of their amused audience of cowboys to let him order her about like a child.

But the granite wall was not about to be pushed aside and she found herself imprisoned by his grip, his fingers digging into the soft flesh of her arms. "You're not getting on that horse!" He ignored her wildly flailing arms and legs.

"If you two are going to fight like that in public," Jack laughed, "you oughta marry her, Morgan."

Morgan swung her over his shoulder, her shrill cry of protest falling on deaf ears as he took long strides toward the arena exit. "I intend to!" he shot back gruffly, to applause and cheers of the audience.

It took a full second for Patty to realize what he had said. Even then she couldn't believe she had heard him correctly or that he had actually meant it. But a spark of hope flickered as her fists stopped hammering his back.

"Morgan—" Her temper dissipated almost as rapidly as it had ignited.

"Shut up!"

He was carrying her through a door into a small office off the arena. As he kicked the door shut with his boot, he swung her to the floor, the momentum nearly carrying her into the wooden desk.

Her anger had vanished, but his hadn't in the least. The blue flame of it was burning hotly in his eyes.

"Whose harebrained idea was that?" Morgan demanded before Patty had a chance to open her mouth.

Her eyes were searching his face, desperately trying to figure out what was going on inside his head.

"What did you say?" Patty asked, holding her breath for his answer.

"I said, whose harebrained idea was that?" he demanded again through clenched teeth, the muscle in his jaw working overtime.

"Jack's," she answered his question absently. "I meant before that. What did you say before that?"

There was a brief flicker of something in his eyes before his look again hardened into an uncompromising mask that told her nothing.

"When?" was his clipped and noncommittal response, impatiently issued.

"Jack said you should marry me and you said that you intended to. Or . . . at least, I . . . I thought that was what you said," Patty said lamely. Her fleeting hope sank with her heart.

"Yeah, that's what I said." His mouth thinned into a hard, taut line.

"But you didn't mean it, did you?" She sighed brokenly, a catch in her throat that bordered on a sob of despair.

"Yes, I meant it." Morgan growled out the admission. "Somebody's got to keep an eye on you, so you might as well get it through your head right now that it's going to be me!"

With a gasp of delight, Patty threw herself into his arms, circling his waist with her own arms and clinging to him. For an instant, his body was rigid against hers, then it relaxed.

"Hold me, Morgan," she begged, not caring how much emotion she was revealing. "Don't ever let me go."

Gently his fingers touched her cheek, then curled beneath her chin to lift her face away from the open collar of his shirt. There was no holding back as Patty gazed into his rugged face, all the love in her heart shining in her brown eyes as she returned his look of wary disbelief with understanding.

"I love you, Morgan," she said simply.

A frown of doubt drew his dark brows together. Then it smoothed away and he bent his head to touch her lips, tenderly at first as though expecting her resistance, then with hungry possession at the unchecked response of hers. She was crushed against him, but Patty didn't care. The feeling roaring through her was a wild song of supreme joy.

All too soon Morgan was dragging his mouth from hers, burying it in her chestnut hair as he cradled her tightly against his chest. Patty smiled contentedly into his shirt at the slight tremor that shuddered through him.

"You'd better not be playing some game with me," he warned her, "because I mean to marry you."

"It isn't a game," she promised. "I would be proud to be your wife."

"How much time have we wasted?" he murmured against her forehead. "How long have you known?"

"I don't know exactly. For a while. I admitted it to myself, but I never dreamed that you might care. Then you left and—"

"I should have stayed." He smiled wryly. "I thought you were beginning to respond to me. I tried to get you to admit it, but you went all cold and prickly again and I gave up."

"I didn't give up on you," Patty murmured. "No matter how unbelievably annoying you were." She snuggled closer against his chest, needing the reassurance of his uneven heartbeat.

He turned her face up to his with loving gentleness. "You do love me?" Morgan asked her again. "And not Lije, right? I don't feel like sharing you. Not even with a figment of your imagination."

"Hey, you are the only man I love, stupid," Patty assured him tenderly. "I hope he's happy, but Lije hasn't meant anything to me for a very long time."

He frowned. "But you kept—"

"No, honey," she laughed easily, "you kept bringing him up. Every time I tried to tell you he didn't matter anymore, you kept insisting I was lying."

"Is this an argument?" He grinned. "Can we stop now?"

"Sure. But I have to say one more thing—"

"No, you don't." Morgan shut her up with a kiss. And then another.

REILLY'S
WOMAN

CHAPTER ONE

The pages of the magazine were flipped with an impatient finger. The articles couldn't hold Leah Talbot's attention as she kept glancing at the clock on the wall above the reception desk.

Through the window, she could see the sun dipping closer to the horizon. Its light cast a pale yellow glow on the wings of the small planes parked on the hangar apron outside.

The faint clatter of the computer keyboard stopped. The dark-haired woman behind the reception desk rose from her chair, turning to her coworker, an older woman.

"Want a cup of coffee, June?" the dark-haired woman asked. The older woman nodded without glancing up from the accounting printouts spread across her desk. With two cups in hand, the brunette walked to the waist-high counter door, deftly swinging it open with her hip.

She smiled politely at Leah. "How about you? Ready for a refill?"

Glancing at the empty Styrofoam cup sitting on

the table in front of her, Leah hesitated, then shrugged. "Why not?" She had nothing to do but sip coffee.

Leah picked up her cup and, sidestepping her luggage, followed the woman.

"Getting tired of waiting?" The woman's question was sympathetic enough.

Breathing in deeply, Leah nodded. "And getting impatient to leave."

The glass coffeepot sat in its heated nest on a table. Several vending machines stood adjacent to it, offering snacks of candy and cold sandwiches that had probably been there for at least a week, if the limp lettuce was any indication.

"You're going to visit family, aren't you?" The woman filled Leah's cup, then turned to the two she had brought.

"Yup. My brother Lonnie." The refill of coffee made her cup almost too hot to the touch. Leah held it gingerly. Her hazel eyes turned to the window and the slowly sinking sun. She flicked her light brown hair behind her shoulder with a restless gesture.

"Maybe you should call him and explain about the delay," the woman suggested.

"There's no need." Leah gave a brief shake of her head. "He doesn't know I'm coming. It's a surprise. His birthday is tomorrow." She glanced at the clock on the wall. It didn't seem to change. "At least I hope it'll be a surprise. First I have to get there."

"What's your brother doing in Austin? I mean," the woman laughed, "it's not exactly the most exciting town in Nevada. Basically east of nowhere, right?"

"He mentioned that." Leah smiled. "He's only

there temporarily. He works for a mining company and they sent him and his team to Austin to do some tests in the area."

The coffeepot was set back in place. "What about the rest of your family?" The woman picked up the cups and began walking back to the reception counter, still looking at Leah.

"There's only my parents. They're in Alaska now." At the woman's curious glance, Leah explained, "Dad's in the Air Force."

"Oh. Guess that's why you seem so at home here." The woman laughed a little. "You must have spent a lot of time around airfields."

"Yeah. Now and then." Leah really didn't want to get into it. "How much longer do you think it will be before we leave?" She glanced at the clock, her impatience returning. The red digital numbers might as well be painted on.

The woman shrugged, setting down one of the cups to open the counter door. "I don't know. As soon as Smith arrives, I guess."

The vague answer only increased Leah's irritation. She had been waiting for the last two hours. His lateness didn't seem to upset anyone but her. However, he was a frequent flyer on this charter.

Settling down on the vinyl-covered couch, Leah reminded herself that it would be even worse if Smith didn't show up at all. Her share of the chartered flight to Austin had maxed out a credit card as it was. Sharing the cost of plane and pilot was the only way she could afford this flight.

Luck had been sitting on her shoulder the day she had called to ask how much it would cost. When she had been told the price, Leah had been ready to shelve the idea as too expensive. Then an inquiry as to when she wanted to go prompted the discovery that a charter flight had already been booked for that Friday with the same destination.

Of course, she'd had to wait until the mysterious Mr. Smith confirmed that he was willing to share the expense. With a sigh, she accepted her fate and the fact that the waiting wasn't over yet.

A connecting door into the waiting lounge opened and a man stuck his head inside the room. Receding brown hair crowned his forehead, creased with a frown of studious concentration.

"Hey, Susan, have you heard any more from Reilly since he called to say he'd be late?"

"Sorry, Grady." The brunette shrugged. "Haven't heard a word."

He sighed. "What about my other passenger?"

"She's here." The receptionist motioned toward Leah sitting on the couch.

His gaze swung the width of the room to Leah. Immediately that distant look left his expression. He stepped into the room, a wide smile on his face.

"Are you Leah Talbot?" His smile deepened at Leah's answering nod. "I'm Grady Thompson, your pilot."

"Hello, Mr. Thompson." Leah winced a little as he wrung her hand in a vigorous shake.

"Hey, call me Grady," the pilot insisted with a bright twinkle in his eye.

He sat down on the couch, adjusting his waistband to accommodate his paunch. He was in his late forties, old enough to be her father, but that didn't stop him from flirting. Yet his good-natured grin made it impossible for Leah to feel offended.

"Okay, Grady." She smiled naturally. Her light brown hair caught the golden fire of the sunlight streaming through the windows.

He studied the streaks of gold for a second, then shifted his gaze to her classic profile, partially outlined as she turned to him. Her features were not that striking, not the arching curve of brow, nor the bright gleam in her hazel eyes or the hazel glow of her complexion. Yet the total picture was decidedly attractive.

"First names are fine with me," the pilot said affably. "Unless you prefer Ms. Talbot."

"Leah's fine."

"Tell me, Leah, are you a friend of Reilly's?"

"Is he Mr. Smith?"

Grady chuckled. "Obviously you don't know him. If you aren't a friend of his, then why are you headed to the middle of Nevada's nowhere?"

"I'm going to see my brother, if your Mr. Smith shows up," Leah said wryly.

"Reilly is not anybody's Mr. Smith."

The dry undertone of his voice aroused Leah's curiosity. "Sounds like you know him well." She might as well amuse herself by asking questions. She had nothing else to do until her fellow passenger showed up.

The pilot took a long breath and leaned against the back cushion of the couch. "Not really. I doubt if anyone knows Reilly well. He's a lone wolf, when you get right down to it. And he's part Indian."

"Oh," murmured Leah. "Why is he going to Austin?"

"Business. He has connections with some of the mining interests around Austin and Tonopah. I usually fly him to one place or the other," Grady replied.

Fleetingly Leah wondered if this Reilly Smith worked for the same company as her brother Lonnie. It was also possible that he worked for one of their competitors. Didn't matter, Leah thought. The only thing she was interested in was when the guy was going to show up.

"Do you live here in Las Vegas?" Grady changed the subject to one that interested him more.

"Yes." Before he could ask the usual question, Leah added, "I'm an assistant to an executive at a local bank." She hoped he would skip the inevitable comment that she would look good in one of the chorus lines of the lavish shows at the hotels on the strip.

"And your brother lives in Austin?"

"Only for the time being." Leah went on to explain his temporary assignment.

"Sounds like it's been a while since you've seen him."

"Well, we were together at Christmas, but tomorrow is his birthday and I wanted to surprise him."

Grady smiled. "You must think a lot of him to go to all this trouble."

"Lonnie and I are very close."

She didn't want to touch on the details of her hopscotch childhood, skipping from one end of the world to another. Under those circumstances, it was natural that she and Lonnie would be as close as twins, though they were years apart in age.

"Hm. What's your boyfriend have to say about all this? And don't tell me a girl like you doesn't have at least one boyfriend," the pilot teased.

"Let's just say that he questioned my sanity." A small smile curved her lips as Leah remembered Mark's reaction.

He worked in the same department of the bank as she did. She hadn't decided yet where their relationship was going, so, for want of a better word,

she accepted the classification of Mark as her boyfriend.

In truth, none of her coworkers or her room-
mate Nancy thought this trip was a good idea.
Besides the cost of a charter flight, they knew that
Leah was taking vacation days to do it. They had all
claimed that they understood, but none of them
seemed to be all that close to their brothers and
sisters. If she had been spending the money to see
a boyfriend, they probably wouldn't have questioned her decision. But a brother?

"Your boyfriend was probably jealous that you
weren't spending the weekend with him." Grady
ran an admiring eye over her features. "I would
be."

Check the box marked Inappropriate Comment, Leah
thought, wishing Grady would shut up. She felt annoyed all over again—and a little trapped. She
darted a look at the wall clock. "I'm beginning to
think I won't be going anywhere this weekend."
She sighed.

"Don't worry, Reilly will be here. If he couldn't
make it, he would've said so when he called earlier," the pilot assured her. "In the meantime, why
don't I take your luggage out to the plane and
stow it in the baggage compartment?"

"Okay," Leah agreed. "At least I'll be one step
closer to leaving."

With a cheerful smile, Grady leaned a little closer.
He seemed to be on the verge of more inappropriate attention. Like patting her on the knee. Leah
scooted down the couch.

But he was only getting up. "Don't worry. We'll
make it off the ground yet."

Then he was picking up her blue duffel bag and
walking toward the door leading to the hangar

apron. With his departure, the minutes started to drag again. She could just about see the remaining coffee in her cup start to evaporate, leaving a thin brown ring.

The outside door opened. Her gaze moved indifferently toward the sound, expecting to see the pilot returning. But a stranger entered.

Her mind had a preconceived idea of what Reilly Smith would look like. She had figured, for no particular reason, that he would be in his late forties, short and stocky like Grady. Only an older, senior member of a mining team would charter a plane.

This man didn't fit that description. He was six foot, leanly built but not slim and probably in his mid-thirties. Jet black hair framed the boldly defined features of his bronzed face, with prominent cheekbones that hollowed to a powerful jawline. It was a face carved by the wind and the sun.

He wore a faded denim jacket with a workshirt, and jeans that were also faded. In all the right places, she noted. Things were looking up. His blue chambray workshirt was open at the throat, revealing a large nugget of turquoise attached to a beaten silver choker around his neck.

Despite the difference between the man and her mental image, Leah was sure that this was Reilly Smith. The quiet pride of his body language, the impression of aloofness, and his effortless, animal stride convinced her she was right.

Susan, the dark-haired receptionist, confirmed it. "Well, if it isn't Mr. Smith." She rested her hands on her hips. "You kept Leah waiting, you know."

For the first time since entering the waiting lounge, his gaze acknowledged Leah's presence.

His eyes were startlingly green, the smooth, impenetrable color of jade.

A disturbing shiver of awareness trembled through Leah as his cool gaze took her in, admired her openly from head to foot, then smoothly looked away to concentrate on the business at hand.

"I was delayed," he said. It was neither an explanation nor an apology. "My cases are outside. Are you ready to leave?" He directed the question to Leah.

After waiting for almost three hours . . . Leah marveled that he had the nerve to ask her if she was ready. She suppressed the impulse to remind him that he was the one who was late, and kept her reply to a calm yes.

But she shot him an irritated look as she rose to follow him. Outside the building, a desert wind tugged at the hem of her skirt, briefly lifting it to reveal a toned leg. Leah held the open front of her jacket together with one hand and tried to keep the teasing wind from taking her skirt any higher. She realized that she probably should have worn jeans. But she had never found them comfortable to wear on planes.

Her shoes clicked loudly on the concrete while the man walking beside her made barely any sound at all. A sideways glance confirmed that her heels didn't gain her much height. The top of her head came somewhere around his chin.

Automatically her gaze slid to the left hand carrying his bags. There was no wedding band on his finger. Somehow Leah had known there wouldn't be—perhaps because of Grady's statement that Reilly Smith was a lone wolf.

Shifting her gaze straight ahead, Leah mused

silently that there were probably a lot of women who would like to change that. He was a compellingly handsome man. Not that it mattered to her. She was making this trip to see her brother.

A few yards ahead, Grady was standing beside the orange-and-white wing of a classic Cessna. The twin engine plane looked sleek and racy. A smile flashed across the pilot's face as he saw them approach.

"Didn't I tell you he'd make it, Leah?" he said in a hearty voice, then to the man at her side, "Hello, Reilly."

"Hello, Grady." Reilly's tone was warm and friendly. A brisk handshake followed the exchange of greetings.

"Let me stow your gear." Grady reached for the two bags Reilly held in his left hand.

"I'll take the briefcase on board." Reilly Smith relinquished only the larger of the two bags, keeping the attache case. His green eyes scanned the darkening sky. A single star winked feebly in the purple twilight. "What's it look like up ahead, Grady?"

The pilot studied the sky, then shrugged and returned his attention to his passengers. "There's a front moving in. We still have a chance of reaching Austin before it does. If not, it might get a little rough, but we'll make it." With his free hand, Grady motioned toward the open door of the plane. "Climb aboard."

The two small steps made it easy for Leah to climb onto the wing even in her skirt. Maneuvering past the front seats to the second seats was more awkward. Reilly Smith followed with an ease that she envied.

He sat down in the seat beside her. Considering

the friendliness between Reilly and the pilot, Leah had sort of expected him to sit in front with Grady. As she fastened her seat belt, she noticed the briefcase he had brought on board and realized that he probably intended to work.

Grady climbed aboard and swung himself into the pilot's seat directly ahead of Leah. His quick look backward encompassed both of them before he buckled his seat belt.

"Did you two introduce yourselves?" The question didn't break the rhythm of his preflight checklist.

"More or less," Leah answered.

"She's flying to Austin to visit her brother."

The first of the plane's engines growled to life, the propeller hesitating, then spinning into a blur.

Leah cast another sideways glance at her companion. "My brother works for a mining company. He's part of a team that's been temporarily assigned to survey the Austin area." She might as well find out if Reilly Smith was a member of the same company or with a rival firm. "Grady mentioned that you had connections with some mining interests. Maybe you know my brother. His name is Lonnie Talbot."

He leveled a look at her with those disconcerting eyes. The grooves at each side of his hard mouth deepened into a faint smile. "No, I don't know him."

The roar of both engines made conversation impossible. Leah was forced to set aside her curiosity for the time being. At least she knew that Reilly Smith didn't work for the same company as her brother.

In the pilot's seat, Grady was on the radio. "Ground Control, this is 92 George requesting taxi instructions."

Excitement coursed through her. After all the waiting, she was finally on the way. Looking out the window, Leah smiled with secret amusement at the thought of Lonnie's reaction when he learned that she had flown to be with him on his birthday.

Blue lights flashed outside her window as the plane taxied to the airport runway. At the end of the runway, the engines roared with thundering force as Grady made his run-up. Then the tower radioed permission for them to take off.

Grady half-looked over his shoulder, a grin on his face. "Now we'll get this bird off the ground."

He pivoted the plane onto the runway, the engines building power. Leah felt the surge of acceleration as the brakes were released and the throttle opened to full power. The nose lifted off the ground. Seconds later the plane was airborne and climbing, the landing gear thumping into the belly.

Outside her window, Leah could see the blaze of city lights piercing the darkness below. The brilliant neon lights of the hotels and casinos on Las Vegas's famous strip were like an iridescently colored ribbon.

Cool night air from the vent above her head ruffled her light brown hair. The infrared lights on the instrument panel cast a faint light in the cockpit and there was a reading light shining down on the seat next to hers.

Her fellow passenger wasn't looking at the diminishing world below them, Leah noticed. His briefcase was open on his lap. Common courtesy ruled that she shouldn't try to chat when he was obviously working.

But she was tempted to look over his shoulder and catch a glimpse of the papers he was studying. She resisted, turning her attention again to the window. Eventually the only thing she could see was her own reflection.

She considered taking out the paperback book she had in her bag, then decided against it. She was too intent on reaching her destination to concentrate on reading.

The airplane leveled off. Grady turned slightly in his seat. "Want to sit up front with me for a while, Leah?"

"Sure. Thanks." She unbuckled her seat belt.

"You don't have any objections, do you, Reilly?"

"None at all." His green eyes flicked a glance at Leah. He seemed to be laughing silently.

Briefly she wondered if Reilly Smith thought she was making a play for the pilot. As if he couldn't see that Grady was old enough to be her father, she thought with indignation.

"Don't bump into any of the controls," Grady cautioned as Leah crouched to negotiate the tiny aisleway to the empty front seat.

A helping hand gripped her elbow. With faint surprise, she realized it belonged to Reilly Smith. His touch was pleasantly strong and reassuring but brief.

Dodging the control panel near the floor, Leah slid onto the right front seat, straightening her skirt over her knees. The change of seat had been accomplished neatly enough despite the close quarters.

"Thanks for the hand," she said over her shoulder. "I hope it won't distract you if Grady and I talk."

"As a matter of fact, I think I'll quit for a while and get some sleep." The snap of the briefcase lid followed his statement.

When the reading light went off, Leah wished

for a second that she hadn't moved from her seat. She would have preferred to talk to Reilly if she'd known he wasn't going to work.

"It's amazing." Grady shook his head, a wry smile on his face.

"What is?" Leah asked.

"Him." With a backward nod of his head, the pilot indicated the man in the seat behind Leah.

She was well aware that Grady's remark carried easily to the man. She glanced over her shoulder to see Reilly Smith's reaction to the comment. He was leaning back in his seat, eyes closed. His chest moved in an even rhythm.

"He's already asleep." Grady sighed. "He just closes his eyes. No tossing, no turning, just sleep."

"Must be nice," Leah agreed, settling back into her seat. She glanced around at the instrument dials illuminated by the infrared light. "Is the plane on autopilot now?"

"Yup." But Leah noticed the automatic way Grady kept checking the panel. "Have you ever been in the front seat of a private plane before?"

"My dad has taken me up several times, but not in a vintage Cessna."

Grady laughed. "It has a few bells and whistles all the same. Might even land itself if I wasn't looking. Don't you worry."

"Okay." Leah hoped she didn't sound as nervous as she felt.

"Got a ways to go," Grady said after a long minute. "So let's talk."

"What about?"

"Gee, I don't know. Your childhood. Considering how young you are, it wasn't all that long ago. Got any good stories?"

Leah laughed. "Well, yeah. A few. My brother and I were definitely Air Force brats." She added a sketchy outline of her childhood life, moving from air base to air base.

"How did you wind up in Las Vegas?"

"The usual way. Dad was transferred to Nellis Air Force Base when I was in high school. I had graduated and just started a business administration course when his orders came through for Alaska. I wanted to finish my training, so I stayed. And it was time to leave the nest."

"What about the lure of the bright lights?" Grady teased.

"Not for me. I'm very happy working in a bank. I have no desire to be in entertainment. Besides, I flunked dance class. Hung up my patent leather tap shoes when I was ten."

"I see," Grady said. "Now let me guess. I bet you never go to the casinos. People who actually live in Las Vegas just don't."

"Not often," she agreed. "But when new shows open or a performer I like is in town, then I go. But I don't enjoy the crowds of tourists and gamblers."

"Say," Grady paused, turning a curious look to her, "did you tell me that you were in the South Pacific for a time?"

"Guam and Hawaii."

"I was there when I was in the service—and I'm not going to tell you how long ago that was!"

A steady flow of banter began as Grady quizzed her to see if she had been to places he had visited, then compared her descriptions to what he remembered.

Gradually they talked themselves out and drifted

into silence. Leah gazed beyond her reflection in the window to look at the starry sky. She felt sublimely relaxed.

"If you feel like nodding off," Grady said quietly, "you can crawl back to your old seat. At least there you can stretch your legs out without bumping into any controls."

With a contented sigh, she agreed. "I think I'll do that."

It was a bit easier getting back through the tiny aisle, although Leah took care not to waken the sleeping Reilly. As she turned to slide into her seat, she noticed the inky blackness of the sky directly ahead.

"It's very dark ahead, isn't it?" she asked Grady softly.

"It must be that frontal system. I'll see if I can get an update on it."

He made the call while she buckled her seat belt. The answering transmission didn't carry clearly to her, but Grady passed the message back.

"Looks like the front beat us to Austin. Better buckle in tight—it might get a little rough." Then he glanced over his shoulder at the sleeping figure. "Reilly!"

"I heard you," came the quiet reply. With calm deliberation, Reilly straightened and tightened his seat belt.

"I thought you were asleep." Leah spoke without thinking.

"I was."

There was not a trace of sleepiness in his voice. She decided that he wakened as quickly as he went to sleep.

CHAPTER TWO

A black void yawned ominously around the twin engine plane. Jagged splinters of lightning rained fire in the sky. Turbulent crosscurrents of air alternately tugged and pushed at the plane.

At each bone-shaking bounce of the plane, Grady throttled back to avoid putting any more stress on the structure than necessary. The buffeting only increased in intensity.

"Reilly!" Grady called for him to lean forward, not taking his eyes off the gauges and dials in front of him, bouncing with the plane.

Reilly loosened his seat belt slightly and bent forward.

"It's only going to get worse," Grady shouted. "I'm going to try to fly around it. Okay?"

"Okay." The voice that agreed didn't sound at all troubled by the weather.

Leah, despite her instinctive trust in the pilot's competency, felt tremors of fear shudder through her. She tried to forestall the guilty feeling for her

cowardice by telling herself that only a fool would-
n't be afraid.

Still, she held her breath as Grady slowly banked
the plane toward the east, trying to outrace the
storm and sneak around it. Sliding a round-eyed
look at the man next to her, she decided that
Reilly must have nerves of steel.

A severe downdraft sucked at the plane, nearly
taking Leah's stomach when the plane groaned
free. The pitch blackness that surrounded them
was only broken by fiery tongues of lightning lick-
ing the air around them. The plane continued
bucking through the turbulence.

"I can't get above this stuff!" Grady shouted. "I'm
going to take her down a couple of thousand feet
and see if it's any calmer."

No reply was necessary. Leah doubted if her dry
mouth and throat could have made any. It felt as if
they were diving, but she knew it was a controlled
slideslip downward.

Through the mirrorlike reflection of the window, Leah watched the pilot gently level out the
wings. Lightning flashed ahead of them, its brilliant yellow-white light lasting for several seconds.

"Sweet Jesus!" Grady's mutter of angry prayer
reached Leah's ears at the same instant that she
saw the mound of solid black rising in front of the
nose.

It was a mountain. She registered the terrifying
fact a second before she was thrown violently to
one side as Grady executed a sharp right turn.

Another flash of lightning clearly outlined more
mountains in their path.

"There aren't supposed to be any damn mountains at this altitude," Grady muttered as he banked
sharply. "This damned altimeter must—"

He didn't finish the rest. A jagged fork of lightning illuminated an escape route—a low saddle-back ridge connecting two peaks. Grady aimed the nose of the plane at where he thought it had been. Leah waited in frozen stillness for the next streak of lightning that would reveal if his aim was true.

It was late. They were nearly there when flashing light revealed that he had misjudged the spot. The plane was going to crash into the side of the mountain.

Quickly Grady tried to correct for his error. Leah gasped silently in horror—*oh, Lonnie!*

Fingers closed viselike on the back of her neck, pushing her head to her knees and holding it there.

"Stay down." Reilly's softly spoken order pierced her terror.

A sickening jolt rocked the right side of the plane. The right wingtip had clipped the mountainside, wrenching and tearing. Half the wing split away.

The plane pitched downward.

"Come on, baby!" Grady urged below his breath.

The belly of the plane bounced and thudded on solid ground. It sliced along for a few rattling feet, then the right wing again met an immovable object. Their speed sent the plane spinning like a top across the ground.

The screaming rip of metal seemed to surround Leah on all sides without end. *Why is it all happening so slowly?* Glass shattered above her head. There were more tearing, crunching sounds of metal from her side.

She felt a faint sensation of pain as blackness swirled in front of her eyes. Yet Leah remained semiconscious, dissociated from what was happening. The roaring in her ears deafened her to all outside sounds.

Then the black mist began to recede. An iron hook of some kind was pulling her upward. A second later she realized it wasn't an iron hook but a muscled arm.

"Come on. We've got to get out of here." The firm voice seemed to come from a great distance.

But Leah knew she had to obey the command. She shook her head to chase away the lingering daze. The trembling awkwardness of her legs made the arm around her ribs provide most of her support.

Taking a shaky breath, she suddenly realized that she was alive. It was Reilly Smith's arm that was helping her through the open door of the downed plane. As she squeezed through the narrow opening, stumbling over the seats, she wondered why he hadn't opened the door wider.

When her foot touched the loose gravel outside the door, she knew. The plane had stopped lengthwise against the side of the mountain. It was the mountain wall that wouldn't allow the door to open another inch.

Wind whipped at her hair as she emerged. She felt the sting of rain against her cheeks while thunder rumbled ominously overhead. She wanted to lean against the body of the plane and quietly sob her relief and gratitude at being alive but the arm around her waist wouldn't let her.

"We can't stop here," Reilly said.

Accepting the wisdom in his words, Leah didn't protest his guidance. The numbness was leaving her legs. Walking was still difficult over the uneven ground because of the high heels of her shoes.

Some distance from the plane, he halted in an open patch of mountain desert—an occasional flash lit up the dark sky and let her see that much.

"Wait here," he ordered. "I'm going back to the plane. And stay down, or you could get hit by lightning."

Leah nodded, then found her voice. "I will." As he turned to leave her, she remembered. "Where's Grady?"

There was no answer as her rescuer glided away into the dark. Perhaps he hadn't heard the question, she decided, or else he was going back to get the pilot.

More lightning crackled. In the illuminating light, she could make out his shadowy outline. Beyond was the mutilated metal body of the plane. She shuddered, knowing that it was a miracle they had survived the wreck.

The tiny drops of wind-whipped rain could hardly be called a downpour, but as Leah waited in the darkness, she could feel the rain slowly soaking her clothes. She pulled the front of her jacket closed.

A shooting pain stabbed her left arm. Her right hand explored the painful area. The sleeve of her blouse was sticky and warm. Then her fingers felt the tear in the material and the gash in the soft flesh of her upper arm.

She didn't remember being hurt. Instinctively her hand clutched the wound, checking the flow of blood. In this darkness, she couldn't see how serious it might be. Only now that she had discovered it was it beginning to throb. Suddenly Leah felt very cold and very alone.

Her gaze tried to penetrate the black curtain of

night for a glimpse of the man who had led her here. She saw only the ghostly shimmer of white from the painted metal of the aircraft.

Thunder boomed. A flash of lightning followed before the rolling thunder stopped. Leah had promised to wait, but if Reilly Smith didn't return soon, she wasn't going to keep that promise.

An eerie pool of light was coming from the direction of the plane, floating along the ground through the desert scrub. Several spine-chilling seconds passed before Leah realized it was coming from a flashlight. A sighing laugh slipped from her throat.

She could distinguish enough of the tall figure to see that he was carrying something over his shoulder. Grady? She waited breathlessly for Reilly to reach her.

Blinded by the light when it picked her out in the darkness, she shielded her eyes from the glare. The light moved away as he knelt beside her, swinging the burden from his shoulder. Leah stared at the bundle—a coat with its sleeves tied together to carry the loose objects inside.

"Where's Grady?" Her eyes searched his face in the dim glow as she mentally braced herself for his answer.

"He's dead." Reilly's long fingers deftly untied the coat sleeves.

"No . . ." she whispered. It couldn't be true. But she knew that it was. She tried to swallow back the tremor in her voice. "You didn't leave him in the plane?"

"Yes. There wasn't anything I could do for him." His face was a mask and his green eyes were expressionless. "Let me see what I can do for your arm."

Absently Leah touched her wound, its throbbing vaguely uncomfortable. It seemed wrong to have left Grady in that frightening mess of twisted metal. It was harder to comprehend the fact that he was dead—that warm, vital man.

"You'll have to hold the flashlight." When his words brought no response from Leah, Reilly frowned. Sooty lashes thickened by the rain narrowed his gaze. "Snap out of it!"

"W-what?"

"I said you'll have to hold the flashlight so I can look at your arm," he repeated curtly.

Her eyes had started to mist with tears. She hurriedly blinked them away as her fingers closed over the cold, wet flashlight. She directed the beam at her injury. Beyond the circle of light, she saw Reilly remove his pocketknife and choose a blade.

"I'm going to rip the sleeve the rest of the way." Explanation given, he sliced a blade through the material's seam. A quick rip and the sleeve was in his hand.

Using it, he carefully wiped away the blood to see the extent of the cut. The jagged rip in her flesh wasn't a pleasant sight and Leah turned her gaze away. She could feel him probing the wound for any splinters of glass or metal. It throbbed with burning fire now.

He turned away, opening the lid of a large first-aid kit he had placed at his side. He took out a bottle of antiseptic and closed the lid before the rain could damage any of the contents. Water droplets glistened like diamonds in his jet black hair.

"This is going to hurt," he warned.

Leah took a deep breath, but she couldn't hold back a choked gasp of pain as her arm jerked to avoid the fiery liquid.

"Hold still!"

"It hurts!" she snapped back, stating the obvious.

Reilly ignored that. "And hold the light still so I can see what I'm doing."

Insensitive pig, Leah thought angrily. At least he could have said he was sorry but that he couldn't help hurting her. Still, at least she was alive to feel the pain. She couldn't complain.

Gritting her teeth, she focused the light on her arm again. This time she didn't cry as he poured the antiseptic on the open wound, although the flashlight beam did waver slightly. Next came the bandage, which was expertly and efficiently applied.

"Thank you." Leah felt the pain begin to recede.

"You're welcome." A distant smile touched his mouth.

He took the flashlight and laid it on the ground, bathing their clearing with light. Unfolding the coat on the ground, he slipped a pistol into the waistband of his jeans and pulled his jacket over it to keep out the rain. A canteen and another small box were set aside along with a folded square of red material. He stood up, shaking out the coat.

"This'll keep the rain off you," he said, holding it out to Leah.

"In case you haven't noticed, I'm already soaked." She hugged her arms tighter around her waist, feeling the biting chill of her damp clothes.

"I don't want the bandage getting wet." He draped a man's raincoat over her shoulders, drawing the collar around her neck. "At night it's cold in the mountain desert—in the spring or any other time of year. It will give you some protection against the cold if not the rain."

What she wanted was some dry clothes, but logically Leah realized that they would soon get wet, too. Gingerly she slid her injured arm in a sleeve and carefully eased her other arm into the second sleeve and buttoned the coat.

"Whose is this?" she asked unthinkingly as the coat drowned her in its looseness.

"Grady's."

Leah paled. Suddenly the coat didn't feel the same. She started to unbutton it.

"You can wear it," she murmured tightly.

"No." His voice was firm as his watchful eyes studied her face. "He isn't going to object, Leah."

Her temper flared at his apparently flippant remark. "How can you be so callous?"

"It's the truth, even if you don't want to hear it," Reilly replied calmly. Her anger flowed over him without denting his aloof composure. "Grady would tell you to wear the damned coat if he were here. But he didn't make it. Nothing we can do about that. Our main concern now has to be ourselves. We have to use what's on hand to survive the night."

His cold logic defeated her. She began rebuttoning the coat. "You could build a fire to warm us up and dry us out," she declared, a seed of rebellion remaining.

"It's raining," he reminded her dryly.

"Right." Feeling stupid, she pushed the wet brown hair away from her forehead. "But you're part Indian. Shouldn't be too difficult for you."

He gave her a measuring look. She nibbled self-consciously on her lower lip, instantly ashamed of what she had said.

"I'm sorry."

"Never mind. You're still in shock."

"What about you?"

"Oh, I'm okay. Indians can survive anything. Guess I could build a fire." There was a hint of cynical amusement in his voice. He reached down and picked up the folded red square. "All I have to do is find some dry wood and kindling. Maybe after a couple of hours, I could get a blaze going. If the two of us don't succumb to exposure and shock, we might enjoy it."

"I really am sorry. I didn't think." Leah lowered her gaze to the ground. She took a deep breath and let it out slowly. "We can't sit out here in the rain. Weren't there survival blankets on board or something we could use to keep warm?"

"I only found one but I didn't want to stick around—" He stopped in midsentence for a second. "I'm afraid the plane will catch fire. It happens."

"Right."

"Besides, the metal of the plane might act like a lightning rod. It's too dangerous." He shook out the square of red, which rustled stiffly in protest. The opposite side of the material resembled aluminum. Its silvery finish gleamed in the circle of light.

"And I saw loose tailings from an abandoned mine higher up the mountain. If the rain brings that stuff down, the door would be blocked by morning. Out here, we might get wet and cold—it wouldn't be any warmer in the plane—but we wouldn't be trapped inside the wreckage."

"Sounds like you thought of everything."

"I hope so," he said tonelessly. "It'll be a while until the sun comes up."

Leah had no choice but to agree. But she was wet and cold, and getting colder. Her teeth had

started to chatter and her arm was beginning to
stiffen and feel sore.

"What are we going to do?' Her gaze moved
wearily to him. Since all her thoughts seemed to
have been wrong, it was time he suggested something.

"Stand up."

His hand was at her elbow, lifting her upright.
Leah stood, waiting uncertainly for his next move.
The thin survival blanket was partially wrapped
around her, rising above her head in a stiff half-
hood.

"Hold the side," Reilly instructed, pushing an
edge of it into her fingers. He hesitated, drawing a
curious look from her. "What we're going to do is
wrap ourselves together in this blanket. Our body
heat will keep us warm and the blanket should
keep off most of the rain."

Leah summed it up. "You're saying we should
sleep together." She was shivering and trying to
keep her teeth from chattering too loudly. "It's the
logical and practical thing to do, isn't it?" she
added wryly.

"Yes." He nodded, a faint smile on his wet face.

She was too cold and wet and miserable to care
what happened.

"By all means. Let's do it." She returned his
smile, a little weakly.

He slid an arm around the bulky folds of the
raincoat at her waist as he drew the stiff blanket
behind and around him. At his signal, they eased
themselves to the ground in unison.

Reilly lay on his back, drawing Leah's head and
shoulders on his chest and curving the rest of her
against his length. Needles of rain struck at the

blanket, but the waterproof material kept them dry.

At first she was conscious of the cold wetness of his hard form, then gradually she felt his body warmth steaming through his soaked clothes and she snuggled closer, shivering uncontrollably. His hands began rubbing her back, shoulders and waist, stimulating her circulation while taking care to avoid her injured arm. It throbbed dully.

"Is that better?" Warm breath stirred the air near her forehead.

"Much better." She inhaled deeply with contentment. The musky scent of his maleness was heightened by the rain.

His hands maintained their slow, steady rhythm. A small fire was glowing inside her. She was beginning to feel human again. Her mind stopped dwelling on her physical discomfort and started to wander on to other subjects.

"A search party will start looking for us tomorrow, won't they?" she said quietly.

"Yes."

"How long do you think it will take them to find us?"

"It's hard to say."

For a minute Leah thought that was the only reply Reilly was going to make, then he enlarged upon his answer. "There wasn't time for a mayday call to give our location. Grady had his hands full trying to keep from slamming into the side of the mountain."

"I remember," Leah said softly.

"If there was a global positioning system or tracking device on board, I didn't see it. The crash completely wrecked the instrument panel anyway.

And if he filed a flight plan, he flew off course try-ing to avoid the center of the storm. A search would initially cover the planned route, then widen its area if the plane wasn't found."

"Then it could be late tomorrow before they find us?"

A moment of slight hesitation followed her question.

"This is rugged terrain. It's not that easy to find people or a plane from the air. And a party on foot would have a lot of ground to cover. It could be Sunday—or Monday."

Leah shuddered, this time not from the cold. "I'm glad I didn't let Lonnie know I was coming. He won't be worrying about me for a while any-way, wondering if I'm dead or alive."

She guessed that the authorities would notify her parents first, who would then contact her brother. With luck, they would be rescued before that.

"You were planning to surprise him?"

Leah nodded, her cheek moving against the damp denim of his jacket. "For his birthday. It's tomorrow." She sighed, then pulled her mind away from the de-pressing thought. "You were expected, weren't you?"

"Yes, by some business friends."

"Who do you work for?" She tipped her head back against his shoulder, peering through the darkness of their cocoon for a glimpse of his face. The intimacy of being in his arms made her bold and a little giddy. "An arch rival of the mining firm that my brother works for?"

"Arch rival? Do you read a lot of comic books, Leah?"

She could sense his smile.

"Anyway, I work for myself," he went on.

"You own a mining company?"

"No." There was amused patience in his low voice. "I design jewelry."

Leah remembered the nugget of turquoise he wore around his neck. "Turquoise jewelry, I guess."

"Or Indian jewelry. Whichever you prefer to call it." The mockery in his tone was unmistakable.

Leah stiffened. "Okay, I admit I wasn't exactly tactful about that. I was cold and wet and all I could think of was a nice, warm fire. I don't know how to build one." She hesitated, irritated by her own defensiveness. "Grady said you were part Indian. That's how I knew."

"Figured that out already," Reilly said.

Leah gave up trying to explain her tactless remark. "Then why were you flying to Austin?"

"There are turquoise mines in the area," he said. "I deal directly with their owners, and buy the stones I want to use from them."

"I didn't know that." She frowned slightly, trying to remember if Lonnie had mentioned turquoise mines in one of his letters. "About the mines being there, I mean."

"There's a line of turquoise deposits that runs almost directly down the center of the state, starting around Battle Mountain through Austin. At Tonopah it curves northwest. The line would look like a J if you drew it on a map."

"I guess I always thought most turquoise was found in Arizona."

"Arizona does produce quite a bit, but mostly as a by-product of copper mining." His fingers gently pulled her long, wet hair free of the coat collar, smoothing it over her back. "And that's the story of turquoise. I think it's time we got some sleep. Got a long day ahead of us tomorrow."

The truth was that Leah didn't want to stop talking. As long as her mind was occupied with other things, it couldn't dwell on the crash.

"I suppose you're right." She sighed reluctantly, adding a silent *again* to the admission. Her eyelids were beginning to feel heavy. "What time is it?"

"About midnight, I imagine. Are you comfortable?"

"Yes," she nodded, nestling her head closer to his chest. "Good night."

"Good night."

Silence closed in. Despite the crash of thunder and lightning and the tapping rain, it was silent and mostly dark. There was none of the comforting background noise of the city, no sounds of cars and people, and no streetlights shining through the windows.

The ground was hard and unyielding beneath her hip. Her pillow, Reilly's chest, rose and fell with his even breathing. The steady rhythm of his heart beat against her ear.

If the unthinkable had not happened, she would have been sleeping in a strange bed tonight but not one as strange as this. And Lonnie would have been in the same house. Her throat tightened as she remembered that Grady would have been alive, too.

"If we'd left earlier," she murmured in a low, choked voice, "we could've beaten the storm to Austin."

"You would be with your brother. I would be with my friends. And Grady wouldn't be dead." Leah could feel the vibration of Reilly's low-pitched voice, unemotional and aloof. "That isn't the way it is. It's best you accept that."

Tears slid down her cheeks. Her emotional numbness from shock—he had been right about that—was wearing off. She had to admit, bitterly, that he was right again. But it didn't make the tragedy of Grady's death any easier to accept. Her lashes fluttered down, clinging to the tears on her lower lashes.

In the night, her troubled and uneasy sleep was interrupted by a rolling roar that seemed to vibrate the ground beneath them. She stirred, her eyes opening halfway. "What was that?" she whispered, bewildered. She tried to raise herself up on an elbow, but he tightened his arm around her and used his other hand to press her head against his chest.

"Nothing to worry about," Reilly answered quietly. "Go back to sleep."

Not fully awake and with her body protesting the slightest movement, Leah obeyed. It was probably just the thunder anyway, she told herself.

CHAPTER THREE

It wasn't thunder.

The morning sun was in her eyes, but the light didn't blind Leah to the mound of chipped rock and rubble in front of her. A landslide had completely covered the plane.

Farther up the mountain slope on a rocky ledge was the black hole of a mine entrance. A fallen timber lay across the opening, supporting only its own weight. Last night's rain had sent the loose tailings from the mine down the slope.

Leah remembered Reilly's warning about it. If they had taken shelter in the plane, they would have been trapped inside or smothered by the debris.

This morning her bones ached from sleeping on the hard ground and her muscles were cramped from clinging to Reilly. Yet somewhere under that mound of rock was the plane—and Grady's body—and her discomfort seemed like a very small thing.

Soberly she watched Reilly carefully working his way over the rubble. At each step, the ground shifted beneath his feet, miniature slides of loose gravel rolling away. Then he stopped, kneeling cautiously to push away the rock.

A patch of white was revealed. He made it larger, using his left arm as a barricade to hold back the gravel that tried to cover the patch again. With painstaking slowness he pushed more rock away with his free hand, digging downward along the side of the plane.

His goal was the baggage compartment in the crumpled nose of the plane. The crash had buckled the door, popping it partly open at the bottom. Leah watched Reilly straining with only one free hand to open it the rest of the way.

When the last fragment of latch released itself, he quickly lifted the door up, using it instead of his arm to hold back the gravel. Reaching inside, he wasted no time in dragging out his suitcase, then Leah's duffel.

Gravel danced around both sides of the door, as if in warning. He shoved the cases away, letting the rolling rocks carry them away from the buried plane. Leah held her breath as he slowly lowered the door. The trickle of rocks grew steadily louder as the angle lessened.

Above him, the rocks shifted but no fresh slide started when the door was down and immediately covered by slow-moving gravel. Turning, he inched his way down the slope in a half-sitting position to the luggage.

When he stood on firm ground again, Leah let out the breath she had been holding in a relieved sigh. Reilly picked up the two cases and walked to where she stood a safe distance away.

"Now we can change." The grooves around his mouth deepened to suggest a smile.

"I can't wait," Leah said. Although she had dried out some from her soaking last night, her clothes still felt vaguely damp against her skin.

"Got a pair of jeans in there?" He set her duffel on the ground in front of her.

"I think so," she told him.

"Better put them on. And some flat shoes."

Leah glanced around. The mountainside was sparsely covered with desert scrub. There was not a boulder or tree in sight large enough to conceal her.

"Where can I change?" she asked finally.

An amused light danced in his green eyes. "Wherever you want." He shrugged.

"I mean somewhere private," Leah retorted. "I don't intend to strip in front of an audience."

"Guess you'll have to crouch behind a bush." His expression turned to one of complete indifference as he bent to unsnap the lid of his suitcase. "I'm more interested in changing my own damp clothes than being an audience for you."

Pressing her lips tightly together, Leah knelt in front of her duffel, holding her injured left arm stiffly across her waist. It hurt badly this morning. She took care not to bump it accidentally as she unlatched the lid and began rummaging through it for fresh underwear, jeans, and a top.

"I wasn't suggesting that you would sit and applaud while I undressed," she muttered tautly.

"Oh? What were you suggesting?"

"I just wanted some privacy, okay?" Leah rolled her change of clothes into a ball and placed a pair of flat-heeled loafers on top.

"Fine." His strong, lean features were impassive.

"Thank you." She zipped up her duffel. Rising awkwardly with her bundle, she marched toward a thick clump of sage, her nose in the air. Damn. She had done it again. She had taken offense where none was intended. Why did she always put her foot in her mouth, she wondered.

"Oh, Leah . . ."

His low voice halted her steps. She turned hesitantly toward him, suddenly wary, knowing he deserved an apology yet still too angry with herself to make one that would sound sincere.

"What?" she asked, somewhat abruptly.

"Before you put on a clean top, I'd like to look at your arm."

"All right," she agreed, and resumed her course to the nearest large bush. Not until she had shed her damp clothes and put on dry ones did she realize that he wanted to look at her wound before she changed her clothes. The ripped sleeve of her blouse would have given him free access to the bandage.

The lacy edges of her bra accented her cleavage too much for her to let him see her only in that. It didn't matter that the bra covered more than her bikini top. She looked at the damp, rumpled, blood-streaked blouse she had been wearing. She couldn't stand the thought of putting it on again.

"The hell with it," she muttered to herself. "Here goes nothing."

Picking up a fresh top, she wrapped it under her arms and around her breasts, holding it securely with her right hand. She looked down, deciding that she was decently covered, and stepped from behind the bush.

The morning air was cool from last night's rain and sharply scented with sage. A shiver ran over her bare shoulders. Leah didn't know if it was from the chilly air or her apprehension.

Reilly was in the clearing where they had spent

the night, his back turned to her. He seemed to be buttoning the clean white shirt that hung down over his dark blue jeans. The sunlight gleamed on his black hair.

"Do you want to look at my arm now?" Leah asked in a faintly defensive tone.

He glanced over his shoulder, then turned slowly, the shirt buttoned halfway. Without finishing his task, he reached down for the first-aid kit. "Yes, I will," he answered smoothly.

Leah walked toward him, holding her head proudly to hide her nervousness. His gaze moved lazily to the white bra straps over her shoulders. A dull red flush crept into her cheeks.

"I misunderstood what you meant earlier. I forgot about the sleeve," she said, feeling like a fool for being so embarrassed. A bra was a bra was a bra. He had probably seen one or two before.

"I realize that." A dark glow entered his jade eyes, but she couldn't tell whether or not he was laughing at her. "I was going to explain before you disappeared behind the bush, but I thought you might bite my head off."

"I'm sorry." Leah lowered her chin a little.

But Reilly was already removing the adhesive strips to examine her wound, accepting her apology without comment. The gentle probing of his fingers made her wince.

"Hurt?" His intent gaze moved to her face.

"Of course." Her teeth sank into her lower lip, nibbling it to distract her mind from the pain in her arm.

"It looks clean. Does it feel as if there's anything in it? A piece of glass?" he asked.

Leah shook her head. "No. It's just sore."

"I'll put a clean bandage on."

She watched as he deftly changed the bandage to a fresh one. Her gaze strayed to the tanned column of his neck and the hollow of his throat where the nugget of turquoise rested. Then she inadvertently looked down the partially unbuttoned front of his shirt where his muscled chest gleamed bronze and smooth like a statue's. It was several seconds before she realized he was finished. Caught staring, she flushed guiltily.

"Thank you." Her fingers tightened on her wrapped top as his gaze moved over her face.

"You're welcome." Reilly turned his back. "You can put on your top now." With definite overtones of laughter in his voice, he added, "As long as you promise not to watch me tuck my shirt into my jeans."

Laughing softly, Leah promised and turned her back to him. She carefully eased her injured arm into the sleeve of her top, then twisted to find the other sleeve. As she buttoned the last button, Reilly asked, "Finished?"

"Yeah. You can turn around now." A wide smile was curving her mouth when he turned around, the dark jade of his eyes brilliantly warm.

"Do you feel better?" He reached down to pick up the denim jacket lying across his suitcase.

"I actually do," Leah said. "The only way I could feel better is if I'd already had breakfast."

"The tin box sitting over there has crackers in it," he suggested. "That's the best I can offer in the way of food until I can collect some firewood and get a fire going. There isn't much water in the canteen, so use it sparingly," he cautioned.

"I will." She knelt beside the box and unlatched the lid. There was more than crackers inside. She saw several packages of dried food that had to be mixed with water and sticks of beef jerky. "I didn't know charter flights carried food survival kits."

"They don't as a rule," Reilly answered. "Grady was just superstitious."

"Superstitious? What do you mean?" Leah frowned.

"He served during the first Gulf war. He flew light reconnaissance aircraft. Survival kits were standard issue," he explained. "One day Grady forgot his and his plane was hit by gunfire. He crashed in the middle of nowhere, up to the windows in sand."

"Oh my God," Leah said. "He didn't mention that while we were trading life stories. You were asleep."

"I heard some of it." Reilly smiled. "Anyway, he was found by our guys, but it took them almost three days. He swore he almost starved to death. After that he never went up without the kit and he was never shot down again. When he got his discharge, he came back to the States and started flying charters. He always took a kit like this for luck."

Leah looked down at the partially unwrapped packet of crackers in her hand. The appetite she'd thought she had receded. "The kit didn't bring him very much luck this time," she murmured sadly.

Reilly didn't comment on that. "I pointed out to him that those dehydrated foods wouldn't be much use in desert country like this. Just add water means you have to find the water. He said that he'd never have to use it anyway, but this way the food wouldn't spoil."

Leah looked at the mound of debris that covered the plane. "Can't we get him out of there?"

"No. It would take men and machinery and a way of holding back the slide."

She had known what his answer would be, but she needed to hear it.

"I'm going to look for wood to build a signal fire," Reilly continued, switching the subject. "You stay here. You'll be all right."

"Yes." Leah was still staring at the gravelike mound that covered the plane.

"Keep an eye out for search planes. I doubt they'll be this far east so early this morning, but keep watch."

His firm voice reminded her that they had to concentrate on their rescue. The pilot was beyond help. Breathing in deeply, Leah said a silent prayer for Grady anyway—and added one for herself and Reilly.

She returned her attention to the small package of crackers in her hand.

"I'll watch," she promised.

"Shout if you need me," he added.

At Leah's nod, he smiled in reassurance and started up the mountain slope toward the abandoned mine. His lithe stride took him in a different direction this time, avoiding the unstable ground of the slide. Leah watched him until he disappeared on the rocky ledge high above.

Taking care not to tear the wrapper, she opened the cracker package. The salty square tasted dry and chalky in her mouth. She ate only one and tightly wrapped the others in the package. As she picked up the canteen, Leah remembered Reilly's statement that water was valuable.

Hesitating, she took a small swig to wash the cracker down, then recapped it. It was ironic, she thought, how she only felt more thirsty knowing water was scarce. The dryness of the landscape made the nearly full canteen seem like it held very little.

Setting it aside, she reached for her duffel bag and rummaged through it for her cosmetic case. Vanity aside, her SPF makeup would provide some protection from sunburn. She creamed her face with cleansing lotion first and then applied the makeup. When her long hair had been brushed free of the snarls of sleep, she decided to wear it down to protect the back of her neck.

Letting her hair spill over her shoulders in a silken curtain of light brown, she felt almost whole again. Her hazel eyes, brightened with renewed spirit, scanned the western sky. Not a single cloud broke the vast expanse of pale blue. The storm clouds of last night had completely disappeared.

A bird soared lazily above the desert valley floor below the mountain. In the far distance, Leah could see the wispy ribbon of a jet trail. The desert seemed to stretch for endless miles. She registered the awesome fact that she couldn't see one sign of human habitation, not a building and not a road.

A tremendous sense of isolation closed over her. The incredible silence of the desert mountains was loud. What if they weren't found? Before her nervousness overwhelmed her, Leah rose to her feet. She was not going to panic, she told herself. There was a search party looking for them. She was not stranded in this forbidding wilderness forever.

She glanced at the rocky ledge where she had last seen Reilly. She wished he would come back soon. *Shout if you need me,* he had said. Right now, she needed to know he was still out there. But she stifled the desire to call out to him.

Activity was the answer. Sitting and doing nothing, she had let her imagination run away with her. The search party would find them. It was only a matter of time. Meanwhile, the best thing was to occupy herself with some small task until Reilly returned.

Feeling a twinge in her injured arm, Leah looked around to see what she could do that wouldn't strain it or open up the cut. Her gaze fell on the damp clothes she had set on top of her duffel.

They would never dry in that heap. Her blouse was on top. Leah picked it up and carried it to a bush, spreading it out for the sun to dry. Then she returned for the next piece of clothing. Deliberately taking her time, she made a project out of it, smoothing out the wrinkles and spreading the garment carefully over the bush. It served to prolong the task.

When her clothes were laid out to dry, she started on Reilly's. She was straightening the sleeves on his jacket when a loosened stone rolled down the slope behind her. Turning, she saw Reilly working his way down, his arms laden with broken chunks of wood. Most of it seemed to be timber from the mine.

"Hey!" Her greeting echoed the happiness and relief she felt at his return. Mostly it was happiness. "I see you found some wood."

"There's more up there, inside the mouth of the mine where it didn't get rained on. We don't have to worry about wood for now." He flashed her a quick smile, his aloofness gone. "I found something else, too."

"What?" Leah held her breath.

She sensed that whatever he had found pleased him. It was responsible for the brilliant light in his eyes that seemed to radiate satisfaction. Maybe he had seen a road or highway on the other side of the mountain.

"Water," Reilly stated, dumping the wood onto the ground near the center of the clearing. He looked back up the mountain. "There's a rocky outcropping on the east side beneath a slight over-hang. It's shaped like a giant basin. Last night's rain filled it."

"Then it's safe to drink?" Okay, so he hadn't found a sign of civilization, but her cottony tongue said it was nearly as good.

"It's rainwater." The corners of his eyes crinkled to match the smile curving his mouth.

"I feel like draining the canteen dry to cele-brate." She laughed.

"Be my guest." He motioned toward the can-teen as he kneeled beside the pile of wood.

"Now that I know I can drink, I don't feel very thirsty."

Reilly picked out a thin plank of wood and used it as a scraper to clear a fire circle. "Can you gather stones for a fire ring? Some of those near the slide will do."

Hampered by her sore arm, she did a slow job of collecting medium-sized rocks to form an outer protective ring. When Reilly had cleared the ground to his satisfaction, he took out his pocketknife and began splintering wood for kindling. The tiny mound of wood chips lay in the center of the circle.

"Do you have any paper?" Reilly asked.

"There's tissue in my cosmetic case," Leah volun-teered.

"That should work fine." While she went to get it, he removed a box of matches from his inside jacket pocket.

She handed him one of the white tissues and

watched him stuff it beneath the wood chips. Removing one match, he struck against the side of the box and cupped the flame protectively with his hand as he carried it to the tissue and kindling. The white tissue charred, then burst into flame. A teasing breeze swirled the tiny fire.

Reilly guarded it carefully so the fire wouldn't be blown out. "Guaranteed, no matter which way the wind is blowing, it will change direction the second the fire has started." He slid a glittering look at Leah, amusement in his crooked smile. "Invariably blowing the smoke at the person who started the fire."

"Is that a bit of Indian lore?" She laughed at the truth of his comment.

"Naturally." As the kindling started to burn, Reilly added slightly larger pieces of wood, stacking them in a pyramid around and above the small flame.

There was only a small breeze blowing, a mere breath of wind. Leah looked around the clearing at the dry-looking sagebrush that stretched over the mountainside. Here and there a pinyon tree dotted the slopes, but they were very few.

"There isn't any chance of starting a grass fire, is there?" she asked, trying not to imagine the horror of trying to escape from that.

"Very little," Reilly answered. "The fire ring will keep the flames from spreading as long as the wind isn't strong. Strangely enough, it's rare to have a fire sweep through the desert, considering how dry and flammable some of the plants are."

"Why?" Leah tipped her head curiously to one side, absently tucking her hair behind her ear.

"Mainly because it's so dry," was his reply. Then he explained, "There's so little moisture in the desert that the plants can't grow close together. Their root systems are wide and deep to absorb every available trace of water, so they choke out any new plant that tries to grow. The distance between plants keeps any fire that starts from spreading."

He sat back on his heels, waiting for the pyramid of wood to catch fire. Leah understood what he had meant last night about it being a slow process to build a fire without the aid of kerosene or starter fuel.

"Now that we've found water, we can mix up some of that dehydrated food," he said.

"I'll see what we have." Leah opened up the metal box and began looking at the packages inside. "Here's some beef stew, but what are we going to heat it in?"

"There's some twisted pieces of metal from the plane wing over by the slide. Maybe you could use one for a makeshift pan."

"I'll see." She started to get to her feet, but he motioned her to sit back down.

"On second thought, I'd better look," he said. "I don't want you accidentally cutting yourself on the metal edges."

He stacked two more pieces of wood, larger than those propped against each other, making sure there were openings at the bottom to circulate the air.

Leah didn't object as he rose smoothly to his feet. With only one hand operating effectively, she had already discovered that she was clumsy and slow.

Within a few minutes Reilly returned with a bent piece of metal. Using two of the rocks around the fire, one as a hammer and one as a hard surface, he beat away the sharp edges around the outside. Then he turned the hollowed center upside down on top of the rock and hammered a flat bottom in the pan. When the sides were fairly straight, he examined it for a moment, then glanced at Leah.

"You're the cook. Do you think it will work?" He lifted a mocking eyebrow in question.

"I don't remember signing up for that."

There was a wicked glint in his dark jade eyes. "Cooking is squaw's work, isn't it?"

Leah smiled and shrugged. He wasn't going to let her forget what she'd said last night, evidently. "I've heard that it is," she admitted.

"Will the pan do, then?" He held it out for her inspection.

"I think so." Leah took the pan and set it on the ground beside her. "Hand me the canteen, will you? I'll start mixing the stew while you get the fire hot."

First, Leah rinsed out the makeshift pan with a little water, wiping it dry with some tissue. By guess, she roughly measured the amount of water required into the pan and added the dried ingredients. She read aloud from the package. "Dried beef. Dried potatoes. Dried carrots. And hydrolyzed vegetable protein—oo, I love that stuff. Salt. Should I go on?"

Reilly made a face. "No, thanks."

"What can I use to stir this?" She glanced at Reilly, her face breaking into a sudden smile. "Better yet, how are we going to eat this without a spoon?"

"Here's my pocketknife." He handed it to her with the blade closed. "I guess we'll have to stab the meat and potatoes with the blade and drink the liquid."

"The pan will have to work as a bowl for two, I

guess." She laughed a little and stirred the dry ingredients into the water.

Almost an hour later, Reilly separated a few glowing coals from the fire to heat the stew. He propped the pan an inch above the embers on flat rocks.

It wasn't long before the liquid began to bubble. The aroma was actually appetizing.

In the meantime, Reilly had banged out two bowls from other fragments of the plane. When the stew was heated through, he took the shirt Leah had draped over a bush and folded it to use as a potholder.

Carefully he poured the stew into the two bowls and handed Leah's portion to her. Leah refused his offer to use the knife, choosing to scoop out the chunky pieces with a cracker. Neither method was particularly efficient, but they managed to eat well enough.

Reilly rolled over on his back to digest, closing his eyes. She realized that he had done all the heavy work on an empty stomach. His tiredness and the hot food were probably catching up with him.

"Okay. Time to wash up. Let's have that dish."

"Go for it." He opened one eye halfway and pushed it toward her. "We might have to use them tonight." His comment drew her attention to the sky, empty of any search plane. "Sand will work better than water to clean."

Drawing her gaze away from the sky, Leah picked up the pan and poured in a small handful of sand. When it was scoured clean she rinsed away the grit with a little water and started on the shallow bowls. Reilly picked up the canteen and emptied it into the pan.

"Why did you do that?" She frowned.

"I'm going to refill the canteen from the basin. While I'm gone I want you to have water on hand to pour on the fire in case you see a search plane," he answered.

"But it will put the fire out," Leah protested.

"It will also make a lot of smoke. With luck the pilot would see and do a flyover to investigate."

"I see." Dimples edged into her cheeks. "The old Indian smoke trick."

"Right." He winked and started walking toward the slope, turning to say one more thing over his shoulder. "Just take a stick and poke a few coals to one side if you have to. We can use 'em to start another fire. You don't have to drown it."

"Okay." She scoured the two bowls clean, rinsing them with a handful of water from the pot and letting them dry in the sun. With that done, she checked the clothes she had draped over the bushes, and found that they were stiff and almost hot to the touch. She folded hers up and put them in her duffel bag.

Reilly's clothes she stacked as neatly as she could on top of his suitcase, smiling a little at how incongruous it was to be folding laundry in the middle of the wilderness. Still, the familiar action was comforting.

With only the partial use of her left hand, the task took some time. The sun rose higher, making its fiery presence felt, yet Reilly did not return. Leah added more wood to the fire and sat down away from the blaze to wait.

Finally she saw him on the ledge above. He started down the fairly steep slope with the canteen in one hand and a four-foot-long board in the other.

"I was wondering what was taking you so long," Leah called when he was halfway down. "You made a side trip for more firewood."

Reilly jumped the last few feet. "No, this board is for something else." He set the canteen beside the box of packaged food. "I'm going to make lean-to poles out of it. We need something to shelter us from the sun."

She watched him as he used his pocketknife as a wedge and split the board down the middle. He whittled each end—four in all—to a point.

"Now what?" Leah asked.

"The survival blanket has grommets in each corner." He picked it up and slipped the grommets over two of the stakes, jamming the ends into the ground. The sandy soil was just damp enough to keep the poles upright. Reilly weighted the other two corners down with rocks.

"Nice. I'm totally impressed."

"Thanks." He grinned. "A strong wind would probably blow it down, but it'll keep out the sun for now." He bent down to enter, then waved to Leah to join him. "Come on in."

She moved eagerly to its shade, reveling in it after a morning of intensifying sunshine. Reilly picked up one of the sticks from the firewood pile and began whittling.

"What are you making now?"

"Thought I'd try my hand at carving a spoon."

"Only one?"

He smiled slightly. "Guess you don't want to share. I'll make two."

"Thanks."

"You're welcome."

Leah stretched and settled down. "I wish I had something to do."

He shrugged. "Hunt lizards. Organize rocks."

She smiled. "That would mean going back out into the sun. No, thanks."

Lying on her back with her arm as a pillow, she watched him shaving away the outer layer of wood with his knife. The steady rhythm of the slashing blade was slightly hypnotic. Soon she found her eyelids growing heavy.

"Why don't you take a siesta?" Reilly suggested when she tried to blink away the tiredness. "I'll keep watch for search planes."

"I think I will." She stopped fighting the drowsiness and closed her eyes.

CHAPTER FOUR

Leah slept through the heat of the afternoon. The same rhythmic sound that had lulled her to sleep was the first one she heard when she wakened. Reilly was sitting in the long shadow of the lean-to, still whittling on a stick that now bore considerable resemblance to a wooden spoon.

Blinking the sleep from her eyes, she started to push herself to a sitting position. Without thinking, she used both arms and gasped sharply at the pain that stabbed like a burning knife in her left one. Quickly, she switched all her weight to her right arm.

"That was stupid," she muttered.

"Is your arm bothering you a lot?" Reilly's green eyes narrowed.

"Only when I do something like that." She sat upright, cradling her left arm in her lap as the shooting pain began to recede. Her mouth felt scratchy and dry, as if coated with wool. She glanced around. "I need a drink. Where's the canteen?"

"In the shade behind you."

Leah had to shift slightly to reach it. Uncapping it, she took a long swallow. The water was warm but deliciously wet. The funny taste left her mouth.

"How's the spoon coming along?"

At her question, Reilly stopped whittling and held it up for her to see.

"Wow. It looks like . . . a spoon."

"That's the idea."

The knife resumed its work. A fly buzzed noisily about her head, and Leah waved it outside the lean-to, looking up to the empty sky.

"No sign of a search plane, huh?"

"No." He didn't elaborate. After several minutes of silence, he set his project aside, folded the knife and slipped it into his pocket. "We'll need more firewood for tonight. I won't be gone long."

As he started up the slope, Leah scooted from beneath the lean-to and stood up to stretch her legs, arching her back to ease the stiffness from lying on the hard ground. The action tipped her head back and a black object in the sky caught her eye.

A buzzard was slowly circling. Leah shuddered, bringing her gaze swiftly to earth to focus on the slide. She was glad that the rock and debris had buried Grady. The desert scavenger was wasting its time.

She didn't want to let her thoughts dwell on its menacing presence, so she turned toward the western horizon. Shielding her eyes from the glare of the late afternoon sky, she studied the empty blueness. There was not a speck of anything. Surely by now, the rescue team would be widening their search grid, she thought.

Her parents had probably been notified that

she was missing—and her brother, too. What a birth-day present for Lonnie. Tears misted her eyes at the dispiriting thought of the agony her family was going through.

An explosive sound ripped the air. A gunshot.

In a flash of memory, she recalled the pistol Reilly carried in the waistband of his jeans. What could he have been shooting at? A snake? Terror gripped her throat. This wild country was probably crawling with venomous rattlesnakes.

What if he had been bitten? The thought was horri-fying. She raced toward the slope. Her wide eyes scanned the rocky ledge where he had disappeared from sight. "Reilly! Reilly!" she screamed.

His reply was instant, and calmly clear. "It's all right," he called.

A few seconds later he appeared at the rim of the ledge, tall and bronzed. Her knees threatened to buckle under at the sight of him. Sweat plas-tered his white shirt against his muscular chest. His hair glistened blue-black in the sun.

"I heard a shot." Leah's voice trembled.

He raised an arm to show a jackrabbit dangling lifeless from his hand. "Tonight's dinner," he ex-plained. "I'll be down as soon as I get the fire-wood."

Then he disappeared again. He had looked so compellingly masculine standing there that Leah sighed when he left. And that wild, proud look in his eyes was almost too much for her. She suddenly began to wonder about the women in his life—and whether there was just one.

Remembering the strong arms that had held her in sleep last night and the hard length of his body lying beside hers, she realized that she envied the woman, if there was one. As a lover, Reilly—she stopped, shaking her head wryly. Her thoughts were becoming too intimate.

Turning away from the slope, she walked back to the clearing. She kneeled beside the box of food supplies, forcing her mind to concentrate on deciding what to serve with the rabbit Reilly had shot. Setting aside a pouch of dried vegetables, she added a packet of peaches to the water left in the pan.

When Reilly came down a few minutes later with an armload of wood, she was still stirring the peaches, pushing them down under the water. It was difficult not to look at him with the new sensual awareness she felt—which Leah did her best to ignore.

"I hope you don't expect me to clean that rabbit," she said. "I never skinned anything, you know."

"Then you can watch me." Reilly grinned crookedly.

"No, thanks." She turned quickly back to her peaches. "I mean, I appreciate you being the mighty hunter and all, I really do, and I know we have to make the dried food last . . . but I'd rather not see what happens next."

He only shrugged and turned away. She kept her attention firmly riveted on her task. Blood didn't make her squeamish, but watching that small carcass being cleaned was just too much for her right now.

"When I heard the shot, I had visions of a rattlesnake attacking you," she said.

"It's too hot for them to be out. They do their hunting just before sunrise and right after sundown," Reilly explained. "Besides, rattlesnakes don't attack. They're relatively peaceful. The only time you have to worry about them is if you step on one."

"Remind me not to go wandering about, then," she said.

Reilly chuckled quietly, a pleasant sound that Leah found she liked very much. She glanced over at his chiseled features when he wasn't looking at her. The words for him were *lean* and *powerful*. Qualities she liked. A lot.

Later, after their meal of roasted rabbit, they sat and watched the orange sun wavering above the horizon. The western sky was painted a brilliant scarlet-orange, the distant mountain range set afire with its flaming light.

The emptiness was overwhelming. It was as if she and Reilly were the only two people on the whole of the earth.

She stared unblinkingly at the sunset. "Do you think the search planes will find us tomorrow?"

"Possibly."

A thin thread of fear stretched over her nerves. She turned. "What if they don't find us, Reilly? What if we're stranded here?"

He held her gaze for a long moment, looking deep into her hazel eyes. Then he smiled faintly and shook his head. "We won't be. We'll get out of here."

"Of course." She sighed, silently chiding herself for giving in to that momentary twinge of fear.

The plane had crashed only twenty-four hours ago, hardly enough time to panic over not being found. *One day,* her mind echoed. It seemed much longer than that.

Standing, Reilly added two more small logs to the dying fire and took down the lean-to so the survival blanket could be used as a cover. While the dwindling sunlight still gave enough light to see, he smoothed away the small rocks on the ground where their bed would be.

With the departure of the sun, the temperature dropped quickly. Leah moved closer to the fire, staring into its flames. Its welcome warmth couldn't reach her back. When she started shivering, Reilly suggested it was time they went to sleep. A blanket of stars was overhead as she curled against him.

The second day was longer than the first. They had already found water, built a fire, improvised cooking things and put up the lean-to. None of that needed to be done on the second day and the time seemed to pass with excruciating slowness.

The heat of the sun seemed more intense to Leah, and sweat made her skin prickle. All day long, her gaze restlessly searched the sky for a rescue plane. The inactivity and the torment of waiting scraped at her nerves, although Reilly's stoic composure didn't seem affected by it.

Only once had she seen anything. Jumping to her feet, she had pointed excitedly to the flash of sunlight on something in the sky. "There! It's a plane, isn't it?"

As he stood beside her, his piercing gaze had searched the sky until he too saw the slow-flying plane far in the distance. "Yes," he agreed calmly.

"I'll let them know we're here!" She had turned to grab the canteen and douse the fire to make a smoke signal that would mark their location.

But strong fingers curled around her wrist, stopping her. "It's too far away now."

Leah had waited, her gaze riveted on the plane, praying fervently for it to fly toward them. But it had continued on a southward course, growing smaller until it disappeared.

"It'll come back," she had declared in a low voice to conceal her disappointment and the fraying edges of despair.

But it hadn't.

That night Leah slept badly. The hard ground was torture for aching muscles already stiffened by two previous nights sleeping in the cold. Reilly slept with infuriating ease, waking only twice to reach from beneath the cover to add wood from a nearby stack to the fire.

Rousing from a fitful doze, Leah discovered it was morning. She groaned at her lack of restful sleep and laid her head back on Reilly's arm to stare disgustedly at the brilliant blue sky. Her left arm throbbed painfully. She shifted against him, trying to ease her arm into a more comfortable and less painful position.

As she twisted onto her side, her gaze focused on his face. She almost hated the way he was sleeping so calmly, tempted to poke him in the shoulder and wake him up. While she was contemplating doing just that, his sooty lashes lifted a little.

"Good morning," he said in a voice that was disgustingly refreshed and relaxed.

Irritation flashed in her eyes. "Is it?" she snapped, and tugged at the stiff edge of the survival blanket to get it out of his hold. "I don't know what's particularly good about it."

When he released it, she hurled the cover aside and scrambled awkwardly to her feet. He rose when she did, but with an ease that showed not a trace of sore muscles or joints.

"You didn't sleep well." He seemed amused.

"That's an understatement. But then you slept

well enough for both of us," she muttered sarcastically.

"I don't think so." Silent laughter edged his voice. "A critter was wriggling in my bed all night. Wonder what it was."

She glared at him, scraping tousled light brown hair away from her face. She was tired and cross and taking it out on Reilly. It was unfair, but she couldn't seem to stop herself.

"You're lucky it didn't bite you," she retorted.

She kneeled beside her duffel, rummaging through it to find a clean top to replace the rumpled one she wore. If he dared to laugh openly, she would throw something at him.

Reilly let it go. "Put some water on to boil so I can shave, okay?" It was more of an order than a request.

Leah couldn't help reacting to his tone of voice. "What a waste of time," she snapped. "And wood. And water."

"We're not going to run out of water. And I'll bring more wood down later. My face itches."

She silently cursed her bad temper. It wasn't his fault she hadn't slept. After all, he had kept doing the heavy work to keep her from having to use her injured arm. Her guilty sideways look caught the sharp narrowing of his eyes. "Never mind," she said. "I'll do it. Guess you have a hot date tonight."

"Maybe I do." Reilly grinned. He walked off into the brush.

She scraped a few glowing coals from the fire and added more wood to the rest. With careful movements, she managed to balance the pan of water on the four supporting rocks around the coals.

That accomplished, she shrugged off her top,

feeling a burning sensation from the bandaged gash in her arm. She eased the clean top over it, buttoning the last button when Reilly returned. Sliding a glance at the pot, Leah saw the water was steaming.

"Your water is hot," she told him curtly.

"Thanks," was his equally indifferent reply. He looked in his suitcase and retrieved an aerosol can of shaving cream. "Can't eat this. Might as well use it."

She didn't bother to reply,

With a handkerchief he took from a side pouch he set the pot off the coals, then paused. "Would you like to wash first?"

Shaking her head, Leah opened her cosmetic case and took out the bottle of cleansing lotion. The mirror in the lid of the case was turned at just the right angle so that she saw not only her reflection but Reilly's, too.

He squirted lather onto his hands, then rubbed it luxuriously on the lower half of his face. It was a curiously intimate experience to watch a man shave. His long, sun-browned fingers gripped the disposable razor, its blade slicing through the foamy lather and one day's stubble. Each stroke revealed more of the bronzed skin below his cheekbones and the strong line of his jaw until his chiseled features were fully exposed.

As he rinsed away the traces of lather, Leah voiced the thought that had just occurred to her. "I thought Indians didn't shave."

"They didn't." Reilly shook the razor dry and replaced it in his suitcase. His vioce was emotionless and distant. "They plucked out the hair from their faces."

"Ouch." Leah winced at the thought.

"So how's your arm this morning?" he asked in the same expressionless tone.

"Hurts."

"Let me take a look at it." He started toward her.

"You don't have to," Leah said, holding up a hand to stop him from getting any closer. "It's sore because it's healing."

Reilly hesitated thoughtfully. "We don't have much bandaging material left in the first-aid kit. I'd rather not change it for a few days if it really isn't bothering you."

"I said it was just healing pains."

"Okay." He accepted her explanation, but not without shooting her a serious look. "I'm going to get more firewood. Have something to eat while I'm gone."

"I'm not hungry."

"It might make you feel better."

Leah's eyes flashed. "You mean, improve my mood? Have you noticed that I'm not a happy camper?"

"Yeah."

"Well, this vacation destination leaves a lot to be desired. Especially the food."

A moment of tense silence followed her irritable remark.

"I realize you didn't sleep well last night, Miss Talbot," Reilly said in an ominously quiet voice, "but I suggest that you stop taking your frustration out on me."

He turned his back on her and his long strides took him toward the slope.

Better shut up, Miss Talbot, she told herself with a dejected sigh. She deserved the put-down, but it didn't make it any less cutting.

She rummaged in the cosmetic case, grateful that she had it. Putting on makeup was her last connection to a safe world that seemed very far away and she needed to do it.

She had been away from civilization for what seemed like an eternity. The desolate country that surrounded her made the thought of Las Vegas's brilliant lights and bustling crowds seem like a surreal dream. Out here there was just . . . nothing.

Leah took her time with the makeup. Then, with her long hair brushed to a silken shine, she slipped off her shoes and shook out the sand. Removing her socks, she grimaced at the sand and dirt that had collected between her toes and on the bottom of her feet. They felt hot and sweaty, too.

The pan of warm water sat invitingly near, flecks of shaving foam still floating on top. She hesitated for only a second. It would be foolish to put on a clean pair of socks without washing her feet.

Treading carefully over the rough ground on bare feet, she retrieved the handkerchief Reilly had laid over a bush to dry. With it as a washcloth and the small bar of soap from her cosmetic case, she started washing her feet in the pan of water. She rinsed the soap away with water from the canteen and wiped her feet dry with the rumpled top she had taken off earlier. She dumped the dirty water on the sand.

It was nearly as good as taking a bath, she thought contentedly. Washing her feet in the same pan they used for cooking was not very hygienic, but Reilly could always bash another piece of metal into shape and make a second pan. She would do it herself if her arm didn't hurt so much.

She would ask him. Nicely. She let her thoughts drift. When they got back to civilization, the first thing she would do was laze in a bubble bath for about two hours. Maybe more. She tugged on her clean socks and shook the sand out of her shoes a second time.

As she slipped on the first shoe, she heard a humming sound. She frowned, listening intently, trying to place it. She couldn't tell which direction the sound was coming from, yet it seemed to be growing louder.

Her eyes widened. It was the drone of an airplane engine. She looked immediately toward the western sky. The plane was unbelievably near their position and flying toward it. The breeze from the east must have carried the sound until it was nearly above her.

With an excited shout to Reilly, Leah grabbed the canteen and dumped the water on the fire. Only a trickle came out, sizzling to a tiny puff of smoke as it touched the fire. She stared at the insignificant puff in disbelief.

"You idiot!" she muttered. "Why did you use all that water to wash your feet?"

The roar of the plane's engines came from overhead. Wrenching her gaze away from the fire, she looked up. There was no indication that they had been spotted as it flew outward to the east into the sun.

"Here we are!" she shouted, running after the plane's shadow and waving her arms frantically. "Here we are! Down here!"

Reilly came racing down the slope, a miniature avalanche of small rocks rolling before him. "Pour water on the fire!" he shouted.

Leah stopped. "There isn't any water. I used it all."

His expression hardened at her statement, but

he made no comment on her stupidity. Without breaking stride, he hit the level ground at the bottom of the slope. He paused long enough to pick up the wrinkled survival blanket and tossed it to her.

"Wave that in the air!" he snapped. "Aluminum side up!"

As she obeyed, she was conscious of Reilly kneeling beside her cosmetic case, but she was more aware of the plane flying away from them. Then Reilly was standing beside her. The rectangular mirror from the lid of her cosmetic case was·in his hand.

While she waved the blanket until she thought her arm would drop off, he wigwagged the mirror in the sun, trying to direct the flashing light at the plane. But the plane never wavered from its course.

"Come back!" Leah screamed. Her right arm hung limply at her side, without the strength to raise the blanket one more time. Her injured left arm was cradled across her waist.

The plane disappeared into the sun. A tear slipped from her lashes, then another and another until there was a silent, steady stream down her cheeks. Her lips were salty with the taste of her tears.

"They didn't see us," she whispered in a choked, tight voice.

Her chin trembled as she turned to look at Reilly. His hands were on his hips in a stance of angry disgust. He was staring into the emptiness where the plane had been. He turned, his stormy green eyes briefly meeting hers before he walked back to the fire.

"I'm sorry, Reilly." Leah followed him. The stiff survival blanket was still clutched in her fingers, trailing along the ground behind her. "It's all my fault. I used the water to wash my feet and threw it away without thinking."

"Your feet?" he repeated dryly, his speaking glance saying all the things he didn't put into words.

"They were dirty," she said, only too aware of how lame that reason sounded.

Reilly began stacking the few remaining logs on the fire. His silence was more crushing than any verbal condemnation. Finally Leah couldn't take it anymore, and her anger at herself erupted like a volcano.

"Why don't you say something?" she yelled. "Why don't you shout at me and tell me what a stupid, idiotic thing it was to do? We both know it was, so why don't you say it! Get angry or something! Don't just keep putting wood on the fire as if nothing had happened!"

"No point in that," Reilly answered calmly, rising to his feet and brushing his hands on his thighs. Except for the grim tightness of his mouth, an impersonal mask had slipped over his face. "I'm going to go fill the canteen and bring down the firewood."

A broken sigh of frustration slipped from her constricted throat.

"What if the plane comes back while you're gone?"

"Wave the blanket and yell for me."

When he had disappeared up the slope, Leah collapsed on her knees. Her fingers relaxed their tight grip on the survival blanket, and it settled beside her, the shiny aluminum side catching the sun's rays. She was exhausted and emotionally drained.

She wanted to bury her head in her arms and cry silently at her stupidity, but she didn't dare.

There was a chance that the plane might fly back this way. She couldn't risk being caught unaware a second time.

Sniffing back her tears, she wiped the salty dampness from her cheeks and started scanning the skies. Her ears strained to hear the drone of an airplane engine. There was only the desert mountain silence until stones rolling down the slope signaled Reilly's return.

After setting an armload of wood on the ground a few feet away from the fire, Reilly handed the canteen to Leah. "Have a drink."

She looked at it as if it were poison. She was hot and tired and very thirsty but no matter how parched her throat might be, she didn't want to drink the water that might get them rescued. Some part of her mind knew that she wasn't thinking rationally, but she shook her head anyway. "No," she said with quiet firmness.

Exasperation straightened the line of his mouth. "Listen to me. You were yelling and jumping up and down in the hot sun, and you have to have some water. Just do it."

Reluctantly Leah obeyed, taking a small sip and letting it roll around to wet her dry mouth before swallowing it. Moistening her lips with her tongue, she handed the canteen back to him, aware of the alert greenness of his eyes watching her, but unable to meet his gaze.

He set the canteen in the shade of the firewood. Without a word Reilly walked over and picked up the stiff blanket lying on the ground beside Leah. She frowned, wondering what he intended to do with it, then saw him erecting the lean-to.

"Won't we need the blanket to signal the plane?"

Reilly didn't turn away from his task as he answered. "It can come down in seconds if we see the plane. In the meantime, we need a sunshade."

Leah stared at the crackling fire. It burned cleanly, a thin wisp of smoke rising and disappearing in the clear desert air almost immediately. Shimmering heat waves danced above the fire.

"The plane flew almost directly over us," she said quietly. "I didn't hear it coming until it was almost here. Why couldn't they see us?"

"In the first place,"—Reilly secured the last corner of the lean-to—"they were flying into the morning sun. They couldn't see much of anything with that much glare. And in the second place, they were looking for airplane wreckage." He nodded in the general direction of the slide. "Ours is buried beneath that."

"They would've seen the smoke signal, though." She sighed, gazing into the morning sky. "It's my fault."

"Stop feeling sorry for yourself," Reilly ordered firmly.

"I'm not!" Leah protested.

"Yes, you are and it's not going to change anything."

"I never said—"

Reilly cut her off impatiently. "Arguing isn't going to get us rescued. Let's concentrate on being prepared in case the plane flies back this way."

Leah paused. Something in his voice made her ask, "Do you think it will?"

"I don't know." Nothing in his expression revealed what Reilly really thought or believed.

CHAPTER FIVE

A cloud blocked out the western sun. A halo of gold formed around its ragged gray-white shape, then streamed to earth to bronze the sage-covered landscape.

Leah's blouse was damp with sweat, clinging to her like a second skin. Her left arm ached with an agonizing throb. The morning's exertion—she had unthinkingly used it to wave the blanket a few times—had increased its soreness.

Wearily she pressed her right hand against her forehead for a few seconds, then lifted her head, her hand pushing the hair away from her face. All day they had waited and the plane had not returned. It was nearing sundown.

Her troubled gaze moved to Reilly relentlessly watching the sky yet seeming to be miles away in thought. "How long do you think they'll continue looking for us?" She voiced the fear that had been haunting her all day.

A remoteness remained in his jade eyes as he glanced at her. "Hard to say. An extensive air search is expensive and time-consuming," he replied. "They'll probably look for a couple more days at most. After that, they'll ask local pilots to keep a lookout for any sign of wreckage and send out one or two search planes of their own."

The knowledge was sobering. Being stranded in this wilderness for more days was a distinct possibility. Leah knew she couldn't think about that without sinking into a morass of guilty feelings. And Reilly was right, that wouldn't change anything.

"I think I'll fix us something to eat," she murmured.

Food didn't interest her. At lunch, she had chewed indifferently on a stick of beef jerky, just to keep her strength up. That, and not hunger, was her motivation for cooking the evening meal. The side benefit would be taking her mind off their situation.

After three days, their choice of dried food dishes had dwindled considerably. Leah glanced through the few that remained, searching for one that at least sounded appetizing.

Out of the corner of her eye, she saw Reilly crouching in front of her duffel bag. Curious, she shifted slightly to see what he was doing and her lips parted in surprise. He was searching through its contents.

"What do you think you're doing?" she said indignantly, getting up and going over to him. He didn't even look up. "You have no right to go through my stuff!"

"Just a routine security check, Miss Talbot," he said mockingly. "Nothing personal."

"Those happen to be my personal things."

He took out a stack of folded underwear and set

it to one side. "So I see." He took out other clothes, also folded. Leah tried taking them out of his hands to jam them back in the duffel, but he took things out and set them aside so fast she couldn't stop him.

"Did you hear what I said?" She was yelling, she realized, but she *was* angry.

"The whole damn desert heard you." He made a sweeping gesture at the landscape. "The jackrabbits have their paws over their ears."

"Very funny!"

He sighed. "I'm looking to see if you have any clothes you can walk in. If you don't mind." He picked out a pair of well-worn jeans and a light, long-sleeved blouse, then threw a bandanna on top of it.

"What?" Leah sat back on her heels, staring at his impassive face bewilderedly. "What do you mean?"

"We're leaving," Reilly announced calmly and turned to her cosmetic case. "Do you have any face cream or sunblock in here?" he asked as he snapped open the lid.

"I have face cream." She reached in and picked up the jar. "Why do you want it?" The answer to that didn't seem nearly so important when his announcement sank in. "How are we leaving?"

"On foot, of course." He flicked a brief glance at her, then looked at the label on the jar. "Okay. This is SPF 30. Good. Your pale face won't fry."

"On foot? You must be crazy!" Leah stared out over the vast expanse of arid terrain.

"It would be crazier to stay here." Reilly set aside the cosmetic case and opened his own suitcase.

"I know you think I'm stupid—" Leah began hotly.

"Actually, I don't," Reilly interrupted her.

"But I do know," she continued with barely a break, "that when you're lost and people are looking for you, you're supposed to stay in one place and not go wandering off. We don't even know where we are!"

He removed two of his dirty shirts from the suitcase and closed the lid. "I have a rough idea."

"Wonderful," Leah said sarcastically. When he rose to his feet, she followed as closely as his shadow. "Does that mean we're somewhere in Nevada? I could have made that guess."

Reilly stopped short, nearly causing her to run into his broad back. His gaze was as hard as steel when he looked at her.

"We're on the east side of the Monitor Range, which would put us roughly sixty miles from the nearest town as the crow flies. In this terrain, on foot, it would probably be ninety miles."

In this emptiness, it seemed impossible that they were even that close to civilization. "We could die out there," Leah argued.

"We could die here," he pointed out.

"Yes, but"—his reply shook her up for a second—"here we at least have a chance of being found, of signaling the next plane."

"When will it come, Leah?" Reilly studied her frightened face. "Tomorrow? The day after? Three days from now? When?"

"I don't know." Her hand lifted to wave the questions aside. "But it will come. My parents and Lonnie won't let the searchers quit. They'll hire a plane and look for me themselves. I know they will!"

"I agree, but time is still a factor."

"Why?" she demanded.

"Because in three, maybe four more days, we won't have the food, water, or the strength to walk out of here." His low voice and his calmness commanded her attention.

She looked up the slope in the direction of the water he'd found. "But—"

"The water I found in the rock basin is drying up," Reilly explained. "I thought it would last longer. But the heat got to it."

A tide of helplessness washed over her. "You should have told me."

"You were already stressed by your injury and Grady's death and everything else. I didn't want you to panic. I was hoping we'd be rescued in time. But that might not happen."

"You still should have told me."

"Maybe so. But I didn't." Reilly's tone was indifferent. What had been done was done, he seemed to be saying. As far as he was concerned, there was no purpose in arguing about the past.

"If we tried to walk out,"—Leah still didn't favor the idea despite Reilly's logic—"how would we know which way to go?"

"We'll go south."

"Why?" she said stubbornly. "Why not west? When we flew off course, we came east. Surely we should go back that way."

Reilly breathed in deeply, as if his patience with her questions was running out. "The mountain ranges run in a north-south line. I don't know how many of them we would have to cross before we reached either a highway or a town. Finding a safe way over them and down would take too much time. That same reason rules out going east. To the north, I can see mountains. If we went that way, we would have to travel along the ridge. But south, we have a valley. The walking will be easier and we can make better time."

"We could also get lost," Leah pointed out.

"I won't get lost," he assured her dryly.

His confidence irritated her. He was absolutely positive he was right. With all of her arguments dismissed, she retaliated with sarcasm.

"Of course not," she snapped. "You know everything. You were sure that we had enough water. So I should trust you on this, too."

His carved features were shadowed by a frown. "Who else are you going to trust?"

She pressed her lips together. Her barb had somehow fallen short of its mark. Exhaling an angry breath, she glanced away. "I don't care what you think," she muttered. "I don't think we should leave here. The search plane could find us anytime."

"We're leaving in the morning at first light," Reilly said calmly.

Leah tossed her head back, defiantly meeting his cool gaze. "You can leave if you want. I'm staying here."

"No, you are not." His jaw tightened.

"And how are you going to stop me?"

He didn't answer.

"Reilly, you can't carry me all the way and I won't go with you willingly. So that means we stay here."

"You're making a mistake." His eyes narrowed into a measuring look.

"I don't think so."

"All right." He nodded curtly in acceptance. "You can stay here. I'll leave in the morning."

Her eyes widened in amazement. "What?"

"I can make better time without you along and you can be here to signal the plane in case it flies over this area again. If it doesn't, then within three day's time at the outside, I'll reach help and pinpoint your location for an air rescue team," Reilly concluded, a satisfied look on his face.

"You mean you'd leave me—here—alone?" Leah said in disbelief.

"It's the logical thing to do. This way we cover all bases." He paused, as if thinking it over more thoroughly. "I'll have to take the canteen with me, but you can use the pan to fetch water. You can keep the dried food since I won't have a dependable water supply."

"Neither will I!"

He didn't seem to hear her. "I'll take the beef jerky, though."

"No!"

A black eyebrow shot up in surprise at her vigorous protest. "Hey, I will need some food," Reilly said. "If you don't mind, that is."

"I don't care about that." Leah frowned. "You aren't honestly going to leave me?"

"Why not?" He tipped his head to one side. "Are you going with me?"

"No."

"Then stay here."

Her fingers closed over the hard flesh of his arm, stopping him when he would have walked away from her. She stared into his impassive face, lean and compellingly handsome in its proud, carved lines.

"You really would leave me here by myself, wouldn't you?" Leah murmured.

A faint smile crooked his mouth, as if he didn't understand why she had doubted it. "Yes," Reilly answered simply.

She fought back the impulse to slap him. "If you go, then I'm going, too."

"But you were going to stay here to signal the plane," he reminded her with a wry shake of his head.

"I'm going with you," Leah said emphatically. "I don't care how practical it is. You can't make me stay here."

The instant the last sentence was spoken, her teeth bit into her lip. Only minutes ago she had been insisting that he couldn't make her go with him in the morning.

"In that case," Reilly drawled, "I guess you'll leave with me."

As he started to turn away, Leah caught the glint in his eyes. "You tricked me," she hissed accusingly. "You never intended to leave me here by myself!"

He paused. "Guess what, Leah. You're not behaving rationally. If one of us gets to make life and death decisions, it's going to be me. And yeah, I do know what I'm doing. You don't."

She let go of his arm and her hand moved in a swift arc toward his face. Reilly didn't attempt to check her slapping swing. He simply drew back so that she missed her target.

When her hand swished by, he captured her wrist in his fingers, smiling in a way that infuriated her. Leah tried to twist free of his steel grip. Her left arm was throbbing too painfully to be of any help.

He held her easily. Her angry struggles only brought her closer to his chest. A throaty chuckle rolled from his lips.

"I don't think it's funny!" Leah glared at him coldly.

He stared down at her. The brilliant fire that leaped into his eyes dazzled her, halting her attempts to pull free. Her heart skipped a beat when his attention shifted lazily to her mouth.

His thumb slowly rubbed the inside of her wrist. His other hand came up to smooth the hair from her face. It stayed to cup the back of her neck. A shiver of anticipation raced up her spine. She was already swaying toward him when his hand exerted pressure to draw her face to his.

His mouth closed over hers warmly, masterfully firm in its possession. Her muscles melted closer to the lean hardness of his body. His kiss ignited a slow-moving fire within her soul.

Yet when the moment came for the embrace to deepen with passion, Reilly relaxed the pressure that had drawn her on tiptoe to him. Weakened by his kiss, her legs couldn't support her in that precarious stance, her breath coming in uneven spurts.

The look in his eyes was gentle—and ardent. There was no other word for it. But he regained his composure all too quickly. The mask was back in place. "We're in this together all the way, Leah," Reilly said quietly. "We both leave in the morning."

"Yes." She nodded.

His hand uncurled from her neck, a finger trailing lightly over her cheek as he smiled, forming crinkling lines at the corners of his eyes. Leah couldn't help wondering if the kiss had been a way of getting her to agree without more arguments.

It was a good thing that they were leaving in the morning. She was definitely attracted to Reilly physically. More days alone in their isolated camp and a few more expert kisses might increase the temptation of night. At least the exhaustion of the trail would dull her awareness of him.

Fortunately, she didn't have to think about that for the rest of the day. The remaining hours were filled with activity.

The three-quarter moon had barely risen when Reilly announced that they should go to sleep early to rest up for the long hike out.

In his arms beneath the blanket, Leah felt the stirring of her pulse in response to the male length of him molded against her. Since the afternoon's kiss, she had expected him to attempt to make love to her tonight.

Expected was the wrong word. She had anticipated that he would make love to her, and with dangerous honesty, she admitted to herself that she was looking forward to it. The even rise and fall of his chest beneath her head was disappointing.

Granted, their situation was extreme. Being thrown together constantly by the isolation, forced to sleep in each other's arms to get through the cold desert nights, and enduring the physical hardship of being lost in the wilderness wasn't exactly romantic. Under the circumstances, she wasn't all that sure that she should want him.

Once they got back to civilization, they would no doubt go their separate ways.

Leah sighed angrily and shifted her throbbing left arm across the muscular flatness of his stomach. She forced her eyes to close and ordered herself to go to sleep. After last night's fitful dozing, she drifted off almost instantly.

Strong fingers pushed the hair away from her temples. "It's time to wake up," a familiar male voice said insistently.

She felt the cover being pulled away from her head. Leah shivered at the intruding cold and tried to snuggle deeper into the curve of Reilly's shoulder. His fingers chucked her under the chin.

"I said it's time to wake up," Reilly repeated with indulgent humor.

Moaning in protest, she peered through her lashes at the outside world. Except for the crackling fire, there was utter silence. Overhead sparkled the brightest stars Leah ever remembered seeing, thousands of them glittering with profound brilliance against a curtain of black.

"It's still dark," she grumbled.

"It won't be for long. Come on." His arm tightened around her side, drawing her into a sitting position as he pushed himself up.

"We're honestly getting up at this hour?" Leah protested, stifling a yawn.

"It's nearly daybreak. You'd better get the water boiling so we can have what's left of that instant oatmeal," he ordered, pushing her the rest of the way out of the bed.

"Who's hungry?" she muttered.

"You will be when we start down the mountain if you don't eat something now."

Leah knew that he was probably right, but she wasn't interested in food. What she really wanted was to go back to sleep. Instead she poured water from the canteen into the metal pan and balanced it on the rocks to boil.

The lonely wail of a faraway coyote echoed through the stillness. Leah huddled closer to the fire, needing its warmth. The eerie call drew her gaze to the landscape. The three-quarter moon frosted the ground with a silvery glow.

Bubbles started to rise in the pan of water, forcing her to leave the fire's circle for the oatmeal, bowls, and the two carved wooden spoons. A glance at Reilly showed him folding the survival blanket into a stiff square. He added it to the other small items they would carry out with them in the backpacks he had improvised from his dirty shirts.

With a few knots in the right places, the sleeves had become straps. The body of the shirt made a capacious pouch. Not surprising, considering the breadth of his chest measurement, she thought. She had to admire his ingenuity.

When the water boiled, Leah stirred the oatmeal into it. It was difficult to gauge how much water was needed without a measuring cup, but this morning the oatmeal was neither lumpy nor runny. With the last portion, she had found the right mixture.

"Breakfast is ready," she called softly, spooning some into her bowl and giving Reilly the largest amount.

While they ate, a pink hue touched the horizon as dawn began its silent appearance. The coppery pink pushed back the night, making way for a golden haze. By the time Leah had cleaned their dishes with sand, the entire sky was bathed in the half-light of sunrise.

Reilly handed her the canteen. "Drink all the water you can hold, then I'll go and fill it up."

After several swallows, she paused. "What are we going to do for water along the way? This canteen doesn't hold that much."

"We'll have to find it." He waited for her to take another drink. "If there's a creek in the desert, it will probably run along the base of the mountains. Once we get down in the valley, we'll stay close to them."

After drinking as much as she could, she handed the canteen to him. While he disappeared up the slope, she changed into the clothes he had picked out for her. She was tucking in her long-sleeved blouse when he returned.

His green eyes appraised her from head to toe. "You're going to need that bandanna I found."

She waved it at him.

"Tie it around your head. It'll give you some protection from the sun."

Leah did as she was told, though it was difficult with the searing pain in her arm. "I don't see what good it will do."

"If you'd ever had your scalp sunburned, you wouldn't say that," he replied dryly.

"What about your head?" She glanced at him pointedly, only to find he was swathing a blue bandanna of his own around his jet-dark hair. He tied his with swift expertise. When he had finished, Leah could see the inherent traces of his Indian ancestry. The stamp of wildness and a natural nobility was more striking than before.

He opened the jar of face cream and offered it to her. "Put it on thick," he ordered.

Again Leah obeyed, surprised to see him doing the same thing. The white cream looked strange against his tanned skin. "Since when did Indians need protection from the sun?" she teased.

"Everyone does." Reilly grinned. "The Plains Indians used to rub sunflower oil all over their bodies just for that reason." He watched Leah smear the cream over her face. "Your nose is already kind of red. Better slap on a little extra."

His carved features glistened like a bronzed statue in the soft morning light. There was nothing to wipe the excess cream from her hands, so Leah did what he did and used the legs of her jeans.

"Anything else you need out of the suitcase?" Reilly asked.

"No."

"I'm going to set them over by the rock slide, then we'll get loaded up."

While he walked to where the plane was buried, Leah carefully touched the area around the wound on her left arm. It was burning as if a hot knife were being held against it and it was sore nearly down to her elbow. Yet it didn't feel as if her arm was swollen. She wondered if she should ask Reilly to take a look at it.

What he'd said yesterday about not having much bandage material left and his intent to get an early start today made her decide not to bother him. The wound was obviously healing, though it had been a nasty gash.

"Ready to load up?" His long, easy strides carried him back into the clearing, his gaze touching her briefly.

"Why not?" Leah shrugged.

The lighter pack, containing the blanket and cooking utensils, he tied on her back. The heavier and more cumbersome one with the first-aid kit, food box, and flashlight, Reilly fastened on himself.

"Here." He handed her one of the sticks that had been used to support the lean-to.

"What's this for?" she asked. "Scaring snakes?"

"Use it for a walking stick. It'll come in handy on the steeper stretches of the mountain." He

walked over to the fire and stirred the ashes with
the other stick, covering the remains with gravel
and sand. "Okay. Let's go."

"Okay." She shifted the pack on her shoulders
to a more comfortable position, then smiled. "I
feel like a squaw carrying a papoose on her back."

Reilly laughed softly, a dark glint in his jade
eyes. "Time to hit the trail."

Waving her stick, Leah motioned for him to
lead the way. Reilly started off, setting an easy pace
that she could easily keep up with.

The level ridge top gave way to the sloping
mountainside. A lean jackrabbit darted swiftly out
of their path while a lizard sunning himself on a
rock stuck out his tongue as they passed. The sun
was a yellow sphere above the horizon.

CHAPTER SIX

Rivulets of sweat ran down her neck to the hollow between her breasts. The straps of the improvised backpack chafed her shoulders, adding to her discomfort.

The blazing sun was nearing its noonday notch and the fiery rays beat down relentlessly. Leaning heavily on her stick, Leah paused, winded, to catch her breath. The backs of her legs ached, protesting the sight of the downhill grade still before them. All morning long they had zigzagged down the mountain and there seemed to be no end to it.

"How much farther?" Leah cried in a tone of exasperated anger.

Reilly halted several yards ahead, squinting his eyes against the sun to look back at her. "It's hard to judge distance in open country. I don't really know." He wiped the sweat from around his mouth with the back of his hand.

"Great," she muttered.

"Do you want to rest here or wait until we get to the bottom?"

That would be by the end of next year, Leah thought tiredly. "How long has it been since we last stopped?" Since starting down the mountain, they had taken a ten-minute rest about every hour.

"Maybe twenty minutes," Reilly answered.

It seemed like a year ago, but Leah gritted her teeth and pushed onward with her stick. "Let's go down."

She wished they could just sit on their rumps and slide down to the bottom. The grade was certainly steep enough, but Reilly maintained his zigzag course, doubling the distance while lessening the strain of walking downhill.

Her left arm was hurting her more now. Its weight swinging freely at her side seemed to increase the pull on the healing wound. She tucked her left hand in the waistband of her jeans to form a natural sling. It helped, though it made balancing on the rocky stretches somewhat awkward.

Both shoes were rubbing against her heels. Leah knew she would soon have blisters to contend with. She lifted the pack on her back, but it slid back to the already chafed area. So she trudged on, putting one aching foot in front of another.

Except for an occasional glance to be sure Reilly was still ahead of her, she concentrated on only the ground ahead of her feet. She tried to blank out all her aches and pains and the dryness of her mouth and throat.

Time became meaningless. Leah didn't know if she had walked for one hour or four when the ground finally leveled out beneath her feet. Reilly was already shedding his pack.

"We'll rest here for a couple of hours and stay out of the worst of the heat," he announced.

If she had had the energy, Leah would have

cheered. Instead she sank to her knees, shrugging one strap of the chafing pack off her right arm and gently easing the other down her throbbing left.

Dully she watched Reilly take a quick swallow from the canteen before handing it to her. The sound of the water sloshing against the sides was beautiful. She was so thirsty she knew she could drink it dry. But her thirst reminded her how precious water was and she settled for a swallow.

Opening her pack, Reilly removed the blanket and picked up the stick she had dropped on the ground. He looked disgustingly fresh, she thought, as if he could walk down ten mountains like that with ease.

"Why don't you look as tired as I feel?" She sighed as he swiftly set up the lean-to.

He smiled faintly. "Probably because I don't spend five days a week behind a desk." The last corner of the lean-to was secured. "Come on, get out of the sun."

Leah willingly crawled into the shade, stretching out on her back. Her only wish was never to move again. Then Reilly was bending over her, his green eyes mocking and gently amused.

"Here, gnaw on this for a while." A stick of beef jerky was in his hand.

"I don't have the strength to chew." She waved it aside with a flick of her fingers.

"Eat!" He put the beef jerky between her parted lips.

Reluctantly she obeyed, knowing he wouldn't leave her alone until she did. Her jaws were weary by the time she finished eating it. Sighing, she closed her eyes to rest and fell asleep almost instantly.

A hand shook her shoulder. She forced her eyes open to focus on Reilly squatting beside her on the right. His pack was again strapped to his back, the canteen in his hand.

"It's time we left. Have a drink first."

Leah pushed herself up, fighting the blackness that swirled sickeningly in front of her eyes. She took a hesitant sip of water and handed the canteen back. While Reilly started taking down the lean-to around her, she pressed a hand to her burning forehead and waited for the dizziness to subside. She felt awful.

Her left arm was worse, but she decided it couldn't be the cause of her nausea. There wasn't a part of her body that didn't ache.

The sun had begun to move west, but the heat, even in the shade, was scorching. If anything was to blame, it was that and not her general exhaustion. She rose slowly, not wanting any quick movement to bring the dizziness back.

Reilly put the folded survival blanket in her pack. While he was adjusting it in place on her back, he accidentally brushed the area near her wound. Leah winced at the knife-sharp pain.

"Does it hurt?" he asked instantly, his alert gaze missing nothing.

"Everything hurts." She grimaced.

He handed her the walking stick. "Are you ready to go on?"

At her brief nod, Reilly took the lead. Although he set the same slow pace as before, Leah had trouble keeping up. At each step, pain jarred through her body. Twice he had to wait for her to catch up.

The rays of the sun seemed to set her skin on fire, burning through her clothes until she felt drowned in a river of sweat. Waves of weakness kept eroding her strength. Her parched throat made swallowing difficult.

The ten-minute rest at the end of the first hour was all too short. The one swallow of water hadn't quenched her thirst and her throat felt as dry as the desert sand. Her mind cried that she couldn't go any farther, but with feverish determination, she forced herself to do it.

In memory, she could hear her brother Lonnie saying something like *I told you girls can never keep up.* His voice sounded so clearly in her mind that she had to brush a hand in front of her glazed eyes to keep his image from dancing before her.

At Reilly's concerned look, she smiled wearily. "I'm all right," she said hoarsely, more to convince herself than him.

"Hold this pebble in your mouth," he instructed as he handed a small stone to her. "It will keep the saliva flowing and help your thirst. You look pretty dehydrated, but we have to ration the water until I find some."

The pebble did help to moisten her mouth as they started out again. She just hoped she wouldn't swallow it. Leah tried hard to follow the path Reilly was taking, but she kept weaving from one side to the other. The fire raging inside her sapped her remaining strength.

She tried focusing her gaze on Reilly, using his broad shoulders as a reference point to guide her onward. The world was spinning before her eyes and she kept losing sight of him in the intermittent moments of reeling blackness. She could feel herself beginning to lose consciousness and was terrified.

"Reilly!" Her cry for help was a croaking whisper, made thicker by the pebble in her mouth. She stumbled and leaned heavily on the stick to regain her balance. Before her reeling senses collapsed under the raging heat and unquenchable thirst, she called desperately to him again. "Reilly."

Then she had no more strength. Her knees started to buckle beneath her and only the stick was keeping her upright. As she fought to keep the blackness away, she sobbed because she didn't think he'd heard her. She had fallen so far behind.

The stick wavered in its support and she began to sink slowly to the ground. A pair of strong arms circled her waist, easing her down gently.

"Reilly," she breathed, unable to see him clearly yet recognizing the arms that had held her in sleep these last nights. "I'm sorry . . . I can't . . . make it . . . any farther."

"Don't talk," was his low reply. He propped her against his chest.

He held the canteen to her lips but most of the water trickled down her chin when she couldn't make her mouth swallow the precious liquid. He started to brush the damp tendrils of hair from her face, then stopped abruptly, his rough hand cupped on her cheek.

"My God, you're burning up with fever," Reilly muttered.

Quickly he stripped the pack from her back and unbuttoned her blouse. The pain was excruciating when he started to pull the sleeve away from her bandaged wound. Leah cried out sharply, a sickening blackness swirling in front of her.

Through it, she heard the angry hiss of his breath. "Look at that," he muttered. "Why the hell didn't you tell me how much this was hurting?"

Her tongue felt thick, but she replied, "It's . . . it's healing."

"Healing? Like hell—it's infected!"

With a groan of defeat, Leah surrendered to the blackness, letting it carry her away to oblivion. The sensation followed that she was floating above the ground, cradled against a masculine chest by a pair of strong arms. Her consciousness returned long enough for her to realize that Reilly was carrying her before she drifted away again.

A beautiful dream world closed around her. She was lying beside a mirror-smooth pool of clear water where green grass grew thickly along its banks. Overhead the branches of willow trees veiled the scarlet fire of a setting sun. Their leaves were green, a more brilliant green than the jade color of Reilly's eyes. A blessed coolness bathed her burning forehead. A trace of wood smoke was in the air.

Then she was being lifted and her blouse removed. She moaned a protest at the interruption of her serenely peaceful vision.

"Hold as still as you can," was Reilly's gentle request.

Her lashes fluttered open, her eyes focusing on his jet-dark head framed by a willow bough. "I'm having the most wonderful dream," she murmured. "There are big trees and water and grass."

"It isn't a dream," Reilly told her as he removed the old bandage from her arm and began cleaning the infected wound with a sharp-smelling liquid from the first-aid kit. She drowsily assumed that it was disinfectant. "Looks like a Basque shepherd dammed this little spring to water his sheep. Can't use the water because it isn't sterile and I want to deal with this right away. Going to sting a bit. Sorry."

So it was real. She felt the cleansing sting, sighed to herself and drifted again into unconsciousness.

The green world vanished and she stumbled over sun-scorched earth. The fiery rays of the sun blinded her eyes and burned her skin, its relentless blaze never once slackening.

Now and then, the coolness of water touched her parched lips. Sometimes it was Lonnie holding the canteen to her mouth, teasing her as he had done when they were children, when her short legs were unable to keep up with his long, lanky strides.

Other times it was Reilly telling her to lie still and rest. He couldn't seem to understand that she was condemned to walking beneath the searing sun. So she kept walking, surrounded by a furnace of heat.

The rising of the moon brought no relief. Its silvery glow burned white-hot from the sky. The desert night did not cool off as it had always done. Sweat seemed to boil on her skin.

The sun was worse. Leah cried aloud when it returned to the sky, yet there was no escape from its fierce heat. The only protection she had to prevent her from being consumed by the flaming tongues was her clothes. To her horror, she felt them being removed and struggled wildly to stop it.

"Leah, can you hear me?" Reilly's firm voice pierced her nightmare world.

"Yes." She sobbed with relief that she hadn't been abandoned. Her glazed eyes opened to discover that she was once again in the green oasis, Reilly bending beside her, stripped to the waist.

His compelling gaze wouldn't let her slip back

into the nightmare. "I have to take off your clothes."
Each word was spoken clearly and slowly.

Her head lolled to one side in an effort to
protest. Being naked would expose her again to the
terrifying sun. "No, you mustn't," she whispered in
a fever-choked whisper.

"You're too far gone to understand. I think
you're delirious." Reilly let that statement settle in
her mind before continuing. "I have to get your
temperature down. The water from the spring is
cool and I'm going to bathe you in it."

The raging fire that engulfed her was caused by
a fever. Leah grasped that thought for a few seconds,
but her dazed mind let go of it again.

"Leave . . ." She was so weak she could hardly
get the words out. "Leave . . . my clothes on." She
felt him smear something cool and gooey on her
wound and trembled.

"That's antibiotic gel. It will help seal the wound
from the water."

"No. No water."

"Don't fight me, Leah. You're going to need
your strength."

Her mind resisted, but her body was pliant
under his expert hands. In a semiconscious haze
she was aware of Reilly lifting her into his arms
and carrying her to the water, her head resting
against his naked shoulder.

Then she was immersed in water, cooling ripples
washing her from head to toe. An arm around her
waist kept her from sinking into the refreshing
depths of the pool. The overhanging branches of a
small willow shaded them from the sun.

Time was in limbo, beyond measurement for
Leah. At some point in her fever-induced stupor,

she became aware that Reilly too was unclothed, but it didn't matter as long as the deliciously cool water rinsed over her fiery skin.

Stirring, she tried to escape the stifling cocoon that held her tightly. She wanted the refreshing water of the pool to cool her again. A hand gently stroked her temple and settled along her neck. She was lying on the ground in Reilly's arms, the survival blanket wrapped around them.

"Sleep," he murmured near her ear. "Your fever has broken. You need to sleep."

With shuttered eyes, Leah relaxed against him. The warmth of his body turned into a safe haven instead of a furnace that she needed to escape. She slept without dreams or nightmares.

Reilly awakened her once in the daylight to feed her some broth. She instantly went back to sleep, noticing the sensation of him lying beside her much later.

The next time she opened her eyes, Leah discovered she was alone under the blanket. The sun was well up in the sky. The snapping sound of a fire drew her attention to the center of the glade. Reilly was crouched beside the fire, stirring the contents of the pit sitting near it.

His bronzed torso was shirtless, his muscled chest and shoulders rippling a golden copper in the sunlight. At least his lower half was covered, in the same jeans he'd worn since the morning they'd started down the mountain. It seemed like an eternity ago.

As if sensing her gaze, he glanced over his shoulder. The boldly chiseled face was more handsome than she remembered. He met her look. "Hello." The grooves around his mouth deepened with the familiar smile that crinkled his eyes.

"Hello," Leah said, feeling self-conscious without knowing why.

"Are you hungry?" He poured the liquid from the pan into one of the small bowls.

"A little," she admitted, and tried to shift into a sitting position, only to discover she was weaker than she had realized.

"Lie down. I'll feed you," he said, rising to walk over to her.

"You cooked, huh? That's squaw work." A wan smile curved her lips.

The line of his mouth crooked in response. "It is, but an Indian has to take care of his woman. Especially when she's crazy with fever."

His woman. The words made her heart lurch. He couldn't have meant her to take it literally. He had responded in kind to her lighthearted question, that was all. Yet what he had said took her breath away.

Setting the bowl on the ground nearby, Reilly took his backpack, cushioned it with the shirt he had been wearing and put it beneath her head for a pillow. Cross-legged, he sat beside her and picked up the bowl.

"How many 'moons' have I been out?" Leah asked after swallowing the spoonful of broth that he put to her lips.

"A moon is about a month. You've been out of it for about three nights, if you really want to know."

He held another spoonful of broth to her lips.

"That long?" she breathed in surprise.

"Try eating without talking," he suggested with amusement. "It'll go a lot faster."

When half the bowl was gone, Leah couldn't manage any more. Reilly set it aside, not forcing her to eat more than she wanted.

"How does your arm feel?" His dark head was tilted to one side, his gaze intently studying her.

Tentatively she moved her left arm, testing it with care. It was sore, but without that aching throb. She smiled with relief.

"Much better." She nodded.

"You'd better let me have a look at it," he said. "I don't trust your opinion anymore." The fond look in his eyes took the sting out of that comment.

Without any protest, Leah began unbuttoning her blouse. She was on the third button before she realized she wasn't wearing a bra. She knew it was ridiculous to blush, but she couldn't help the involuntary reaction.

She turned crimson.

"Do you remember that when you were delirious with fever I undressed you to bathe you in the pool?" A black eyebrow arched briefly with his question.

Her fingers fumbled with the buttons, neither undoing them nor buttoning them back up. "Yes, I remember. Sort of."

"Your shoulders were chafed from the backpack, so I didn't put your bra back on," he explained. "Not like it's something you needed to wear, anyway."

"I see," she murmured.

His thumb and forefinger captured her chin and lifted her head to meet the gentle amusement dancing in his eyes. "So did I. Everything there was to see. You okay with that?"

Leah's answer was to unbutton her blouse the rest of the way, heat flaming in her face. While Reilly eased her left arm out of the sleeve, she automatically shielded her breast with her hand. The blood pounded in her ears.

Expertly and impersonally, he examined the wound and bandaged it again, helping her back into the blouse.

"This time I think it will heal," he announced, turning away while she rebuttoned the front. "I could wring your neck for not telling me it was bothering you."

"I guess I got used to the pain," Leah said. "And I really did think it was healing."

"From now on, let me be the judge of that." He picked up the bowl and rolled to his feet in one fluid movement, reminding her again of his animal grace. "You'd better get some more rest."

"I've been sleeping for days as it is. I think I should get up and see if I can still walk." But she had to fight a wave of weakness just to sit up.

"Stretch your legs while you're lying down to get the circulation going. Rotate your ankles. That's enough for now," Reilly insisted.

Leah didn't argue. She didn't have the strength to get up on her own. She had to lie back down. Despite the hours of sleep she'd had, she was soon dozing off again.

A purple dusk had settled overhead when she awoke, casting its violet color on the still surface of the pool. Chunks of meat sizzled on a spit above a low campfire. Again Reilly's sixth sense alerted him to Leah's awakening.

"The food is about ready," he said. "Do you want to sit by the fire?"

"Yes," she answered emphatically.

When he lifted her to her feet, Leah's legs nearly crumpled beneath her. She wavered toward the fire. She doubted she could have made it even that short distance if it hadn't been for the support of his steady hand at her waist.

Shakily, she sat cross-legged in front of it, realizing the full extent of her weakness. Even her hand trembled when she took the bowl of greens Reilly offered her.

"What is this?" she asked.

"I found some rushes growing on the far side of the pool," he answered, spooning the rest into his bowl. "They may be a bit stringy, but they're edible and nourishing."

Actually, Leah thought the rushes were quite tasty, if stringy as Reilly had warned. But it was the tender white quail meat, roasted to perfection on the spit, that really aroused her appetite. She felt positively stuffed as she finished the last piece and licked her fingers in satisfaction.

"That was delicious." She sighed.

"You liked it?"

"Mmm, did I ever." Leah pressed a hand against her full stomach. "How did you manage to catch the quail? Did you set a snare?" Unless she had slept very soundly, she hadn't heard a gunshot. Not that you could kill a little bird like a quail with a pistol, she thought suddenly. It would be blown to bits.

"Quail?" A crooked grin lifted one corner of his mouth.

"That's what it was, wasn't it?" She eyed him curiously.

"No-o," Reilly drawled the word. "I don't mean to ruin your meal, but it was rattlesnake."

Closing her eyes, Leah swallowed a lump that had suddenly risen in her throat, then took a couple of shaky, calming breaths. Slowly the color returned to her face as the brief nausea passed. "All right. It was protein. I'm just going to think of it as protein."

"Is the meal still delicious?" He had been watching her changing expression with laughter in his eyes.

"Maybe not as good as it was when I thought I was eating quail," she admitted.

Reilly smiled and poked the fire. After the shock of finding out that she'd eaten snake wore off, Leah wanted to change the subject and talk about anything but food.

"Do you know that in all the time we've been stranded, you've hardly told me anything about yourself? I've rattled on—ugh. I need another verb."

"How about talked," he said, chuckling.

"Yeah. That'll do. I talked about my parents and Lonnie and my vagabond childhood, but I know very little about you, except that you design turquoise jewelry."

There were plenty of things she had observed about him—his calmness in a crisis, his knowledge of the desert—but she had no actual facts about his life.

"What would you like to know?" he asked dryly.

"Oh, whatever." In truth, Leah wanted to know everything, but she tried to sound nonchalant. "For instance, how did someone who's part Indian get a name like Reilly Smith?"

"You were expecting something more like John Black Feather, right?"

"Yeah. That kind of suits you, by the way."

"My mother was half Indian. My father was Irish-American."

Leah shot him a quizzical look. "I guess I don't think of the name Smith as particularly Irish, though I suppose it could be."

Reilly smiled. "It's not particularly anything. Years and years ago, men who came West to escape their pasts often changed their names. That's what my father's father did. My father never knew what his real name was, but family rumor said that my grandfather had killed a man in a barroom brawl back East. No one ever proved whether it was fact or fantasy."

"Well, it's a good story," Leah said.

"One fact is that he married an Irish girl named Maureen O'Reilly, who was my grandmother. My father left off the *O* when he named me."

"Are your parents alive?"

"No. My father was killed in a car accident shortly after I was born. And my mother wasn't able to keep me with her, so I was raised by her parents on a reservation. She died when I was eight." Reilly studied the fire and poked it again. "Anything else you want to know?"

Leah shook her head. Remembering Grady's comment that Reilly was a loner, she was surprised that he had already told her so much about his past. But his last question had invited her to ask more and she definitely wanted to know more.

"What was it like growing up on a reservation?"

"The rez? Home sweet home. Life was simple enough." He continued, "I went to school with other Indian children, took care of my grandparents' sheep, and helped with other chores. Their house was pretty isolated. We were way out in the desert."

"That explains a lot of things," Leah said.

"Yeah, I guess it does." He smiled at her. "Anyway, my grandfather made turquoise jewelry as a hobby and a way to earn a little extra money. Whenever my work was done, he would let me help. Mostly I did cobbing."

"What's that?"

"Separating the turquoise from the surrounding rock with pliers or a hammer and lead block,"

Reilly explained. "My grandfather got most of his ore from an abandoned mine in the hills. You had to be patient to find good stones and he was."

"So that's how you got interested in jewelry."

"Yup." He looked up at the first timid stars in the night sky. "In many respects I grew up thinking like an Indian with some of the old customs and traditions, but I always knew I was mostly white. I never really belonged."

When he paused, Leah didn't fill the silence but waited.

"I've never decided whether it was my Indian blood wanting freedom that made me leave the rez or the materialistic white part of me that gave me driving ambition and the desire for a different life."

"You can't divide yourself," Leah murmured. "You're the end product of both worlds, whole and complete."

In her mind, she added more. He was a strong and gentle man, creative and intelligent, resourceful and proud. Sewing all those qualities together was a strain of unshakable confidence in himself that gave him an inner peace.

"Uh-oh. We're getting philosophical," he told her firmly. "I think it's time we went to bed. I'll move the things a little closer to the fire."

While he retrieved the blanket a few feet away, Leah stared at the fire only inches from her knees. "Why do you always make such a small fire? Wouldn't it be warmer if it was larger?"

Reilly spread the blanket beside the fire within arm's reach of the woodpile.

"The white man makes a big fire and then has to sleep several feet away because it's too hot. The

Indian makes a small fire and lies down beside it."
He held out his hand to help her to her feet, the
flickering reflection of the blaze dancing in his
eyes.

CHAPTER SEVEN

The serenity of the pool was soothing, clear and cool without a ripple to disturb its smoothness. The small water willows curved above it to admire their reflection on the surface. A faint breeze stirred the rushes at the far end while water giggled over the dammed side of the pool to follow the course of the narrow silver stream.

Leaning against a slim tree trunk, Leah plucked at a blade of grass. It was about all she had the strength to do.

A string rested in a curved line on the water, made of unraveled threads from one of Reilly's shirts that he had braided together. The string was attached to one of the lean-to poles and a pin from the first-aid kit was fashioned into a hook on the other end.

A slight smile touched the edges of her mouth. "Do you really think there are fish in the pond?"

"No." Reilly darted her a sideways look. "But it's an excellent place to sit and think."

"Think about what?"

"Things." He shrugged with one shoulder.

"What things?" Leah prompted.

His mouth tightened, leading her to believe that his thoughts were serious ones. He didn't answer immediately.

"This is a good place." His alert gaze swept the area. "There's plenty of water, and firewood, too, from that deadfall over there."

"And it's peaceful and beautiful," Leah added to his practical assessment. "We were lucky to find it. Well, you found it. I don't remember getting here."

"Against the desert, a patch of green stands out for miles. And where there's green, there's water," he replied. "I noticed it when we were almost at the bottom of the mountain."

Turning her gaze to the mountains that ringed the glade on three sides, Leah tried to locate the saddle-backed ridge on which their plane had crashed. But one ridge was much like another and she couldn't find it.

"Where were we?" she asked.

"About thirty miles back and up." Reilly pointed toward a mountain peak that didn't seem very far away. "Do you see the small dip on the other side of that peak? That's where the plane crashed."

Sighing, she leaned back against the tree. "I guess we've been given up for dead after all this time."

This was the eighth day. It seemed like such a short amount of time, yet conversely, it seemed like forever. "It'll be another three or four days before you have the strength to walk out of here," he said grimly.

"At least here we won't have to worry about a supply of water," Leah offered. "And there's plenty of firewood to boil it. We'll just have to find more food."

That morning Reilly had announced that the three remaining packets of dried food would be used only as a last resort. They would eat what they were able to forage. He had placed snares along the game trails leading to the watering hole. If that failed, he would hunt with his pistol and there was no shortage of snakes. Leah shuddered a little. But she would eat one again if she had to. She didn't have a choice.

"With the two of us, the food we have now would only last three days. It would last six days, if there was only one," he said quietly, trailing the string through the water.

Something in his tone made her stiffen. "What's that supposed to mean?"

His impassive face turned to meet her challenging look. "That you stay here while I go for help."

"We've been over that before," she said tautly.

"Things are different now. You aren't capable of traveling, not for several days." Reilly turned his attention back to the fishing line. "I noticed a dirt track about ten miles from here. It heads down the center of the valley floor. It will either lead to the highway or a ranch house."

"How far?"

"I don't know. I haven't seen any smoke to the south in the morning that would indicate a ranch house," he answered thoughtfully. "The second day that we were here I walked over to the track. There wasn't any sign that it had been used for a long time. It might have been abandoned when the mine up there was. But it leads somewhere."

"I won't stay here alone, Reilly. I mean it." Her teeth were clenching in determination.

"The longer we stay out here, the more risk

there is that both of us will get too weak to get out. You'll be safe enough here by yourself."

"You said we were in this together," Leah reminded him. "I won't let you leave without me."

"You're too weak to go now."

"I am not!" she protested vigorously, even though she knew that what Reilly said was true. "I can walk just as far and just as long as you can! There's nothing wrong with me. My fever's gone and I'm as healthy as a horse!"

To prove it, she rose swiftly to her feet and took a quick step toward him, but the sudden movement instantly made her dizzy. She pressed a hand to her reeling head and swayed unsteadily.

In a split second, Reilly was on his feet, hands gripping her waist. She leaned heavily against him, fighting to regain her sense of balance. He lifted her in his arms and sat her back against the slim trunk.

"Now will you admit I'm right?" His green eyes moved over the pallor of her face. "You are too weak."

"I moved too quickly, that's all," Leah said defensively, resting her head against the tree to gaze at the man kneeling beside her. "I swear that you're not leaving without me, Reilly. If you go, I'll follow." There was a tight lump in her throat as she spoke, but her voice was otherwise controlled.

"I believe you mean that." He started to rise and move away.

But Leah needed assurance that he had changed his mind and wouldn't leave her. She clutched at his shirt to stop him.

"Reilly?" She leaned forward, looking into his eyes.

Motionless, he held her gaze, revealing nothing of his thoughts or decision. A smoldering light burned in his eyes and his hand slid slowly, almost unwillingly, along the back of her waist.

Her heart fluttered uncertainly, excited and afraid. Then his mouth took hers in a passionate kiss. Reilly intensified it, making Leah feel like she was melting against the solid wall of his chest.

The weight of his body pressed her backward, pinning her on the carpet of grass while he continued to explore her mouth with sensual thoroughness. Shudders of thrilled rapture made her body tremble. She had not guessed that his masterful kiss would be as glorious as this. Her senses were overwhelmed by the force of his desire.

His caressing fingers explored her neck and shoulders, blazing a trail that his mouth followed. Gasps of air were all she was allowed before a new shiver stole her breath.

In a mindless haze, she knew she had lost control and was powerless to regain it as long as his lips kept returning to dominate hers. Unexpectedly, Reilly rolled onto his back, pulling her on top of him. There he cupped her face in his hands.

Her parted lips were swollen and tender from his kisses. She knew her eyes had darkened from the desire he had aroused. Her lashes fell to veil the completeness of her response. Yet she couldn't deny the truth of what she felt.

"I want you . . . so much." Her voice shook.

"Leah." His husky tone betrayed his inner passion, too, yet his voice was controlled. "Don't say that. We shouldn't."

The gently spoken words frightened her as his embrace had not. The silken curtain of her hair had fallen forward. It concealed the crimson blush in her cheeks as she drew away from his unresisting hands and scrambled to her feet.

She could feel his piercing eyes watching her, but she was unable to meet them. Keeping her back to him, she stuffed her trembling hands deep into the pockets of her jeans and drew a quivering breath. "What are you afraid of?"

"Nothing." The answer came from directly behind her, his animal silence bringing him to his feet unheard by her. In the next instant, his hands were resting lightly on each side of her waist. She breathed in sharply to keep from turning and seeking his embrace.

Reilly had wanted her—she knew that. But he had rejected her. Why?

She turned around to face him, but pushed his hands away. "I don't understand you, Reilly Smith!" Leah rubbed the back of her neck in frustration and tried to check the welling tears as she stormed away.

A sigh came from Reilly. Grass whispered beneath his feet as he walked toward her again. His hands touched her shoulders and Leah shook them off. He simply grasped them more firmly a second time.

"Please don't try to convince me that you're a saint," she declared, tossing back her head to glare at him through her tears.

"Okay, I won't. I'm not. But you've been through too much in the last few days. You've been hurt and you're vulnerable. I can comfort you but that's all. I have to say no . . . to anything more."

A tremulous smile touched her mouth. His words chased the clouds away from her heart and let a little joy shine through.

"Was that what that kiss was? Comfort?"

He smiled a little. "Well, it's proof that I'm no saint."

"Yeah. True enough."

Reilly smiled but there was a sad look in his eyes. Slipping her arms around his middle, she sighed and nestled her head against his chest. She was thoroughly confused but if comfort was what he was offering, that was what she would take.

His arms tightened to hold her close, a strong hand slowly caressing her shoulders and back as his mouth roughly moved against her hair. His fingers stroked it, then drew her head back. His mouth closed over hers again in a lingering kiss.

Second meltdown in a day, Leah thought. Damn him.

When he released her at last, his eyes were smoldering. "I think it's time we did something else."

Her heart skipped a beat.

"You take charge of the fishing and I'll check the snares," Reilly said huskily.

"Let me go with you," Leah whispered.

His fingers covered her lips as he shook his dark head. "I want to be sure you get plenty of rest so you'll be able to cook dinner tonight." He pushed her gently to the ground near where his pole lay.

"Reilly, are you trying to distract me?"

His answer was swift. "No. I'm trying to distract myself."

Leah watched him walk away. She knew she was falling in love with him, if she hadn't already. Was it because she couldn't have survived in this desert wilderness without him? She thought it over. She admired his competence, resourcefulness, and strength, but her feelings for him went well beyond that. Nor was what she felt strictly physical.

So, eliminating all the other possibilities, she *was* in love with him. She tried to tell herself that eight days was a very short time to fall in love with someone. Her heart answered that she and Reilly had been through more than some couples experience in a lifetime together.

The only uncertainty that remained was how Reilly felt about her. Was it more than physical attraction for him, too? Leah sighed, knowing that no one could get an answer out of him that he wasn't prepared to make. But for the moment, the knowledge of her love for him was enough.

One of the snares had trapped a rabbit. Reilly cleaned it and showed Leah how to roast it on the spit. Again, their menu had a side dish of greens, an item that Leah decided they needed.

The exertion of doing their few dishes left her slightly weak. She set them near the fire to dry. Brushing a hand wearily through her gold-brown hair, she wished longingly for a hot bath and a shampoo.

"Tired?" Reilly asked gently.

"A little," Leah admitted. She sat down beside him in front of the fire, curling her legs beneath her. "Mostly I was thinking that I was a mess."

An arm circled her waist and drew her against his shoulder, locking his hands over her middle as he kept her faced toward the fire. Leah stared into the flames, a feeling of intense bliss stealing over her.

"Aren't you going to say that I'm not a mess?" she teased with a soft sigh of contentment.

"You are, though." Reilly chuckled.

"Now that's a tactful reply." She shook her head with pretend exasperation, but his honesty made her smile.

A coyote sang his lament to the winking eye of a crescent moon. On a faraway hill another coyote joined in the chorus. Overhead, the stars blazed brightly in the velvet sky.

His chin brushed the top of her head. "Did you want me to say that your hair is perfumed with sage and smoke? That its color reminds me of the dappled coat of a fawn in the morning sunlight?" The husky murmur of his voice quickened her heartbeat.

"Is that really what you think?" Leah held her breath. She could feel Reilly smile against her hair.

"Your eyes are the color of the fawn's, round and trusting, fringed with fantastic lashes." His hand circled her wrist to make her arm join his as he held her more tightly. "Your ankles are as dainty as a doe's."

"Wow, the Compliment Shop is open." She knew he was putting it on thick, but she enjoyed it all the same.

"I mean every word."

"I think"—she was sinking in a quicksand of heady emotins, yet didn't exactly want to struggle free—"that one of your ancestors kissed the Blarney Stone, Reilly Smith."

"Do you?" he mused softly against her hair. "It runs on both sides of the family then. Some of the greatest orators in our history were Indians—Red Cloud, Spotted Tail—if only someone had listened."

There was no bitterness in his statement and nothing that required a response. The desert silence moved in, drawing them into its magic circle of ageless enchantment.

It was a long time before either of them moved. Then Reilly finally decreed softly that it was time they got some sleep. The only thing that made Leah willingly agree was knowing that she would return to his arms beneath the blanket.

This night, as he cradled her in his arms, she lifted her head for a kiss. The firm pressure of his mouth on hers started a slow glow of warmth through her body. The feeling remained even after he had dragged his mouth from hers, leaving it tingling and moist from his kiss. The steady beat of his heart beneath her head soon lulled her to sleep.

Cool air invaded the blanket cocoon. Leah frowned at its chill, keeping her eyes tightly shut, and tried to snuggle close against Reilly's muscular length. He wasn't there.

She was immediately awake. Soft morning light filled the camp. The flames of the campfire were hungrily devouring the fresh wood that had been added. Throwing back the cover, she sat up. There was no sign of Reilly.

The canteen was gone. Her gaze flew to the waterhole several yards away, thinking Reilly was there filling the pot to boil water for the canteen. He wasn't. Scrambling to her feet, Leah scanned the area around the campfire again.

A cold dread filled her heart. "He couldn't. He wouldn't!" she murmured aloud, protesting against the chilling thought.

But it was entirely possible. Reilly was nowhere to be seen. That left only the desert. Shuddering, Leah realized that he had not promised he wouldn't leave without her. In fact, he'd never said that he wouldn't go.

Her gaze shifted toward the center of the valley.

He had sneaked away at first light, probably thinking she would be too weak and frightened to follow.

Leah scowled. "You're in for a surprise, Reilly Smith!" she muttered.

Deciding that he couldn't be very far ahead of her, she kicked sand onto the fire, quickly stirred the smoldering embers, and kicked on more sand. If she hurried, she could catch up to him.

There was no point trying to carry the few items with her. Their weight would slow her down. Reilly had the canteen and that was the important thing.

Not allowing herself time to question the wisdom of her impulse, Leah abandoned the campsite without a backward glance. Her only thought was to catch up with Reilly as quickly as possible. She started running, wanting to make up the distance that separated them.

The desert brush whipped at her legs and thighs. A startled flock of mountain bluebirds skimmed the bush tops in flight. All her attention was focused on the land ahead of her.

Leah's scream ripped the air as an unknown force yanked her backward. Her motion stopped with an impact against a hard, immovable object.

"Where the hell do you think you're going?" Reilly demanded, shaking her by the shoulders.

She stared at his angry face in disbelief.

"Reilly!" She started laughing and crying at the same time, ceasing her instinctive struggle of self-protection.

"Answer me!" His eyes were cold.

"I thought . . ." Her breath came in short, relieved sighs. "I thought you'd gone for help. I thought you'd left me."

"You crazy—" Reilly snapped off the rest of the

sentence, leaving it dangling unfinished in the air. "And you were coming after me?"

Leah bobbed her head, trying to calm her shaky breath. "I told you I would," she reminded him.

His fingers loosened their grip. "You might have checked to be sure I was gone," he replied tightly, "instead of racing off into the bush like a mad-woman."

"I looked for you. The canteen was gone," she said. "Then I kicked sand in the fire and took off. Where were you?"

"Checking the snares." He released her entirely, standing in front of her, his hands on his hips, still unsmiling.

She had completely forgotten about the snares in her panicked certainty that he had left her. "I didn't remember them," she admitted.

Reilly breathed in deeply, his expression letting her know what he thought of that. "Let's go back to camp and restart the fire." His mouth thinned. "Since you were so intent on following me . . . would you like to follow me back to camp?"

Leah nodded. There was no doubt he was angry with her. In retrospect, her action was foolhardy and impulsive. She could have gotten lost very easily.

"How . . ." She had to hurry to keep up with his long strides. "How did you know where I'd gone?"

"I didn't," he replied curtly. "But I heard the racket of something charging through the bush and I decided it was you or a stampeding herd of cattle."

"I was stupid."

He slid her an icy look. "If you expect me to dis-agree, woman, you're wrong."

Until his anger cooled, Leah decided it was bet-ter to keep silent. It became an oppressive silence, as he patiently rebuilt the fire. When it was burning freely once more, he began cleaning a game bird he had caught in the snare. Not a word or a glance did he direct at Leah.

There was little for her to do but sit and watch him, squirming inwardly at the uncomfortable silence. The feeling kept growing that she was being unfairly punished. Finally she decided that it was time for a truce.

As Reilly started to put the cleaned bird on the spit, Leah stepped forward. "Let me do that. It's squaw work." She tried to lessen the crackling tension by using their standby joke.

"You aren't a squaw." The aloof indifference in his voice cut like a knife.

"Reilly, I'm sorry. What more do you want me to say?" she demanded.

With the bird secured on the spit, he stood up, his face set in hard lines. "Do you realize you could have gotten yourself killed out there? If not from snakebite or a broken neck, then from thirst or starvation. You didn't take anything to protect you from the elements. You didn't even take any food or water!"

"I wanted to catch up to you!" Leah shouted in answer to his loud, accusing voice. "I didn't want to be slowed down carrying things. Besides, you had the canteen! Was I supposed to go racing through the desert carrying a pan of water?"

"You shouldn't have been racing anywhere. And if I had left, then you should have stayed here. Don't you trust me at all?"

"No! I didn't know any of that," she protested angrily.

His eyes narrowed as he let out a long, exasperated breath. "I ought to take you over my knee," he declared through gritted teeth. "Except it wouldn't do any good."

"That's right," Leah retorted. "Next time notify me before you disappear. Is that too much to ask?"

"Not at all. Next time I'll leave a detailed memo. And a map with my coordinates. That way if you follow me again, you'll have some chance of surviving. You would have been lost or dead before the day was out," Reilly said harshly.

"At least then you would be rid of me and not have to think about me anymore!" she cried. "Aren't you sorry you went after me and brought me back?"

He pulled her against his chest in one fluid motion. Her startled mouth flew open to protest and it was covered with his. Love rushed, unchecked, to respond to the ardor of his kiss.

Her senses whirled in the vortex of Reilly's embrace until she didn't know up from down and didn't care.

Then his mouth traced the sensitive cord along her neck. "You would try the patience of a saint," he muttered against her skin. "And you already know I'm not one."

His warm breath was a disturbing caress as she wound her arms tightly around him for support. The wild tempo of her heart made clear thinking difficult. She inhaled deeply of his intoxicatingly male scent and sighed. "That's right," she murmured. "And neither am I."

His hands set her firmly away from him. The dark fire glittering in his eyes did nothing to steady the erratic beat of her heart. His mouth crooked wryly.

"Don't remind me." There was no more cold anger in his expression. "See what you can do about keeping our breakfast and lunch from being burned up while I wash. I guess we're both freaked out by this point."

The fire was trying to char one side of the dressed fowl. Leah rescued it as Reilly walked toward the narrow stream formed by the water spilling over the dam's walls. As she turned the spit, she watched him crouch beside the stream, splashing the cold water on his face and the back of his neck.

Smiling at his action and feeling a little of the tension ease, she glanced at the sun. Its fiery heat hadn't yet begun to scorch the ground. In fact, it was only pleasantly warm.

CHAPTER EIGHT

After they had eaten, Reilly suggested that Leah rest in the shade through the hot hours of early afternoon. She tried, knowing that it was important to regain her strength, but she couldn't relax.

A fever burned inside as she watched him repairing one of the snares. It wasn't a fever caused by infection, unless love was infectious. If it was, she hoped Reilly caught a worse case of it than hers.

No matter how often she closed her eyes, they opened again and her gaze strayed to Reilly. Her senses tingled with awareness of him. The ache to be in his arms would start and all thought of rest immediately vanished.

It was no use. She stopped trying to force inactivity upon herself. She recognized the inherent temptation of their present situation, what with the two of them alone in an isolated paradise. The only thing missing was the succulent apple. There were snakes to spare.

Pushing herself up from the cool grass, Leah

rubbed her hands over her hipbones. Reilly's questioning look flickered over her.

"I'm going to wash my clothes down at the stream," she announced. "If you want, I'll do your shirt." She tried to sound offhand and almost succeeded. "I'm not in the mood to lie around doing nothing," she explained. At least it sounded sort of like an explanation.

His shirt was already unbuttoned and hanging loose in front. With a nod of acceptance, he slipped it off and tossed it to her, immediately returning his attention to the damaged snare.

"You can wear one of the shirts we used for a backpack while you're washing your clothes." His dark head remained bent over his task.

"Thanks."

He seemed not to hear her reply.

Behind the screen of a thick bush, Leah stripped off her outer clothes and donned the shirt. Its tails reached halfway down her thighs, providing relatively decent coverage for her underwear. Rolling back the sleeves, she set to work rinsing and rubbing to try and wash their clothes minus the assistance of detergent.

Finally she decided they were as clean as they were going to get under the circumstances. With the back of her hand, she wiped the sweat from her forehead, then picked up the wet clothes and carried them to the sunlit brush on the edge of the glade.

The sun would dry it all in minutes. She smiled, feeling its scorching rays the instant she stepped out of the shade. More sweat collected between her shoulder blades as she spread the clothes over the bushes. She glanced longingly at the pool of water, saying a silent thank-you to the unknown shepherd who'd built the dam.

She retreated into the shade. "Reilly? Would it hurt anything if I got my arm wet?"

"Why? Did you get it wet?" He frowned but didn't glance up.

"No," Leah said quickly. "I just wanted to take a dip in the waterhole to cool off."

"You'd better let me look at it first." As he lifted his head, his gaze slid over her in absent appraisal.

"Just a minute." She turned her back to him and slipped her left arm out of the rolled shirtsleeve, wrapping the left side of the shirt in sarong fashion across her front.

Leah saw a flicker of amusement in his green eyes. He rose to his feet to examine the wound. His touch against her skin was strictly impersonal when he eased the bandage away.

"You're going to have a scar from this, you know," he commented, putting the bandage back in place.

"It doesn't matter." Leah shrugged. It was difficult to breathe calmly with Reilly standing so close. Just looking at his bronzed chest ignited all sorts of wayward thoughts. She tried to shut them out as she tossed her head to look at his face. "So I can get it wet?"

His gaze moved to her mouth. For a heart-stopping moment, Leah felt herself start to sway toward him, aching with every fiber of her being to feel his caress. The silver and turquoise necklace gleamed dully against the tanned column of his neck.

Briskly he turned away. "I wish you wouldn't. Why risk a recurrence of the infection? The waterhole isn't deep and you can keep the bandage dry."

"How do you know it isn't deep?" Leah arched a curious eyebrow, frowning slightly.

"I bathed you in it once to bring your fever down, remember?" Reilly bent his head over the snare again. "And I've used it myself a few times—in the mornings before you were awake."

No wonder he always looked relatively clean, she thought. But she decided not to compliment him on it.

"I'll be careful not to slip," she promised diffidently.

At the water's edge, Leah glanced over her shoulder. Reilly's back was turned toward her, deliberately or indifferently, she didn't know which.

Removing the shirt the rest of the way, she stepped into the pool, using an overhanging branch of a willow for balance. The deepest point, near the far end of the pool, brought the water to her waist. The temperature of the water there seemed to be several degrees cooler than the rest of the pool. She figured that she was near the spring's inlet.

It was awkward keeping her left arm out of the water while she tried to rinse the upper half of her body and her hair. It was a slow process, but refreshing. She resisted the impulse to linger, splashing and playing in the water, and waded onto the bank. Reilly was still working on the snare.

She patted the moisture from her skin with the shirt she had been wearing, blotting the dripping water from her underwear. The rest of her clothes should be dry by now. Slipping the damp shirt on, Leah retraced her path to the bushes, collected the washed clothes, and changed swiftly into her own.

The seams of her jeans were still damp, but that

coolness and her damp underwear countered the sunbaked heat of the dry things.

"Here's your shirt," she told Reilly as she returned to the circle of their camp.

"Hang it on the lean-to."

Leah hooked the collar over one of the poles. "Haven't you fixed that snare yet? You've been working on it all afternoon."

"Whatever it was that got caught in it worked on it all night," he replied absently.

Kneeling beside the stack of their few belongings, she looked impatiently through it all, finally sitting on her heels and glancing at Reilly.

"Do you know where the comb is?" she asked.

"In the food box."

"Ick. I hate finding a hair in my food."

"Not a problem. There's hardly any food left."

She found it and began raking it through her snarled hair. The sun had bleached pale streaks in it, and the light brown had turned almost golden. As she tugged the comb through her hair, she watched a cloud shadow racing across a distant mountain slope. A ghost moon occupied a corner of the daylight sky.

There had not been a sign of a search plane in the last two days. There couldn't have been one previously or Reilly would have mentioned it. There was no one who knew where they were or that they were alive.

Leah thought of her father, stern but compassionate, but always correct in his military-man way. His air of reserve was a contrast to her mother's warm, outgoing personality, which helped her make new friends with ease every time her husband was transferred.

With his cold logic, her father would have calculated Leah's chances of surviving the plane crash and nine days in a desert wilderness. She guessed that he would conclude there was little hope that she was still alive. He would be devoting himself to consoling her mother. Lonnie, she knew, would never give up the search until he found her. He did not accept the inevitable as their father did.

Her father's calculations did not include the Reilly factor, of course. Even if her family had been told a few things about Grady's mystery passenger, Reilly had no living relatives to reassure her dad about his knowledge of the desert or his knack for surviving under primitive conditions.

A smile curved her lips as she visualized her parents' reaction if they could witness this scene— Reilly sitting there trying to repair a broken snare to catch their night's meal and herself combing her hair after washing in a stream and bathing in a pool.

The clock could have been turned back a hundred years. The only modern possessions they had brought down the mountain were a flashlight, emergency rations of food, the survival blanket, the first-aid kit, a pistol and a few rounds of ammo, and a pocketknife. Everything else they had made or improvised—the pan, the bowls, the snares, the lean-to.

"Why are you smiling?" Reilly was studying her, his head tipped to one side in idle curiosity.

"I was imagining what my parents would think if they could see us now."

He nodded understandingly, his gaze briefly sweeping the sky before returning to the snare in his lap. His action wiped the smile from her face.

"Not much hope that a plane will find us, is there?" Leah asked. "We'll have to walk out of here."

"That's right."

She looked away, over the sage-colored valley and the mountains that enclosed it. The valley seemed to run forever. It was difficult to remember that somewhere beyond the horizon was a world with highways and cars and buildings with electricity, running water, heat, and air-conditioning. The neon splendor of Las Vegas seemed more than ever like a fantasy in the lonely beauty of this wilderness.

A snarl at the back of her head caught the comb. She tried working the teeth through the matted hair and she gasped at her inadvertent yank on her scalp. The sound drew a look from Reilly.

"A rat built a nest in my hair," she answered the silent question in his green eyes.

While she tried to work out the snarl, she watched him set up the snare to test his repairs. At the first pressure, it snapped at the very place he had mended. Reilly made a disgusted sound and tossed it in the banked fire.

"Can't you fix it?" Leah asked as a tiny flame licked greedily over the snare.

He shook his head. "The other three will have to be enough." His sideways glance noted her struggles with the comb. "Want some help?"

"Please," she sighed with frustration. "I can't see what I'm doing"—she rubbed the tender part of her scalp—"but I can certainly feel it."

Rising, he walked to her, taking the comb from her hand as he knelt behind her. With gentle care, he worked the hair free of its snarling knot strand by strand, then smoothed the hair into the rest curling around her shoulders. He offered the comb to Leah.

"Would you comb the rest of it . . . to be sure there aren't any more knots?" It was only an excuse to keep him near. The breathless tremor in her voice must have betrayed her inner wish.

"Leah, no."

He tossed the comb on the ground in front of her. She turned sideways, her hazel eyes wide and shimmering with aching need. The parted softness of her lips issued an invitation that his jade eyes couldn't ignore.

His narrowed gaze moved from her mouth to look deep into her eyes. "You're playing a dangerous game, Leah," he muttered.

"I know," she swallowed hard, her voice unreasonably calm, "but—"

"This situation provides enough temptations without you offering more," he added flatly.

Leah lowered her gaze and looked at the ground. "You're right, of course," she admitted, but it didn't soothe her wildly leaping pulse.

A sun-browned hand lightly cupped her chin, tipping her face up again. Desire smoldered in his eyes as they swept possessively over her.

"I should have left this morning and gone for help."

She rubbed her cheek against his fingers, her lashes fluttering briefly from the magic spell of his touch. "I would have followed you."

"I know." His lips curved into a sexy smile.

An irresistible force bent his dark head toward her. At the touch of his mouth against hers, Leah turned into his arms, sliding her hands around his neck into the black thickness of his hair.

The demand of his kiss tilted her head backward while his powerful hands arched her against him. A fire to equal the burning rays of the sun flamed through her body, the roar of its blaze raging in her ears. The male scent of him was intoxicating fuel to the fire that consumed her.

She gasped as his mouth explored the hollow of her throat, sending shudders through her from his sensually arousing caress. Pushing aside the collar of her blouse, he kissed her shoulder, trailing up the sensitive cord of her neck to nibble at her earlobe. Then he teased the corner of her mouth until her lips sought his kiss.

The iron band of his arms eased her to the ground. Leah's hands slipped to his muscular shoulders to bring him close, then remained to revel in the nakedness of his hard flesh. She could hardly breathe from wanting him. Never before had she been so completely alive.

The sun blazed white-hot in the sky. Behind her eyes the light of love was as intensely bright as the sun, searing in its insatiable fire and illuminating every corner of her heart. It was beyond physical.

Wordlessly, she responded to his embrace, body and soul. The soaring joy within her lifted her to a world without horizons. Reilly's kiss deepened as if he had been carried there, too.

Then, just as suddenly, as if the height was too dizzying, he rolled on his side, his hand slipping away from her breast. His other arm didn't let her go. She was still held against his chest.

In a sensual daze, Leah could only listen to the beat of his heart and the raggedness of his breathing. Much more slowly, she descended to the physical reality of their nearly consummated embrace. The wonder of it kept her silent for several minutes.

"Reilly." Her voice was warm and throbbing.

His hand stroked her cheek, a thumb touching her mouth to ask for silence again.

"Leah"—she could hear his physical need in the roughness of his voice—"be still."

It would have been easy to do exactly what she wanted to do. The delicious temptation teased her thoughts, but she lay unmoving in the crook of his arm until she felt the tension easing from his muscles and knew he was again in total command.

"Tell me about your boyfriend."

"Who?" Leah blinked.

"Mark. The man you've been dating."

She frowned. "How did you know about him?"

"You mentioned him when you were delirious." He smiled but it didn't reach his eyes.

It was strange but she couldn't remember what Mark looked like. It seemed years ago that she had seen him. The vague image she could summon was of a pale, insignificant man compared to Reilly.

"He works at the same bank I do," she answered indifferently. "I went out with him several times. So I guess he falls into the category of boyfriend. What did I say about him?"

"Nothing."

She believed him. There was little she could have said about Mark except that he was nice enough and possessive in an irritating kind of way. A sudden flash of jealousy shifted her thoughts to an adjoining track.

"Okay. Truth or dare. You must have a girlfriend."

"Truth. I don't." He rolled onto his back and stared at the pale blue sky.

"Yeah, right," she scoffed.

"I work hard. Haven't had the time. Don't need the aggravation."

His reply seemed to say that she, Leah, might be

just as aggravating as the unknown others. The thought was upsetting.

"You . . . you once mentioned you lived in Las Vegas," she murmured, hoping to change the subject. "Where?"

"I have a house in the foothills outside the city."

"Why . . . er . . . did you pick Las Vegas?" Leah tried to sound nonchalant.

"It's centrally located for my work. I'm not far from the mines or the outlets for my jewelry in California and Arizona."

"Do you spend much time at your home?"

"Yes," he answered simply.

Leah tipped her head to see his face, smiling bravely, even though she could feel the beginning of stupid, pointless, unwanted tears. His life was none of her business, obviously. "When we get back . . . um . . . will I see you?"

The pause before he answered was electric. His jade gaze revealed nothing to her searching eyes. "Sure. We'll have dinner. To celebrate our safe return. I'll call you. We'll figure something out."

I'll call you. Famous last words. But better than nothing. Maybe he even meant it. Averting her gaze, she slid her hand over the sexy flatness of his stomach. "I'd like that," she said, trying not to sound pathetically eager.

He seized her wrist and jerked her hand away. The motion continued, turning her onto her back, her arms pinned above her head as Reilly hovered above her, dark anger flashing in his eyes. "Don't do that. I'm not made of stone."

"Sorry." She knew she should be frightened by his reaction, but she wasn't. "I can't help it, Reilly, I—"

"Yes, you can!" Abruptly he released her wrists and got to his feet. His expression was forbidding as he towered above her. "You know as well as I do what's happening between us." He turned away, roughly rubbing the back of his neck. "We've been out here alone for too long. The real world doesn't seem real at all. There's just this . . . hostile emptiness." He gestured toward the endless desert landscape. "And you. And me. But we're going to make it back and when we do, it'll be the days we spent together that will seem unreal."

"Is that what you think?" Leah's tone was calm. Having concrete instead of desert sand beneath her feet would not alter the love she felt for him.

"It's the way life is." It was a statement, not issued to be debated. Reilly grabbed his shirt from the lean-to pole. "I'm going to check the snares."

Was he telling her something, Leah wondered as she watched him go. Was he warning her not to fall in love with him because he was not in love with her? She picked up the comb from where he had tossed it and began running it through her hair, feeling numb.

By early evening, Reilly hadn't returned. But she knew he hadn't left her to walk for help. And he was too wise in the ways of the desert to get lost checking the snares he had set some distance from the waterhole.

As dusk settled over the sky, Leah clutched the flashlight tightly in her hand. If he wasn't back by the time the setting sun touched the rim of the mountain, she was going out to look for him. She added another log to the fire and glanced at the horizon.

There wasn't a whisper of a sound, yet something made her spin around. Where there had been nothing but cobweb shadows cast by the willows, Reilly stood, returning to the camp with the animal silence of his ancestors.

Only when she saw him did Leah realize how worried she had been—and how much she had wanted him to come back. Relief weakened her knees, keeping her from racing into his arms. That, and the withdrawn expression in his face. He studied her for a long moment, finally looking at the flashlight in her hand.

"I . . . I was coming to look for you," she explained shakily. "I thought you might have been hurt."

His expression didn't change as he slipped the pistol from his waistband and returned it to the first-aid kit. Then his swinging strides carried him to the fire. He offered no explanation for his long absence.

"Where did you go?" Leah asked.

Except for the sweat stains on his shirt, there wasn't a mark on him. His quietness chilled her to the bone.

"The snares were empty." He took a long drink from the canteen, avoiding her searching eyes. "I went hunting—unsuccessfully."

Leah hugged her arms about her to ward off the sudden attack of misery. "I'm not hungry." She stared into the fire.

"You're going to eat anyway," he said firmly.

A sighing laugh escaped her throat. "Right. I have to get my strength back so we can get the hell out of here."

"Yes, you do." His gaze narrowed on her huddled form.

Leah looked at his profile, so aggressively male. His black hair had grown longer since the crash and curled over his collar. The shirt was open, revealing the hard, bronzed chest. His muscles rippled as he recapped the canteen.

Her desire to touch him was almost painful. "Reilly . . ." Her voice was soft with need.

Was it her imagination or did his face grow paler beneath his tan? A muscle in his lean jaw twitched, but he didn't glance at her.

"I'll refill the canteen. Did you boil more water?"

"Yes," she whispered. "It's in the pan."

"You decide which one of the food packages you want to fix tonight." He turned away from the fire.

His movement brought Leah to her feet. "I'm not hungry now. Reilly, please listen to me."

He was pouring water from the pot into the canteen.

"Reilly, I'm in love with you."

Her statement brought no reaction. He didn't even blink. He just watched the water flowing into the canteen. Somehow Leah had to make him understand that she meant it.

"I know what you think," she hurried on. "But what I feel for you *is* real. When we get back to civilization, the way I feel about you isn't going to change. Ever. I really do love you."

He capped the canteen and straightened. "We're leaving in the morning," he announced without emotion.

Leah tensed at his unexpected response. "Okay, that was my big speech. Glad it meant so much to you. I was going to say thanks for saving my life, but I guess you do stuff like that all the time."

"Yeah." He didn't look at her. "Listen, we can't risk another day here."

"If you think I can walk out, then I guess I can," she said, keeping her tone as unemotional as his.

"If I have to, I'll carry you out."

She shook her head. "I just wish that—you know, I don't think you heard one word I said."

He looked at her with cynical amusement. "I heard you. What do you expect me to say?"

What had she expected? Filled with white-hot humiliation, she didn't know. She hadn't thought he would suddenly admit that he cared for her, too. But his indifference to her declaration of love hurt more than anything she had ever experienced. The only thing she knew was that she wanted to hurt him back.

Her open hand swung in a lightning-fast arc, striking his lean cheek with stinging force. He caught her wrist.

"You're hurting me!" she cried out.

"You started it." His fury was clear. And he didn't let go.

Tears swam in her eyes. "All I wanted was to—"

"I know what you wanted. I'm a man. I wanted it, too." He released her with some force, almost pushing her away from him. "But I didn't want—that—to be something you would regret. Or forget. Guess no one ever said no to you before."

"I've heard the word," she snapped.

"That's hard to believe sometimes, Leah."

An ominous silence fell between them. She knew she had gone too far, and said too much. But so had he.

"Listen up," he said at last. "We have to think about staying alive. Nothing else. Got that?"

"Got it."

Later, with shoulders hunched to conceal her inner anguish, Leah ate the tasteless food. Her hurt and anger kept her from making any attempt to break the silence.

When the scarlet sunset gave way to night, she crawled under the stiff blanket. She didn't ask Reilly if he was coming to bed. She knew without being told that she wouldn't sleep in his arms that night.

Tears washed her face as she turned her back on the fire and Reilly. Even though her pride had taken a hit—a major hit—she knew nothing had changed. She still loved him just as deeply.

The swan dive of a falling star arced across the heavens. Leah didn't feel like making a wish. She watched it fall until the crystal brightness of a tear got in the way. She shivered and pulled the blanket tighter around her shoulders, but the chill she felt was from the inside.

CHAPTER NINE

Leah's knuckles whitened around the end of the lean-to pole, now a walking stick. She felt a poignant tightness in her throat as she gazed for the last time at the place where she had admitted her love for Reilly.

Dawn's light had lengthened the shadows over the pool, making it look dark and mysterious. It was almost as if the doors were closing on paradise.

The campfire was drowned and the ashes scattered. Soon the desert wind would wipe away any trace of their presence and the waterhole would once again belong to the wild creatures who needed it.

"Let's go," Reilly said flatly, adjusting the pack on his back with a shrug of his shoulders.

Forcing herself to turn away from the scene, Leah nodded in agreement. She didn't look at him—she avoided it whenever she could. The voltage in his green eyes jolted her. But other than that, he was aloof.

Reilly probably felt none of the sadness she did

about leaving this place where, for a short time, they had been so close in body and spirit. Her family would be waiting at the end of their perilous journey, but Leah knew that if she had been given a choice, she would have stayed here with Reilly.

Yes, it was a romantic fantasy that was neither logical nor practical. But she loved him. Oh, God, how she loved him, she thought dispiritedly.

As before, Reilly led the way. The pace was slower than last time. She knew he was doing it to conserve her strength. She wasn't even carrying a pack. Everything they had with them, Reilly carried.

The first few hours of walking, each one punctuated by ten-minute rest stops, Leah felt quite good, not tiring as quickly as she had feared. Then the sun reached its zenith and the heat began prickling her back.

Reilly set up a noon camp in the middle of the desert valley along the rutted dirt road they had been following for the last several miles. Exhausted, Leah tumbled beneath the lean-to he put up, swallowed a mouthful of water, and closed her eyes.

The nap helped a little. Before they started out again, Reilly inquired distantly as to how she felt. Leah shrugged aside his indifferent question with a stiff, "I'm fine."

For a while she was, but her energy dissipated sooner than it had in the morning. Each step seemed to jar her teeth. The ten-minute rest stops seemed to get shorter. She could feel the encroaching weakness, but she gritted her teeth and pushed on.

Reilly stayed close to her, never more than a few paces ahead. The spring in his stride goaded Leah to keep walking, reminding her that she was holding him back. If she hadn't been injured—if she hadn't had to recover—if she hadn't been afraid of being alone, he would have reached help by now. Bitterly she reminded herself of Reilly's determination to survive. He didn't want to spend an hour more than he had to with her.

Turning an ankle on a rock, Leah stumbled and fell to her knees. His hand was under her arm to help her to her feet. She wrenched it away from his hold.

"I can make it," she insisted sharply and pushed herself upright. Dirt and grit were embedded in her palms. She rubbed it off on her jeans.

"Did you twist your ankle?" Reilly studied her, waiting for her to take a step.

Leah did, gingerly. The ankle supported her with only a twinge of protest. "It's fine," she answered woodenly. "Let's go."

Reilly handed her the stick she had dropped and started out.

Just before sunset, they stopped for the night. Leah collapsed onto the rutted track, wearily resting her head on her drawn-up knees. Reilly pushed the canteen into her hand and slipped out of his pack. Her hands were shaking too badly from exhaustion to get the canteen to her mouth without spilling the contents. Finally Reilly had to hold it to her lips.

From the backpack, he handed her a stick of jerky. "We don't have enough water to fix one of the packaged meals."

"I'm not hungry." She waved it aside.

"Eat it anyway," he ordered.

"I'm too tired," Leah grumbled, but she took it, reluctantly.

"I'm going to see if I can find something for a fire."

She chewed on the jerky, finishing it before Reilly returned. She stretched out on the hard, uneven ground, not opening her eyes when she heard his footsteps. He threw the blanket over her, but Leah was certain her aching muscles wouldn't notice the night cold. She heard Reilly starting a fire and guessed he had found fuel of some sort. Then a horrible burning stench filled her nose.

"Whew! What's that?" She rolled over, wrinkling her nose, as she glanced at Reilly.

"There wasn't any wood, but I found some cow chips. They smell but they burn and we need the fire to keep warm."

Leah pulled the blanket over her head to try to shut out the stinking smoke. Eventually she was simply too tired to care. She didn't even remember the sun sinking below the horizon.

A hand gripped her shoulder. Leah reluctantly opened her eyes, her vision blurring from heavy sleep. A pair of boots was near her head, topped by dusty jeans. Her gaze moved upward over muscular thighs, narrow hips and waist to wide shoulders, finally stopping as she gazed into a pair of green eyes.

"It can't be morning," she mumbled. But the sky was light.

"Come on, get up," Reilly said. He didn't offer to help.

Every muscle, nerve, and sinew in her legs was cramped with stiffness. Reilly, she noticed, was beginning to show signs of fatigue, too, but there was small comfort in that.

Within a few minutes the pack was on his back and they started out again. Her stiff muscles didn't loosen. Each step made her wince. Leah relied on the walking stick to keep her upright when her legs wanted to buckle.

At the second rest stop, she was afraid to sit down for fear she couldn't get up. She leaned heavily on the stick, exhausted nearly beyond the point of endurance. "How . . . much farther?" It took an unbelievable amount of effort to even speak.

Reilly's hands slipped under her arms, lowering her to the ground. "I don't know."

"I don't think I can get up," Leah protested, but she was already seated. Of its own accord, her body stretched out on the hard ground, her muscles quivering with fatigue.

"You're doing fine," he replied.

"Am I?" Her laugh was choked off by a lack of breath.

Her lashes fluttered wearily. When she opened them, Reilly was crouching beside her. "Where am I? What are you doing?"

"Where you were. You haven't moved for an hour. I was just waiting for you to wake up. Lots of things happened while you were sleeping."

"Really? Like what?"

"I'm kidding. Nothing happened. Nothing at all."

Strange, Leah thought as she looked up at him. They just said more to each other in less than a minute than they had during all of yesterday. Were they both too tired to be angry anymore?

"Ready?"

She nodded.

Reilly lifted Leah to her feet. She couldn't prevent herself from leaning weakly against him. He stiffened away from her, supporting her with his hands and not his body. She knew that not all the barriers had crumbled between them. He shoved the walking stick into her hand and she shifted her weight to it.

They set out at an ambling pace, yet each dragging step was an effort for Leah. Her lungs were bursting with exhaustion, making each breath a sob of determination that pushed her on.

Reilly stopped ahead of her. "Look!" His voice held an undertone of excitement. Leah paused beside him, forcing her eyes to focus on the direction of his gaze. Flat, sage-covered land stretched endlessly in front of her eyes but the mountain corridor had widened somewhat.

"Where?" she said hoarsely, seeing nothing to give them hope.

"Off to the right, near the foot of the mountains, there are some buildings. Ranch buildings, if I'm not mistaken." His gaze was riveted on the distant point.

All she could make out were some dark squares. She marveled that he had noticed them at all. Reilly tugged at the shoulder straps of his makeshift pack and shot a glance at Leah.

"Let's go."

He altered their course to angle across the open country toward the buildings. For a while, the knowledge that they might reach help at last gave Leah a fresh spurt of energy, but too soon it was spent, taking what remained of her strength and coordination. Her legs became like soft rubber. Without warning they collapsed beneath her and not even the stick could hold her up.

In a haze of total exhaustion, Leah felt Reilly try to lift her leaden weight.

"It's no use," she breathed. "I can't make it any farther."

"Yes, you can." His voice rang harshly in her ears.

He pulled her to her feet, drawing one arm across his shoulders and around his neck, while his other arm supported her waist. Half carrying and half dragging Leah, he started forward. She tried to make herself walk to help him, but her tired legs wouldn't obey.

The next thing she knew Reilly was swinging her into his arms. Her head lolled against his shoulder. She felt like a limp rag doll without a solid bone in her body, her mind swimming with extreme fatigue. Distantly, Leah could sense the strain of his rippling muscles carrying her dead weight.

"Leave me, Reilly," she pleaded.

"I'm not leaving you," he refused unconditionally.

Waves of tiredness washed over her and she hadn't the strength to protest anymore. She let herself drift away, semi-aware of the arms that held her and the walking motion that carried her across the ground.

The angry bark of a dog finally dragged her eyes open. Her head stirred against his shoulder, turning slightly so she could see ahead of them. Reilly's steps had slowed. A large dog was squarely in their path. Beyond it was a dusty white house with curtains at the window and wash hanging on the clothesline in the yard.

Leah looked at every detail of the scene with dizzy amazement. It seemed so weirdly . . . *normal.*

The screen door on the porch slammed. "Laddie! Come here!" a woman called and the dog stopped barking and retreated to the porch steps. The woman stepped out of the shadows, shielding her eyes against the sun. A small child clung to her legs. "Who are you?" Her voice was friendly but vaguely unsure.

Reilly stopped several feet short of the porch and the dog. "Our plane crashed eleven days ago in the mountains," he explained calmly. "My woman needs water and a place to rest. May we come in?"

"Yes, yes, of course!" she exclaimed. She clapped her hands at her dog. "Laddie, go lie down. We were notified of the search, my husband and I, but we had no idea the plane had gone down anywhere near here. Come in, come in."

Leah didn't hear half of what was said. Her heart was still singing from Reilly's words. *My woman.* Her hazel eyes lovingly searched his face, dusty and lined with weariness yet indomitably strong. Had he meant that?

"Are you hurt?" The ranch woman rushed to open the screen door for Reilly, the wide-eyed little girl still clinging to her legs. "Should I call a doctor? Or an ambulance?"

"No, just exhausted. The hike out was grueling." Reilly stopped inside the door. "Where can she rest?"

"There's a sofa in the living room. This way." The woman brought them into the living room, hovering uncertainly for a minute. "I'll get some water." She walked swiftly out of the room, the little girl hurrying in her shadow.

Gently Reilly lowered Leah onto the sofa, plumping pillows beneath her head. "Comfortable?"

She nodded, smiling wanly. "I didn't remember anything could be so soft. Reilly—" She didn't finish the sentence as the woman returned carrying a pitcher of water and glasses on a tray.

Leah drank thirstily from the glass Reilly held to

her lips, then sank back against the pillows as some of the strength ebbed back into her weary limbs.

The woman disentangled the little girl from her legs, bending slightly toward her. "Go out to the barn, Mary, and get your father. Tell him to hurry." She turned to Reilly, who was pouring a glass of water for himself. "Is there anything else I can get for you? Whiskey? Food?"

"Black coffee, if you have some." He straightened away from the sofa. "And would you show me where the phone is so I can notify the authorities?"

The little girl named Mary had shyly inched past Reilly, then dashed out of the room, the screen door banging as she ran for her father.

"The phone is in the kitchen and I do have some coffee on." The woman smiled.

Reilly glanced down at Leah lying on the couch. "You'll be okay. I'll only be gone a few minutes."

"I'm fine," she assured him softly, warmed by the concern in his green eyes.

As Reilly and the woman left the room, Leah relaxed against the cushions and pillows. It seemed so strange to have four walls surounding her and a ceiling instead of the open sky above her head. Tonight she'd be taking a hot bath, changing into clean clothes, and sleeping in a soft bed. She'd willingly trade it all . . .

Light, quick footsteps came into the living room. "Here's your coffee," the woman said. "It's hot and black and sweet, the way your husband ordered it. He said to drink it all." She smiled brightly, her plain features, freckled by the desert sun, suddenly taking on a rare beauty.

Leah struggled into a sitting position, using the pillows to help prop herself up. A hint of pink brought color to her cheeks as she held the mug of coffee with both hands.

"Reilly . . . isn't my husband." Much as she wished she could say otherwise.

The woman looked surprised. "I thought . . . that is . . ." She laughed to cover her confusion. "I guess I just assumed you two were married without thinking. I'm sorry."

"It's okay," Leah said, carefully sipping the hot coffee, some of her weakness easing as the sweet liquid traveled down her throat.

"I'm Tina Edwards, by the way," the woman said.

"Leah Talbot," supplied Leah.

"This must have been quite an ordeal for you."

Ordeal. How could she explain to the woman that it hadn't been an ordeal? Despite the shock of the crash, the days she had been delirious with fever from her infected wound, Leah couldn't think of the time she had been alone with Reilly as an ordeal. It had been a primitive idyll in many ways. The most important ways.

"It wasn't really too bad," she answered, choosing her words carefully. "The worst was today and yesterday." When Reilly had withdrawn from her, she added to herself.

"I can imagine." The woman nodded. "Walking in this heat even a short distance can be exhausting."

The screen door slammed and the little girl came racing into the living room to stand beside her mother, peering curiously at Leah. There were other footsteps, then the sound of a strange man's voice speaking to Reilly.

"That's my husband Mike. He was doctoring one of the horses in the barn," the woman explained.

Leah swallowed more coffee, the sugar and the caffeine stimulating her senses. She glanced up when Reilly entered the living room, accompanied by a shorter man wearing a cowboy hat and sunglasses. Intense weariness was etched around Reilly's eyes and mouth. She marveled that he could still keep pushing himself on.

"Mike's offered to drive us into Tonopah," said Reilly, the same tiredness in his face lacing his voice. "Your family will be there to meet us. They know you're safe and well."

Thinking about how worried they must have been almost broke her heart. "Are we leaving now?"

"As soon as you finish your coffee."

Concealing a sigh of regret, Leah brought the mug to her lips. She had hoped for some time alone with Reilly, but he seemed to be avoiding any opportunity for a private discussion between them. She couldn't exactly object to his plans. Later, at some time, she would speak to him and she wouldn't allow him to stop her. She swallowed the last of the coffee.

"I'm ready," she said. When Reilly bent to lift her into his arms, she shook her head. "I'm a little wobbly, but I think I can walk."

His fingers closed over her elbow to help her to her feet. She swayed unsteadily for a moment, then found her balance. But Reilly didn't release his grip on her arm, his touch impersonal and cool, as he guided her toward the door.

"Thank you, Mrs. Edwards." Leah smiled when they paused near the screen door. "For everything."

There was a brief exchange of good-byes before they went out to the car. Leah sat alone in the backseat, so she could stretch out and rest, Reilly had said. She was still exhausted and did rest, but her thoughts kept straying to the man in front of her. Although she tried, she couldn't concentrate on the welcome she would receive when they arrived.

Several miles from the house, the ranch road joined a county road that led to the highway. Mike Edwards's foot was heavy on the accelerator and the utility poles whizzed by the car window in a blur. Yet it was more than an hour before they reached the outskirts of Tonopah, Nevada.

They stopped in front of the building housing the sheriff's office. Leah straightened in her seat, wincing at the soreness of her muscles. Her stiff fingers closed over the door handle, but Reilly was already out of the car, opening the door for her. Once she was standing on the sidewalk he took her elbow again to keep her steady. She resisted when he tried to lead her toward the building.

When his cool jade eyes glanced questioningly at her, Leah spoke in a low voice so Mike Edwards couldn't overhear. "Reilly, please, we have to talk."

"About what?" His face seemed deliberately expressionless.

She swallowed nervously. "About us."

"Leah, I don't see—" Reilly began, with an arrogant kind of patience.

"Leah!" A familiar voice calling her name interrupted him. "Leah!"

She turned slightly in the direction of the voice and a smile of growing joy curved her mouth as she recognized the tall, lanky man half walking and half running toward her.

"Lonnie!" Her happiness made her brother's name a choked sound, so Leah said it again. "Lonnie!"

She took one step toward him. In the near distance, she caught a glimpse of the blue Air Force uniform that her father wore, and both her parents emerged from a car. Her vivacious mother waved eagerly, but Lonnie had gotten there first. His hands were on her waist, lifting her into the air and hugging her tightly as he swung her around.

"You're all right! You're all right!" her brother kept repeating, as if to convince himself. He buried his face in her sun-streaked hair.

"Yes," Leah whispered sobbing with happiness. "We made it."

He finally let her feet touch the ground and leaned back a little to look at her, tears in his brown eyes. "You're crazy, you know that?" His teasing only reinforced the affectionate bond between them. "What were you doing on that plane in the first place?"

Tears flowed down her cheeks. "I was coming to see you—to surprise you for your birthday."

"Leah, my baby!" At the tearfully happy voice of her mother, Lonnie released her, letting her turn to meet their parents.

Leah was immediately engulfed in another tight embrace, her arms winding themselves around her mother and feeling the shudders of relief and happiness that coursed through her.

"My baby, my darling," her mother whispered over and over. "We were so worried. They gave you up for dead. But we—"

"I'm all right, Momma." Leah slid one arm around her father's waist as he stood beside them, unable to express his relief and joy with her mother's openness. Her father's hand tentatively stroked her hair as she buried her face against the buttons of his uniform.

"You gave us quite a scare, child," he said tightly.

"I know, Daddy," Leah whispered. She tossed back her head and gazed into his face, seeing the love shining in his eyes that he couldn't express in words.

"Oh, heavens, just look at you!" Her mother brushed the tears from her face, then shakily tried to do the same for Leah. "You're a sight, Leah Talbot! You must have lost ten pounds and you look as brown as an Indian."

Leah stiffened, moving away a little from her parents and glancing frantically over her shoulder. Reilly wasn't standing beside the car where she had left him. Her heart leapt in fear. Then she saw him, very close to the building's entrance.

"Reilly!" She pulled the rest of the way free of her parents' arms, ignoring their confused frowns. Taking a quick step to follow him, she called again. "Reilly!"

She could see his wide shoulders tense as he hesitated, then stopped. He turned back abruptly, impatience underlining his reluctance. She knew instinctively that he had hoped to slip away unnoticed during the reunion with her parents.

"Reilly, don't leave—" Her voice lilted upward as she nearly tacked on "me." She tried to cover her lack of pride. "I want you to meet my family."

His long strides covered the distance that separated them with a speed that said he wanted to get this over with and be on his way. His features could have been carved out of hard granite. He looked noble and proud, but without feeling.

Leah was almost afraid that if she touched him, she too would turn to stone. Quickly she introduced him to her parents, her heart freezing at the distantly polite smile he gave them.

"This is Reilly Smith. We shared the charter of the plane," she explained, feeling nervous and awkward. "I wouldn't be here if it wasn't for him." Her voice sounded brittle with its forced cheerfulness.

A brief exchange of courteous small talk followed the introduction. Then Reilly took a withdrawing step backward. "It was a pleasure meeting all of you," he said politely. "But you'll have to excuse me. I have a lot of things to attend to, and I know you'd like to be with your daughter."

As he started to turn away, Leah caught at his arm. "Where are you going?"

Reilly barely looked at her. "To the sheriff's office. I have to give him a report on the plane crash, and fill out the FAA forms that were faxed in, too."

"I should go with you." She didn't want to let him out of her sight. If she did, she was afraid she would never see him again.

"I can answer the questions myself," he said firmly. "If the sheriff needs to corroborate my story, he can talk to you after you've had some time to rest. Right now you're too tired to think straight, let alone know what you're saying."

Leah knew what he was implying—that she only imagined she was in love with him. She bit tightly into her lower lip to hide its tremor.

"I do know," she insisted in a choked murmur. Before he could stop her, she slid her arms around his waist and clung to him, burying her head in his chest to hear the beat of his heart and make sure he wasn't made of stone. In a voice so low that only he could hear, she cast aside the last shred of her pride. "When will I see you again?"

His hands hesitated on her shoulders for an agonizing moment, then slid down to grasp her arms and push her away from him. Her eyes were bright with tears as she met the unrelenting indifference of his.

"Go with your mom and dad, Leah. Get some food and some sleep." His hard mouth moved upward at the corners in what was supposed to be a smile, but it left her feeling chilled. "We'll have dinner sometime and talk about our wilderness adventure."

His cool gaze flicked briefly to her parents, then he released her and left. She watched him striding easily away from her and felt an emotional pain so intense it just about shattered her. Self-consciously she turned back to her family, glancing first at Lonnie.

Her brother focused on the man's shirt she wore and the thrust of her breasts against the material. It was obvious that she wasn't wearing a bra. Quiet speculation was in his eyes as he met hers before swinging to look at their father. His calculating gaze was directed at Reilly disappearing into the building.

Leah could guess what was going through their minds. They had just realized that she had spent eleven days alone with the man. Now they were wondering how she had spent the eleven nights.

Lonnie's arm curved around her shoulders and he hugged her against his side. "Let's take her back to the motel where she can clean up." He smiled at his parents, but there was a challenging glint in his eyes when he looked at his father. "Then we'll eat, since Leah owes me a belated birthday dinner."

CHAPTER TEN

A hand brushed the hair away from her cheek, tucking it behind her ear, then coming to rest gently along her cheek.

"Wake up, Leah," a male voice coaxed softly.

Her lashes fluttered but didn't open. "Mmm." Contentedly she rubbed her cheek against the masculine hand. "Have I told you I love you?" she whispered with a blissful smile.

"Not lately," was the mocking reply.

"I love you, Reilly Smith." Her voice vibrated huskily with the depth of her emotion.

The hand was instantly withdrawn. "Wake up, Leah! You're dreaming," the voice ordered tightly.

With a start, her eyes flashed open. Bewildered for a moment, Leah realized that she wasn't sleeping in Reilly's arms. She was in a bed, with a pillow instead of his shoulder beneath her head. And her brother Lonnie was standing right there, his hands shoved deep in his pockets, and a troubled frown on his face.

Hot color flamed in her cheeks as she realized

she had mistaken her brother for Reilly and guessed the conclusion Lonnie must have jumped to. She rolled onto her back, turning her head toward the window and the heavy drapes that had been drawn to shut out the sunlight.

"Is it time for dinner already?" Leah blinked, as if unaware of what she had revealed.

"Dinner? You've been asleep for more than twenty-four hours."

"I have?" She looked at him with bleary disbelief.

Leah started to sit up, then remembered she wasn't wearing anything and quickly drew the covers up under her arms before shifting into a half-sitting position. It seemed only a little while ago that her mother had suggested she take a nap after her bath.

"Mom was going out to buy some clothes for me." She nervously ran her fingers through her hair.

"They're over on the chair." He nodded his head toward the pile. "I'll go next door to the folks' room while you get dressed." Lonnie paused at the door, his hand on the knob. "Leah . . ." He seemed to hesitate.

"Yes?" She held her breath.

"Never mind." He gave an impatient shake of his head. "See you in a bit."

She watched him leave and turned to the clothes on the chair, picking a ladylike dress with a back zipper. Her mother's taste in clothes was as conservative as ever. But Leah wanted to please her.

Afterward, Leah wished Lonnie had asked the question that had been uppermost in his mind. It would have eased the strange tension that suddenly sprang up between them. She tried to be bright and cheerful, the way her parents expected her to be, when they breakfasted together later, but she kept lapsing into moody silences, her thoughts wandering to Reilly—where he was—what he was doing—when or if she would see him.

When they went back to her parents' room, the conversation was all about the plane crash, though she would not talk about Grady's death and they didn't press her on that subject. But they were naturally interested in a first-hand account of what she had done during the eleven days she was missing.

But she couldn't relate the story without explaining the large part Reilly had played in her survival. The more she repeated his name, the more she thought about him. She only had to close her eyes for a fraction of a second to see him in her mind and remember what it was like to be in his arms.

"We made a doctor's appointment for you this afternoon," her father said.

"What for?" Leah asked defensively, then blushed at her brother's warning look.

Her father frowned, his eyes narrowing. "To verify that the gash on your arm is healing. It's probably too late to have it stitched properly, but the doc will make sure there are no signs of infection."

Maybe she shouldn't have told them about her injury or the fever. Absently she touched the clean bandage on her left arm that her mother had applied.

"It's fine. There's no need to see a doctor," she murmured self-consciously. She moved away from the motel room window.

"Really, honey." Her mother laughed, unaware

of the tension that enveloped her daughter. "It's amazing that you didn't catch pneumonia, considering how cold it gets around here at night."

Leah flinched. Her mother had not meant her remark as a subtle question about what had happened with Reilly. But Leah knew she had been carefully sidestepping any comment that might reveal what she felt. She had basically never kept anything from her family before, and her lack of openness was making her feel guilty when there was no reason for it.

"Actually, Mom, I didn't get all that cold." She lifted her chin with unconscious defiance. "Reilly and I slept together to stay warm. Whoa. Wait a minute." A charged silence followed her statement. "I didn't mean that the way it sounded."

"Leah . . ." Her mother hesitated, searching for the right words. "We honestly weren't thinking anything like that."

"I know, but—" Leah pressed her lips together.

"But." Her father picked up the unfinished part of Leah's sentence, his hands clasped behind his back as he stared out the window. "It's what you were thinking."

Leah looked everywhere but at him. "Okay. I'm in love with him, Dad."

"I see. And how does Reilly Smith feel about you?"

"I don't know. He . . . he didn't call while I was sleeping, did he?"

"No," her father answered.

"Leah, are you sure you know what you're saying?" her mother asked gently. "Maybe the emotion you feel is only gratitude. Like when patients fall in love with their doctors."

"No." Leah's sun-streaked hair swung about her

shoulders as she shook her head and laughed without humor. "It definitely isn't gratitude."

Her father turned away from the window, his gaze piercingly intent. "You barely know the man, Leah."

"I can't accept that argument, Dad," she replied calmly. "I spent eleven days alone with him in the wilderness. In conditions that would show anyone's true colors. I do know him. But you don't and I . . . I don't know how to explain everything that happened."

It was becoming painful to talk about Reilly. Leah didn't know how long her shell of composure would last before it cracked. She didn't exactly want to share her uncertainty over whether he loved her or would love her, not even with her mother.

She ran a hand nervously through her hair. "Okay. I'm going to my room and lie down, if nobody minds."

She wasn't surprised when her parents nodded their agreement, guessing that they wanted to discuss the situation in private. For sure, they didn't want their twenty-something daughter to fall in love with a man who was a complete stranger to them.

In her own room, Leah leaned against the door she had just closed and tried to think of a way to explain feelings she couldn't even explain to herself. She was almost grateful when her reverie was immediately interrupted by a knock on the door. Almost.

"Who is it?" she asked impatiently, suddenly wanting to be alone.

"It's me, Lonnie. Can I come in?"

"Of course." With a sigh, she shot back the bolt

on the door and opened it. His eyes flicked thoughtfully to her tense expression as he wandered into the room.

"What did you want?" Leah asked with forced nonchalance.

"My company gave me a leave of absence while you were missing. Now that you've been found, I have to report back to work." Her brother frowned. "First thing in the morning. Whoopee."

"Oh. I wanted to spend more time with you," she said wistfully.

He shook his head. "Can't. Dad's made arrangements for the three of you to fly back to Vegas tomorrow. He's going on to Alaska from there and Mom will join him in a couple of weeks."

Leah waited without commenting on the news. Her brother was obviously leading up to something, but she didn't know what.

"Nice write-up in the paper about your Reilly Smith," Lonnie went on in the same casual tone. "He's quite well-known in his field."

"He's not my Reilly Smith." She stared at her clasped hands, feeling more nervous than ever.

"But do you want him to be?" Lonnie asked quietly.

"I love him, Lonnie, more than I ever thought it was possible to love a man," Leah answered, then laughed bitterly. "For all the good it does me."

"Why do you say that?" He brushed back a lock of sandy brown hair that had fallen across his forehead.

"Because he said nearly the same thing Mom and Dad just said. Only in a different way." She walked agitatedly to the dresser mirror, pausing to gaze at her brother's watchful reflection. "He said that the time we spent together would seem unreal, like something that never really happened, once I got back. He meant that I would forget him when I was surrounded by the civilized world again."

"But you haven't."

"No." She turned away from the mirror. "Lonnie, do you know where he's staying?"

"You want to go see him, is that it?" He smiled understandingly as she nodded. "I don't know, but it shouldn't be too hard to find out in a town the size of Tonopah. Let me make a few calls."

When he located the motel where Reilly was registered, Leah asked him to take her there. Reilly hadn't bothered to contact her. But she wanted to make one last effort to see him before she resigned herself to the fact that he didn't care about her.

"You don't need to come in with me, Lonnie," she said when he got out of the car to walk with her to the motel entrance.

"He wasn't in when I called. He might not be in yet. I don't want to just drop you off." Her brother smiled, linking his arm in hers.

"If Reilly isn't here, I'm just going to wait until he comes." Her chin lifted with determination. "I won't leave Tonopah without seeing him."

Inside the motel, Lonnie asked her to wait for him at the entrance door while he checked at the desk. A few minutes later he was back.

"Come on." His hand gripped her elbow as he guided her past a row of rooms.

"Is he in?" she asked anxiously.

"No." He dangled a key in the air. "But you can wait for him in his room."

"Pretty slick. How'd you get the clerk to give you the key?"

"Easy. Fifty dollars makes a lot of things happen." Lonnie grinned cheekily. "I couldn't have my sister waiting in a motel lobby for a man."

"Gee whiz. You think so highly of me. Gets me all choked up."

He squeezed her hand and laughed. Then his gaze shifted to the numbered doors. "Here's his room." He unlocked the door and opened it for her. "Good luck, Leah. Behave yourself. And if he doesn't, call me."

"Oh, are you going to beat him up? He's a lot bigger than you."

Her brother puffed up his chest and thumped it. "I don't care. I'm your brother." But Leah knew his comical protectiveness was for real, and she did get a little choked up. "Thanks, Lonnie. For everything. What would I ever do without you?" She gave him a huge hug.

"You'd manage." His voice was muffled against her hair as he gave the top of her head an affectionate kiss. "But if you love him as much as you say you do, make sure he gets that. Guys can be a little dense."

"No! Really?" she said with mock surprise.

"Yeah. Take care of yourself, kid."

"I will."

Then she was alone in the motel room and the sound of Lonnie's footsteps faded away. The clock in the room was broken, so she had no idea how long she waited for Reilly to return. It seemed like hours. She wandered aimlessly from the bed to the lone chair to the window and back to the bed. She thought of countless arguments that she could make and rehearsed them until she was sick of hearing herself obsess.

When she heard a key turn in the lock, Leah forgot everything. She stood frozen beside the chair as the door opened and Reilly walked in. He didn't see her immediately as he shut the door and tossed a jacket on the bed, so she had a few precious seconds to study his tired face.

His sun-browned fingers had just impatiently unbuttoned the top buttons of his shirt when he saw her. He stopped short, his green eyes narrowing. Leah had hoped that surprising him might make him reveal his true feelings. She was disappointed.

"What are you doing here, Leah?"

Her throat went dry. Suddenly her big idea seemed ridiculous, even hopeless. "I came to see you. I want to talk." She moistened her dry lips. "I've been waiting forever. Where were you?"

"I had to show the sheriff the location of the crash." Reilly took a deep breath. "We took off-road vehicles, but it was still slow going. I stayed around until they uncovered Grady's body from the wreckage, then came back to make arrangements to have the body sent back to Las Vegas for burial. He has relatives there, but no close family. One of the sheriff's men will take your luggage and anything that looks like your stuff to your motel."

Although she said a silent prayer for Grady's family and felt a familiar flash of grief at the memory of his death, Leah knew she didn't dare let Reilly sidetrack her from the reason she had come.

"You could have brought my things to the motel," she said. "Why didn't you?"

He rubbed a hand wearily over his jaw. "Because I didn't want to see you," Reilly answered with brutal honesty. "Look, I'm hot and tired. I need a shower and some sleep. So why don't you say whatever it is you came here to say . . . and leave."

Leah flinched. "I love you, Reilly."

"Damn it, Leah, we've been over that before," he growled beneath his breath.

"And you believed once I was back with my family in the so-called real world, what I felt for you would fade like some crazy dream. Guess what. It didn't." The corners of her mouth lifted in a sad smile. "Because I'm still me and you're still you. And I still love you, more than I did before, because I found out how empty I feel not waking up in your arms."

A tense silence enclosed them. His level gaze held hers. His impassive face, austerely handsome, might as well have been a mask carved by the desert wind. Abruptly he turned away, his impatient stride carrying him to the dresser table.

"You don't know what you're saying," Reilly muttered. Ice from a Styrofoam container clunked into a plastic glass, joined by the water in the container.

Leah reached behind and unzipped her dress. "I told you once that if you left me, I would follow." She slipped her arms out of the sleeves. "I meant that, Reilly. If you don't want me as your wife, then I'll stay with you as your woman. As goofy and old-fashioned as that sounds, that's what I want. And I want you." She stepped out of the dress as it slid to the floor.

"Will you—" Reilly turned toward her. His eyes flashed over her semi-naked state. Whatever he was going to say was never finished. "What the hell are you doing?"

He banged the plastic glass down on the table, sloshing water over the sides. In lightning strides, he closed the distance between them, tearing the bedspread from the bed and throwing it around her.

Calmly Leah met his fiery gaze. "You've seen me in less than this. Why should I be ashamed if you see me again?"

"Different circumstances," Reilly snapped, drawing the spread tightly around her like a cocoon. The sensation was familiar. Leah smiled.

"How are they different?" she challenged, swaying toward him, her lips parting in a deliberate invitation.

He gripped her upper arm, preventing her from leaning on his chest yet not allowing her to move away. His gaze was riveted on the shimmering moistness of her lips, his breathing suddenly not as controlled and even as it had been.

"They just are."

"Meaning that you want me. And you don't have to stop this time," Leah whispered.

Suddenly and hungrily, his mouth devoured hers, crushing her against the hard length of his body. His hands roamed possessively over her, fighting the folds of the bedspread that he'd wrapped her in, but he didn't let her work free of its protective covering. Leah had to be satisfied with returning his passionate kiss.

"You need more time, Leah." His voice was husky and rough.

"Time won't change how much I love you or how much I want you." She finally got an arm out and used it to bring his head to hers for another hot kiss.

"How can I make you understand?" Reilly groaned, his mouth moving over her forehead and eyelids. "If I make you mine, Leah, I could never let you go. You're not ready for that kind of commitment."

"Reilly!"

"What?"

"Get me out of this damned bedspread!"

"Okay!" He unwrapped her but not all the way. "Put your dress back on. Then we can go talk to your parents."

"About what?" she asked cautiously.

"Ah—getting married."

"I happen to be over twenty-one. And it's my decision. Not theirs. I suggest you talk to me."

Reilly sighed. "It's really, really hard—to just talk to a woman who looks like a movie star even when she's wearing a motel bedspread. But I'll try. Leah . . . I love you."

She threw her arms around his neck. The bedspread fell off. Reilly took her in his arms again and looked deeply into her eyes. "You be my wife, then I'll make you my woman." His dark head bent toward hers and she lifted her mouth for his kiss.

A Behind-the-Scenes Look at
Six White Horses and *Reilly's Woman*

Dear Reader,

Growing up, I was something of a cross between a tomboy and a bookworm. As the youngest of four girls, I was my parents' last try for a boy, so I guess I tried to fill the bill. And because I was the youngest by nearly seven years, my older sisters often resorted to bribery to stop me from tagging after them. Their most effective ploy was to promise to read to me, and so my love of books was born.

After my dad died when I was five, we left the farm and mom moved us to town. All the kids on the block were boys, which suited me just fine. When I wasn't outside playing softball or football or playing cops and robbers or cowboys and Indians, I was inside with my nose in a book. Our little town had a library that was open two days a week. It was in the same building as our local movie theater, where they showed westerns on Saturday afternoon. Hopalong Cassidy, Gene Autry, the Cisco Kid, I saw them all, but my favorite was Roy Rogers. Like most young girls, I was soon horse-crazy. Living in town, owning a horse was out of the question, but I made friends with everybody that had one. I got doubly lucky when my sister married a man who soon bought a yearling colt. Duke looked like he was white, but he was really the palest yellow on the color scale. As soon as he was broke to ride, I was on him. Alec might have had his Black Stallion, but I had a white one.

During the summer between seventh and eighth grade, my mom remarried. Suddenly I had four brothers. Like my sisters, they were all older than me and were already married, living on their own. Still, I was excited to have brothers, but I can't begin to describe how excited I was to discover that new brother Bob rode in rodeos. If he was competing anywhere close to where we lived, I always wanted to go watch him ride. In my eyes, he was a real cowboy.

The first lure of wanting to watch him ride the broncs and bulls was gradually replaced by the discovery that he worked for the stock contractor who supplied the steers and bucking stock. It was the first time I had ever thought about how the rodeo animals got from one rodeo to another—or even where they came from. Curiosity took over (a writer's greatest gift) and I wanted to know more.

That long ago seed became the inspiration for *Six White Horses*. When we attend rodeos, we seldom think about the organization that's required to stage it—the livestock, the judges, the announcers, the clowns—and the entertainment, whether that entertainment consists of some music star, trick rider or clown act. That was the behind-the-scenes look I wanted the reader to have when I wrote *Six White Horses*.

When Bill and I traveled to Oklahoma to research possible locations for an Oklahoma book, one of our stops was in Oklahoma City. For me, the highlight of that visit was the National Cowboy Museum. I remember standing next to the grave of the legendary bucking horse Midnight and recalling my fascination with the rodeo and all its facets. There had always been the vague thought that someday I would write a story centered around the rodeo. Suddenly it was no longer vague; it was definite, and I was going to set it in Oklahoma.

Story ideas come from so many different sources. Sometimes they can be sparked by something you read in a newspaper or magazine; other times it might be a particular place or historical event; and occasionally—just occasionally—you pull it from your own life. Which is exactly what happened with *Six White Horses*—a stepbrother who rodeoed and an almost white stallion named Duke who was my love as a girl.

I'm always asked where I get my story ideas, but few ever ask how I choose the backgrounds for the stories I write. That probably doesn't sound important. In theory, you can take most story ideas and alter them so that they can be set anywhere you choose, but it would be next to impossible to have a cattle ranch in Illinois. A cattle-feeding operation, yes, but a cattle ranch of the kind you find in the West, no.

There is always an ideal setting for a story idea, one that enhances it, one that makes fiction seem absolutely plausible. A good story is one where the reader can easily "believe" something like this could happen.

I have always had ideas for stories that haven't been written yet—mostly because I haven't found the backdrop that makes them come to life. Such was the case with *Reilly's Woman*. The first time Bill and I ventured into the Southwest, I fell in love with the turquoise and silver jewelry. As always happens when something grabs my interest, I wanted to know more about it, meet some of the silversmiths who create these exquisite pieces. And, as usually happens when I learn more, new questions are invariably raised: Where do you get the turquoise? How is it mined? What does it look like in a raw state? What do you mean, different mines produce different shades of green or blue turquoise? Before I realize it, my own curiosity leads to a story idea, which leads to more research.

I always expected a setting for this idea would be easy to pinpoint. After all, I had my pick of states in the Southwest that I could use, yet nothing ever gelled. I never had that "Aha" moment when I knew this was where the story belonged. So I kept the idea tucked in the back of my mind. That's where it stayed until one day Bill and I stopped at a campground outside of Elko, Nevada, around midafternoon, intending to only spend the night and get back on the road the next morning to head to California.

The campground was located outside the city limits, surrounded by the scrubby desert landscape you expect in Nevada. It was too windy to extend the awning on our trailer, and there was way too much dust blowing around to want to sit outside and relax, but our little dog, Mandy, needed to go for a walk, so Bill and I took her. As we were strolling along, I looked at the terrain and wondered aloud whether there were any turquoise mines in the area. When he asked why I wanted to know, I told him about this story idea I had that just wouldn't come together. His reply seemed to make no sense—he suggested that I should have a small plane crash like the one that had once happened to us. How or why he ever thought a plane crash had any relationship to a turquoise mine, I'll never know. But it didn't really matter because my mind grabbed his suggestion and showed me how to make these two seemingly disparate thoughts come together. Just like that, *Reilly's Woman* was born.

And the plane crash he was talking about goes back to the years before I ever started writing. Bill's construction company covered a nine-state area, and the sites were often not easily accessible to commercial airports. He decided he needed to learn to fly and get his own plane so he could cut down on the lengthy travel time. He talked me into attending ground school with him so I could help him study. Then he talked me into taking the written private pilot's test when he did, so I would know what was in the test in case he didn't pass his the first time. I passed the written exam without ever being in a cockpit. Then his instructor urged me to at least learn how to land a plane in the event of an emergency on those occasions when I did accompany him to a construction site.

That first moment when the instructor turned the controls over to me was all it took for me to become addicted to the thrill of flying. Bill and I went from getting our private pilot's licenses to going after commercial licenses. One of the requirements for a commercial license was a long cross country flight. And it was on that flight that the crash happened. The plane developed ice in the carburetor, which wasn't at all unusual, but when Bill pulled on the carburetor heat control, the cable crystalized. He tried descending to warmer air, but that didn't work and the engine quit. I spotted a small field that was long enough to land in. Unfortunately, there was a cross wind and without power to compensate for it, when the plane touched down, the wind caught a wing and cartwheeled us. It all happened in slow motion. We finally came to a stop upside down, still strapped in and without so much as a bruise.

Any landing you walk away from is a good one. It is in *Reilly's Woman,* too.

Catch up with the first book
in the Bannon Brothers series,
HONOR!

There was no shortage of gorgeous women at the reception, but not one was in her league, in his opinion. Kenzie was his definition of perfect. Smart. And sexy, with a superfit, petite body that looked fantastic in a plain white T-shirt and camo cargos—her version of fatigues, now that she was no longer a soldier.

A female guest strolled nearby, trilling a hello to a friend a few tables away. Linc looked idly at them as the woman stopped to chat, then realized she was holding a tiny dog wearing a ruffled collar in the crook of her arm. He'd taken it for a purse at first. Her pampered pet blinked and yawned as the woman moved away.

He shook his head, amused. Not Kenzie's kind of dog, that was for sure.

She'd been a K9 trainer for the army, on a fast track right out of basic. Kenzie wasn't one to brag, but Linc had been able to fill in the blanks from the bare facts she'd offered. Her knack for the work had gotten her quickly promoted to a position of critical importance: training military handlers assigned to new animals and developing new skill sets for the experienced dogs to keep up with what was going on in country.

Then something had happened, she wouldn't say what. She didn't seem to want to reenlist. She didn't seem to want to do anything but work. A lot.

Which was why he was solo on his brother's wedding day.

Two weeks ago he'd stopped by the JB Kennels and seen her out in the field with a half-grown shepherd. Their jumps and leaps looked like pure joy, but he knew she was testing the pup's reflexes and instincts. In time, under her tutelage, the young animal would learn to turn play into power. The sight of the two of them, twisting and turning in midair, was something he would never forget.

Hell, Kenzie looked good even in thick bite sleeves and padded pants. But he let himself imagine her in something close-fitting and classy, her hair brushed to a silken shine and her head tipped back to gaze up at him as they danced to a slow number. Like the one the band was playing right now . . .

"Linc. You with us?"

He snapped out of his reverie and looked up at his younger brother. "Just thinking."

Deke took hold of a bentwood chair, spun it around with one hand and sat on it backward, resting his arms on the curved top and stretching out his long legs.

"About what? Or should I say who?" he asked shrewdly.

"Give me a break, Deke." Linc took a sip of champagne and set the glass aside.

His younger brother wasn't done ribbing him.

"You've got someone on your mind. I can see it in your eyes."

"What are you talking about?"

"That moody, distracted look is what I'm talking about."

"You're imagining things, Deke."

His brother only laughed. "Am I? Just so you know, one wedding per year is all I can handle. I'm not ready to see you walk down the aisle."

Linc smiled slightly. "If I found the right woman, why not?"

Deke was tactful enough to quit at that point. He surveyed the crowd. "Look at all these gorgeous babes. How come you're not dancing?"

"I'm waiting for a song I like," Linc parried.

Deke gave up, shaking his head. "Okay. Have it your way." He returned the inviting smile of the brunette on the other side of the dance floor. She brightened, but stayed where she was, smoothing the brilliant folds of her taffeta dress. "There's my girl. I think she likes me."

"Go for it. You're not taken."

"Neither are you."

Linc only shrugged.

Deke turned his head and studied him for a long moment. "C'mon, bro. You can tell me. What don't I know?"

"Nothing."

Deke didn't seem to believe that reply. "Wait a minute—there was someone. Her name was—it's coming back to me—Karen, right?"

"Who?"

For a second, Linc drew a blank. Then he remembered. Months ago Kenzie had used that name when she'd showed up at Bannon's door with a guard dog to loan him as a favor to Linc.

"Karen," Deke said impatiently. "You know who I mean."

Linc smiled. "Oh, yeah. Her. Ah, we're just friends."

Deke shot him a knowing look.

"If that changes, I'll let you know," Linc said calmly.

His brother lost interest when the brunette seized her chance and swept across the dance floor as the band paused. "I do believe she really is interested." Deke ran a hand over his brown locks and asked, "How's the hair?"

"Looks great. Very natural," Linc teased, echoing the photographer's comment.

"Shut up." Deke straightened his lapels.

The two brothers rose at the same time, but Linc turned to go before the brunette arrived. He wandered away down a carpeted corridor, feeling a little lonely. Without intending to, he ended up in the hotel's bar. It was mostly empty. There was only one other customer, an older man having a beer, but no bartender. The distant noise of the reception was barely audible in the dim, luxuriously furnished room.

He slid onto a stool, folding his arms on the counter and looking around idly while he waited to be served. The liquor bottles arrayed in ranks behind the bar reflected blue light coming from an unseen source. The bar was dark otherwise, but he didn't mind.

The bartender appeared from a door at the end of the polished counter and took his order, exchanging a few words with Linc as he set the drink on a napkin. Then he turned away to prepare for the evening rush, setting clean glasses of various types on trays and filling up a compartmented container with slices of lemon and lime and bright red cherries.

Linc barely noticed. He took one sip and set the drink down, intending to make it last. He had nothing to do and nowhere to go except back to the reception.

Later for that. He was truly tired and it was catching up with him. Being the best man was serious work. Linc had rolled out of bed at six a.m. and barely had a chance to catch his breath since.

Zoning out over a cold drink felt fine. The TV over the bar was tuned to the local news, on low. Good. He didn't really want to listen. The weatherman was saying something about clouds rolling in by nightfall.

So be it. The perfect day was over.

Linc undid his black silk bow tie, taking a deep breath or two as he eased the collar button open next. He wasn't made to wear monkey suits.

He half heard the reporter going on and on about an accident on I-95 just outside of a town with a name he wasn't going to remember. Not a pileup, not a jackknifed semi, just a solitary car.

Filler. News shows made a huge deal out of a fender-bender when there wasn't anything else to yap about.

Then the live feed crackled and filled the screen behind the guy and Linc winced. The accident wasn't minor. It looked like a rollover. Smashed frame, crumpled black chassis scraped to the gray undercoat in a lot of places, back wheels high in the air.

Linc could just make out an ambulance, a red and white blotch in the background, and activity around it, a stretcher being loaded. He got a glimpse of what looked like a head-and-neck stabilizer frame attached to the stretcher.

Fatalities got a body bag, not that rig. He automatically wished the injured person well—he or she was lucky to be alive.

He scowled when the cameraman evaded the highway patrol officer's gaze and moved around for a close-up of the nearly totaled vehicle. The reporter on the scene dogged him, trying to stay in the frame and not always succeeding. They both knew what would get on TV: a dramatic shot, preferably with blood.

Good thing there were a few seconds of lag time before any broadcast, Linc thought. Imagine the shock of someone recognizing a victim of a bad accident or identifying detail—

He pushed away his barely touched drink. Linc *knew* that license plate. There was only one word on it.

KENZYZ.

Ready for more from Janet Dailey?

Read on for a peek at her new book,
TRIUMPH,
available in June 2013.

Kelly St. Johns smoothed her suit, waiting for the countdown in her earbud mic as a cameraman a block away prepared for a long establishing shot. Seventeen stories of open concrete floors towered behind her, next to a huge crane and flatbed trailers laden with rebar. The construction project had been idled, its dirty-money financing gone and its site locked down by the feds. The deserted streets around it were silent, ideal for taping.

"Three, two, one."

Kelly straightened and spoke the sentences she'd memorized before the shoot, gesturing to the unfinished structure.

"Another scandal-ridden project shut down by the authorities. Millions of dollars—your tax dollars—lost to kickbacks. When will it end?"

"And . . . cut. Back to you in a minute, Kelly," the cameraman said. "We want to see how that looks."

Kelly barely registered Gordon's comment. She could hear Laura, the segment producer, discussing the footage with him. She turned and looked around at the building and construction site, searching for a different visual. They were sure to ask for additional takes. There was no point in removing the small wireless mic clipped to her lapel or the earbud.

Today's tape would be digitally edited at the news studio and used as an opener for her previous reportage and interviews on corruption in the building industries. Not her first feature story, but it was an important one. Atlanta was growing faster than ever, crowded with gleaming skyscrapers and world-class hotels that overshadowed the quiet, idyllic neighborhoods surrounding the metropolitan hub.

She ignored a faint tremor of unease. Laura had decided to film at the end of the day to take advantage of the dramatic shadows, getting clearance to use the construction site, abandoned months ago, for a location and obtaining keys to the padlocked gates. Supposedly, there was security somewhere around.

Kelly reached into her pocket and took out her laminated press pass. If anyone stopped her, it would come in handy. She walked through the half-built structure, her heels echoing on the dusty concrete, going around pillars and avoiding the deep hole for the elevator banks.

No safety cones, no nothing. No graffiti either, and no signs of squatters, both of which struck her as odd. A management company had to be maintaining the unfinished building—what there was of it. But the researcher assigned to the story had it on good authority that the owners had fled the United States without bothering to declare bankruptcy.

She could see clear through to the back of the site, greened by tall weeds growing in the gouges left by the treads of heavy machinery, now gone. Kelly continued toward the open area, stopping at the edge of the unfinished floor and looking out, her arms folded over her chest.

"Kelly?" The cameraman's voice crackled in the earbud. "Where'd you go? We can't see you."

"I'm at the back," she answered. "It doesn't look like anyone's been here for months, but it hasn't been trashed. Kind of weird that I don't see any footprints besides my own."

Gordon's reply was cheerful. "Okay, we'll follow them. Laura wants another backdrop, same lines. Anything fabulous where you are?"

"No." Kelly didn't elaborate, noticing a car on the other side of the chain-link fence behind the weeds. It was the sole occupant of the parking lot, a wasteland of cracked asphalt and stomped beer cans.

The car's tinted windows and gleaming black finish seemed out of place in the desolate setting. There was no sign of life that she could see, but maybe that was because of the slanting angle of the late-afternoon light.

She heard Laura and Gordon enter and follow her trail, their sneakered footfalls quiet on the concrete. Kelly turned toward them. The segment producer was carrying Kelly's bag and her own, and some of Gordon's equipment.

Laura, a short brunette in no-nonsense jeans and jacket with the station logo, stopped several feet away beside Gordon. The burly, older man hoisted the camera and looked through the viewfinder. He took his time about focusing and adjusting the lens. Kelly waited, distracted by sounds coming from the parking lot.

Car doors opened and closed softly. So there was someone in that car. Had the three of them been noticed? She didn't like the feeling of not knowing what was behind her.

"Ready for your close-up?" Gordon said finally.

That old line. Always the joker. "Yes," Kelly snapped.

"I say we get a shot of you picking weeds and call it a wrap."

Laura was craning her neck to get a glimpse of the viewfinder that jutted out from the side of the videocamera. "Gordon, do you want that car in the background?"

"The editor can zap it out," he said absently. "Kelly, we're rolling. Three, two, one—"

"Who are all those guys?" Laura demanded. "Wait, there's a woman, too. In the other car."

Kelly whirled around. A second car, a near twin of the one she'd seen, pulled into the parking lot behind the chain-link fence. Two men had gotten out of the first car and stood behind the open rear doors, as if they were shields. A woman gestured from the rolled-down passenger side window of the second car, saying something, not in English.

Instinct made Kelly step back into the shadows.

"Hey," Gordon said. "Not there. We're losing the light. Kelly, move back where you were—"

"Shut up!" she hissed, walking quickly toward him.

The cameraman looked up at her, baffled. "What's the matter? Want me to stop?"

Laura's eyes widened, taking in whatever was happening on the viewfinder. Something was radically wrong, Kelly knew that much.

"Get down! *Down!*"

Not Gordon's voice. Deeper. Urgent. Kelly spun, too startled to figure out more. She heard a muffled *crack* and the faint, unmistakable *zing* of a bullet.

Someone shoved her behind a pillar and held her there.